DESERVEDLY DEAD

B.J. Oliphant

FAWCETT GOLD MEDAL • NEW YORK

A Fawcett Gold Medal Book
Published by Ballantine Books
Copyright © 1992 by B.J. Oliphant

Library of Congress Catalog Card Number: 91-92397

ISBN 0-449-14717-7

Manufactured in the United States of America

First Edition: June 1992

1

WHEN THE PLANE came in over Denver, Shirley McClintock refused to look out the window. City lights made her think of sequins, of carnivals, of those banks of shimmering votive candles she remembered seeing in Catholic churches before they'd all seemingly gone electric—pretty things all. What was below was juvenile gangs, drug problems, pollution from the Rocky Mountain Arsenal, nuclear waste from Rocky Flats, a lung-clogging layer of brown air, and a downtown district so dead after six P.M., you could use it for bait. All the pretty lights in the world wouldn't change that. Sparkling up cities didn't hide their essential nature, and she'd lately had her fill of them.

Grump, growl, grump. She glanced guiltily at her seat mate, who'd been dozing on and off since Chicago. Though her subliminal snarls had seemed loud enough to keep the entire nonsmoking section alert, he'd remained impervious. Which meant she hadn't been as obviously obnoxious as her mental state indicated. And a good thing, too.

The plane tilted, swinging the city lights up beside her left cheek. Umpteen miles of Colfax Avenue, straight as an arrow shot from the eastern plains to the mountains. Broadway crossing it north to south, the crossing marking the center of a grid that marched militantly off into an explosion of curly suburbs. Everything straight and square except in the northwest quadrant, where downtown streets plunged off in surprising diagonals amid a glimmer of tall buildings whose lights shone on mostly empty streets. At least annually the mayor talked of revitalizing the downtown area. He'd be closer to the truth if he spoke of resurrection. Everything that wasn't an office building was a parking lot, neither very attractive at night. Shirley's first husband, Martin Fleschman, had remarked on occasion, "You build a ghetto, you *got* a ghetto." Marty had been right. Downtown was a nine-to-five ghetto, one more piece of evidence of the stupidities so-called urban renewal could commit without half trying.

Yawning, she ran her fingers through her short gray hair, making it stand up in unruly spikes. The flight had been an hour late out of D.C. She'd turned time back two hours in Chicago to be on Mountain time, which, according to her watch, was eight-fifty. J.Q. was meeting the plane. She'd told him not to bother; she'd stay at an airport hotel tonight, and he could pick her up in the morning. Silly to come all the way into the city this time of night. If the baggage was as slow as departure had been, it'd be midnight by the time they got home.

She smiled ruefully, shutting down the pro forma politesse. J.Q. was meeting the plane because he knew she was dying to get home. A month away from the ranch was twenty-nine days too many, and she'd practically drooled in his ear the last time they'd talked. Even though she'd lived in D.C. during all of her first and part of her second marriage, the place had always felt like an assignment: temporary, not unamusing, but definitely involuntary. Now, of course, D.C. was what almost every city was becoming: frightened citizens being ground up between conservatives who were determined to force people to be good and liberals who didn't think it was right to force people to do anything, while the drug disabled subclass went its own ugly way.

2

"You, of course, would do something about it," Roger Fetting had challenged her in the middle of a noisy cocktail party. Roger was her former boss, and he'd always enjoyed being the agent provocateur.

Well, she'd told him. Compulsory schooling for all illiterates and quasi-illiterates—sex-segregated work camps until they could read, write, and speak standard English, plus sterilization for all drug dealers and addicts.

Some of her ACLU-type friends had taken umbrage.

"It's still a free country, Shirley. You can't just abrogate people's civil rights!"

"I'm all for allowing *human* rights to every unfeathered thing that walks about on two legs," she'd snarled. "But *civil* rights can only apply to civilized people, and children aren't born civilized. They're born barbarians. The whole task of parenthood is to civilize kids by compulsory, coercive training and education. Every good parent does just that! And if parents can't and the state won't, you end up with barbarian tribes warring through the streets of your cities!"

That had started an argument that had gone on most of the evening, with several parents indignantly asserting they did not coerce their children while others pointedly asked them whether they had ever held a child until a tantrum wore out, or made a child sit in a corner, or trained a child how to behave in traffic, or made their kids turn off the TV until after homework—and wasn't that coercion?

It had been a pretty good brouhaha, probably more fun than the evening would have been otherwise.

Her ears popped. The plane leveled, heading for the runway lights and the still dimly backlit line of the Rockies on the western horizon. A clear Sunday night in July. Probably still hot. It'd been in the nineties all week. No rain. J.Q. had fussed about that. The hay was baled and in the barn, so now he wanted rain to green up the pastures. "Settle the dust," he said. That was what he always said. What he really wanted was what she wanted: green. Any color green in this arid land. Grass green, scrub-oak green, pine green, willow green. Even sage green if nothing else offered. Green at the

3

foot of red sandstone cliffs against a sky of western blue with piled white clouds sailing overhead in endless processions. Ducks muttering to each other in the pond. Herons croaking down along the creek. Coyotes yipping their heads off at the moon. Bulls bellowing. Home.

She swallowed and blotted her eyes, overcome by a wave of homesickness almost like grief. Where had that come from?

When they taxied to the gate, the air-conditioning shut off and everything went into slow motion. People stood up, muttering and stamping like a herd of cows about to stampede, totally destroying the illusion of breathable air in the cabin. Shirley had never been able to figure out why it took an objective five minutes to taxi to the gate and a subjective half hour after that to get the doors open. Invariably she sat there feeling claustrophobic, trying not to hyperventilate, and suspecting some joker from a rival airline had Super-Glued the doors shut before they took off. They'd all die in here, gasping for air, entombed like sardines.

She actually sighed with relief when the standing mob began to move. Once there was air, she could survive, but at six-three she was too damned tall to stand up until she had somewhere to go. After the first rush had subsided, she pushed past her sleeping seat mate to the aisle. Maybe he was going on to Seattle, Tacoma, Anchorage. Maybe he needed to get off here. If so, no doubt some helpful airline employee would wake him. Her own helpfulness account was overdrawn.

Jacket and briefcase came down from the overhead. Presents for J.Q. and Allison in the briefcase. Other baggage checked through. J.Q. would meet her downstairs at baggage claim. Even back in the days when non-ticket-holders could go directly to the arrival gate, he'd always met her in baggage claim. J.Q. traveled by Amtrak himself, being convinced that airport metal detectors would eventually turn out to cause cancer, diabetes, ingrown toenails, and the common cold.

She had just laid hands on her second suitcase when he reached past her and took it from the carousel.

4

"Evening, lady."

All she could do was stand there, grinning at him. He looked so good. So J.Q. Mustache brushed. Face browner than when she'd left. Might have lost a pound or two. Always did when she went away, even now that he had foster daughter Allison to cook for.

"You're thinner," she said. She always said that.

"Lost my appetite," he said in return. "I can feel it coming back."

She admired him, head to toe. "New boots?"

"Yeah. Treated myself. Ostrich. Whadda you think?"

"*Pink* ostrich?"

"Sunset," he said, extending his right foot to examine its blushing toe. "That's what the salesman called it, sunset. Besides, they were on sale. Allison picked them out. She's out in the car, listening to space music on the radio."

"She didn't come in?" That was odd for Allison. "Well, then," she said, seizing one of the cases back from him. "Let's go."

Twelve-year-old Allison didn't look thinner. She looked brown and smooth, like a well-fed cat, though there was something a little . . . Shirley couldn't identify it. Preoccupied, maybe. Whatever it was vanished as Allison's questions and comments came in a flood. Shirley had to tell her all about Washington: Had she seen the President? Had she seen anybody famous? Had she gone to the Lincoln Memorial? Had she gone to the Library of Congress?

"I told you everything I did on postcards," Shirley complained after the twentieth question.

"It sounded pretty dull," Allison rejoined. "I thought you must've done something else."

There had been something of politeness in the whole conversation. The questions had sounded more rehearsed than spontaneous. Allison was acting the part of a child being good. What was going on here?

"I didn't do much else," Shirley confessed with a sidewise glance at J.Q. "It actually took most of two weeks to go over those two properties Marty left me. I hadn't looked at either of them for years, and there were some problems. I'm going to sell them both. They're supposedly worth a lot, but by the time I pay the mismanagement company for screwing up everything from the leases to the plumbers' bills, I only get a pittance in income. Since I'm not willing to go back there and manage them myself, they'll have to be sold, and that means tax problems."

"Does tax problems mean lawyers?" Allison asked, actually sounding interested.

"Probably. Unfortunately. Lawyers or not, I'll be glad to be rid of the buildings. They've been a headache for the last five years. So, besides taking care of that, I visited with Martin's family. I went to a Bar Mitzvah and a wedding. I wrote a little paper for my old boss, Roger Fetting, just to pass the time between tax consultants, and he took me to a cocktail party where I got into a fight."

"Fight!"

"She means an argument," said J.Q. "If she'd meant a fight, she'd have said a confrontation."

Shirley gave him a look. "I took a few very early-morning walks, after the muggers had gone to bed and before it got hot. I spent an afternoon at a bookstore buying presents for you and J.Q. and me myself. And I went to the zoo once. That's about it."

"Doesn't sound like much fun, except for the zoo."

"Well, that was the high point of the month," she admitted, feeling guilty. She might have enjoyed the family gatherings more if her membership in the group had been as herself rather than as Marty Fleschman's widow. As it was, she'd spent most of two parties listening to Great-Aunt Sophie shriek in a cracked treble, "Isn't he darling!" or "Isn't she adorable!" coincident with the arrival of each unmarried offspring: toddler, teenager, or twenty-year-old. The strident exclamations were identical on the successive evenings; so were the young people apostrophized. Nobody paid much attention, least of all the children. The whole business had the inexorability of ritual, but it had stung Shirley like a grabbed thistle, perhaps because she had no children to be

6

praised. Young Marty and little Sal had died before Martin himself, their deaths no doubt hastening his own. She wondered now if she'd have felt differently if it had been Marty Junior and Sal Aunt Sophie was greeting with that aged shriek: Isn't he handsome; isn't she beautiful! They had been lovely children. Better-looking than Shirley herself was. Better than Marty had been.

The darkness fled by outside the windows of the Wagoneer, and she blinked away another wave of suffocating melancholy as she felt J.Q.'s hand on her own. He could always tell what she was feeling.

"Another thirty minutes," he said. "There's no traffic. Lean your head back and relax. It's after midnight, Eastern time."

She put her head against the seat back and closed her eyes, comforted by finding reason to be weary and weepy. He was right. She was tired. She'd been up since five.

"We made soup, Shirley," said Allison, that strange tone back in her voice once more. "Refrigerator soup. It's got leftover beef and tomatoes and everything in it except J.Q. said no anchovies, but after we strained the stock, we put in new noodles. J.Q. says you can slurp it even if you're too tired to eat."

"You're both very thoughtful," she said, ashamed of herself for her sadness. She didn't need to grieve over family. She had family. Even though Allison didn't sound quite like herself.

When they turned off the highway onto the gravel of County 64, she sat up in anticipation. They were headed northeast and uphill. A mile or two ahead, just past Indian Bluff, where 64 bent eastward toward Allison's school and the Cavendish place, Old Mill Road swooped down to the left, westward, into the valley the McClintock ranch shared with other residents: wild, domestic, and human. As a child, coming home after dark, she had always waited for the turn and watched for the first glimpse of the McClintock porch lights across the darkness of the valley. Other homes in the valley were screened behind ponderosas and scrub or by the willows along Big Cawson Creek.

"How's Mrs. Bostom?" she asked, suddenly remembering that Oriana Bostom, her nearest neighbor, had been diagnosed as having cancer.

J.Q. sighed. "Saw Neb in town last week. He says she's failed a lot."

"She's dying," Allison said soberly. "That's what he said." Allison, who had lost both her parents to murder a little over a year ago, had had more experience of people dying than had most twelve-year-olds. She tended toward an accepting point of view. "He said she's going to die."

"Well, yes," J.Q. said judiciously. "That is what he said."

"I'll have to get over there to see her," Shirley murmured. Oriana and Nebraska Bostom had lived in their low log house south of Old Mill Road as long as Shirley could remember. They had been friends of Shirley's parents and were both well into their eighties by now.

As they passed Indian Bluff, a darkness against the stars, Shirley looked westward, waiting for the moment she'd see the lights at the McClintock place, like little stars, shining miles away in the darkness.

They crested the hill. Light blazed in her face: light that had no business being there, light that didn't belong.

"Damn," she cried. "What the hell!"

"Sorry," J.Q. cried. "I forgot to warn you."

"What the hell!" she demanded again, blinking the glare out of her eyes as they turned to the left off 64 and started the long slope down Old Mill Road toward the McClintock place, the sudden flash fading behind them. "J.Q., that was Hi Jewell's place!"

"Hi sold it, Shirley. You remember that. Sold it to a man named Azoli. Couple months before you left. Azoli's bought part of the old Stenger place, too."

"That's right." She had forgotten. "If he bought some of the Stenger place, he must have a couple thousand acres."

"About that."

"So, what's all that light?"

"Azoli's moved all the ranch buildings that were scattered all over; he's put them down there next to the house."

"All right, so?"

"And he's lined 'em all up. About four, five barns and a couple silos and toolsheds, all the buildings Hi had scattered around. Plus the new cattle sheds he's built."

"And!" she demanded impatiently.

"And he's painted 'em all and put new tin roofs on 'em. Not colored metal. Nothing easy on the eyes. Daytimes, with the sun on 'em, they hit you even worse than when that light's on at night. Like mirrors."

That was what she'd seen. Light reflected off a whole row of tin roofs. The place had looked like an industrial park! "What's he growing? Marijuana? He lighting up gun emplacements or something?"

"Not growing anything except cows, he says. Those long-legged foreign cows that don't take to hills too well. He has some kind of timer to turn those lights on sometimes at night to discourage prowlers, so I hear. He tells people he likes his privacy."

"My Lord," she sighed, shaking her head at the welcome darkness down in the valley. "That's what people have dogs for, to discourage prowlers."

J.Q. kept his mouth shut on the topic of Mr. Azoli's two groveling retrievers, which had been, so the local vet had informed J.Q., debarked. The vet had been pinch-lipped about that, and so had J.Q.

Shirley sighed. "Well, it's sure a punch in the eye when you're not expecting it."

J.Q., who hadn't told her half of it yet, felt what he had said was enough for one night. Allison had her mouth open, but she caught his slightly shaking head and subsided.

Down among the trees, dim squares of lighted windows in the Ramirez house said someone was staying there.

"Joe and Elena came home for the funeral," said J.Q. "I told you about Mrs. Ramirez on the phone last week."

Shirley nodded; yes, too many neighbors getting old, get-

9

ting arthritis, getting cancer, dying of this or that. Shirley remembered the Ramirez kids as children, as teens: solid Joe, fiery Elena. She'd had a crush on Joe in the third grade, even though she'd towered over him. All that black hair and smooth, olive skin. Hector Ramirez had transferred the property to his kids years ago, but their stepmother had gone on living there until her death last week. J.Q. and Shirley had speculated as to whether either of the kids would come home, maybe to live on the place.

They rumbled across the bridge over Little Cawson Creek, then turned a hard right between the old gateposts and under the creaking McClintock Ranch sign, invisible but audible in the darkness above them. To their left a few tumbled stones from the long-ago mill lay among the willows along the drive. The wheels clattered across the cattle guard, then crunched on gravel once more. At the top of the hill the lights were on at the ranch house, and the bunkhouse, and the barns.

"You've lit up the place," she cried.

"We wanted to say welcome home."

"It looks pretty," said Allison.

It did look pretty, the soft glow of lamps and lanterns marking well-loved places. From here she couldn't see the lights back on the Jewell place—the Azoli place. Thank God for small mercies.

"How much hay did we get?" she asked, suddenly voracious to hear about everything she'd missed while she was away.

" 'Bout forty tons."

"We'll need to buy some."

"Not much. And not until spring."

"Forty tons sound like a lot," said Allison. "Looks like a lot, too. The whole barn's full."

"Yeah," agreed J.Q. "But it's a little barn." The size of the barn was cause for recurrent conversation. Shirley's father had planned to build a new hay barn after the dilapidated old pole barn had collapsed, but he'd never gotten around to it, and Shirley kept changing her mind where she wanted it. Anyplace sensible and easy to get to would block a treasured view. Anyplace not sensible would be a pain in the wintertime. The little barn had started life as a stables cum equipment shed, and its roof was too low for the bale stacker to back in. Every time J.Q. hired a man or two to help him stack hay, he spent the next several days making pointed remarks about hay barns.

When they pulled up in front of the house, Dog came to the top of the steps, grinning and wagging. Along the wall behind her, Shirley could see the barn cats, crouching shapes, watching intently, waiting to see who was coming and whether anybody had anything good to eat. From the horse shed came a contented whicker: Zeke, probably. Speaking of horses . . .

"How's Beauregard?" Shirley asked Allison.

"Beautiful." Allison gave her a quick hug. "He's the best thing I've ever had, Shirley. He's the nicest horse."

"So everything's all right." Shirley sighed. "All's well with the world." She heaved one of her bags out of the backseat and started up into the house.

Behind her, Allison gave J.Q. a troubled look.

"Tomorrow'll be time enough," J.Q. whispered, laying a finger on his lips. "Let her get a good night's sleep first."

She woke on Eastern Daylight time with first light barely graying the skies outside her window. The clock, half-hidden behind a mostly eaten bowl of Allison's refrigerator soup, said five-thirty. Contentment said go back to sleep. Homecoming euphoria said no point lying about. She showered, combed her wet hair, put on jeans and a shirt, carried the soup bowl to the kitchen, where she scraped the remnants into a bowl for the cats, then made a pot of coffee, put it on a tray along with milk, sugar, and half a dozen oatmeal cookies, and carried her prebreakfast snack onto the porch.

She leaned on the rail, hearing the lovely liquid fall of a meadowlark's call repeated, the sound evocative of endless childhood summers when time had no end. The sound had always fascinated her: the three tentative flutelike tones, as though searching for the pitch, then the fall of tones, tum-

11

bling over one another like water into a fountain. Whenever as a child she had read fairy tales about nightingales, she had imagined their song being like that of the meadowlark.

From the porch she could look southward and to either side across nine hundred sloping grassy acres dotted with white-belted cows. Behind her lay another seven hundred McClintock acres in folded hills thickly forested with ponderosa and fir and scrub. Mill Creek—sometimes called County Line Creek since its flow marked part of the line between Ridge and Granite counties—glittered by on the right, into and out of the duck pond, down the long grassy hill into stair-stepped beaver ponds, under the road and into larger beaver ponds across the Bostom place and on into the Stengers'. The line of the stream arroyo was softened by low willows and taller cottonwoods, a gentle green that darkened into cattail swamps at the bottom of the hill.

As she watched, a flight of mallards took off from the uppermost beaver pond, circled with wings flapping frantically, then landed again with a great silver splash. Ducks were so urgent about everything. Nothing lazy about ducks. Great blue herons were a different matter, as the two who flew down the creek past her demonstrated, lazing along, huge wings slowly flapping, legs trailing, heads folded back on their shoulders as they croaked at one another. When they landed in the pond, they made no splash at all. The wide wings went up; the long legs inserted themselves into the water; the wings folded softly around attentive gray statues. There were four of them fishing the pond. No. Five.

Shirley counted again. Rare to see five of the big birds feeding in such close company. The ponds down Mill Creek and the ones up on Hi Jewell's place—not Jewell anymore, but Shirley was blocking the new person's name—were big enough to let the valley's heron families spread out. She turned to look east, down the long meadow to the Jewell property line, and beyond it to the ponds along Little Cawson Creek, and was momentarily blinded by the sparkle of tin roofs, like a monstrous junkyard. Damn! She hadn't realized she'd be able to see them from here! She shouldn't be able to see them from here! Something wrong.

Plenty of sparkle from tin, but none from water. She stared, squinting her eyes, then went in to get the field glasses, unable to believe what she was seeing.

J.Q. was in the kitchen. When she went out again, he followed her with his coffee cup and filled it from the pot she'd left sitting on the railing.

"My God," Shirley said. "My blessed God. He's cleaned out the scrub and drained the wetlands. Everything's all brown."

"Ayup," said J.Q., returning into the laconic New Englander persona he sometimes affected.

"When did he do that?"

"Right after he killed off all the willows and cottonwoods with herbicide. Which was the same time he used a helicopter to spread herbicide over all the scrub oak on the place."

She turned back to the glasses, examining the landscape with more care. J.Q. was right. All the hills that had been green with scrub were now either scraped raw or brown and dead. She turned back to J.Q., mouth open. "All the scrub? Why?"

"He says he doesn't like it and it gets in the way of his raising cows."

"But, my God, J.Q., that scrub is habitat for most of the wildlife that lives out here! If he wanted plain grasslands, why buy up here in the foothills? He could've had all the grasslands he wanted over near Elizabeth! Or in Wyoming. Or Montana. Cheaper than here, too. He didn't need to come here and destroy hundreds of acres of wildlife habitat."

"Thousands," said J.Q. "I told you he bought part of the Stengers' place, too. It wasn't all scrub, but when you kill the cover, you mostly eliminate the grazing, too. At least so far as deer and elk are concerned. To say nothing about bears."

"And he's killed everything on it but grass?"

J.Q. sighed. "Well, I can't say whether everything's dead, but I'd venture to say when he's through there won't be a wildflower left on the place, and I doubt if there's a bird there now. I know for sure there's fewer snakes than there used to be, because I saw him and a hired man beating a bull snake to death out at their gate the other day.''

''What's he going to do with that dead scrub?''

''Some of it he bulldozes. For the rest, he's got a machine. Something out of science fiction. Great enormous thing with multiple wheels and jaws. It crawls along and chews the scrub to pieces. When it passes, nothing's left but chewed-up ground and kindling chunks. 'Course, the scrub comes up again, but then he flies a helicopter over and sprays herbicide.''

Shirley sat down with a thump. ''What does he think's going to grow on the tops of those rocky hills?''

J.Q. shrugged. ''Grass, no doubt. And if it doesn't, he'll import topsoil until it does. The man's made of money. Some say he was with the mob or the mafia or whatever you call it back East, and this whole thing's some kind of money-laundering scheme, or he's setting up a guest ranch for wanted men and cutting all the brush so nobody can sneak up on him. Personally, I think his daddy died and left him a lot of money; he's seen too many John Wayne movies, and he thinks he's bein' macho.''

''Is he married?'' She lifted the glasses to her eyes again and began to scan the eastern fence line. Everything J.Q. said was true. The new neighbor had raked a channel down through the wetlands and riprapped it with stone. The stream trickled down this channel like a sewer through a junkyard, not a shred of green beside it. Everything else was brown and chewed except for the meadows.

''He's got a woman he says is his wife, if that's what you mean. She doesn't say much.''

''What did you say his name was?''

''Azoli,'' J.Q. said. ''Eleazar Azoli. Around here, me and a few of the boys call him El Assholy.''

The best Shirley could manage was a twitch of the lips. She was as angry as she could ever remember being, but the anger was so mixed with grief, it was hard to know what to say. The Jewell place had been a delight to the eyes, colorful in all seasons, home for a varied population of birds and beasts and critters, long owned by a family who, like the McClintocks, had cared intensely about the land. To see it raped and riven in this way was like seeing someone you loved killed before your eyes. "We'd better check our fence," she said wearily. "Dad always told me it didn't matter what the poet said, bad neighbors make good fences."

"The bad neighbors already did that. Assholy put in new fence all the way from Old Mill Road up the side of Ramirez's place, where the Ramirez land goes around the old gravel pit. When I saw them doing that, I hired a man and went out and checked our fence that runs from Ramirez's up into the forest, put in a dozen new posts, mended some wire, and stretched it tight. Since I'd already heard what kind of guy he is, I closed up the gate you and the Jewells always used to get back and forth on horseback. Figured we didn't need any source of disagreement."

Shirley put the glasses back to her eyes, following the line of Little Cawson Creek in its southwesterly flow, unable to stifle an exclamation. "He's killed all the willows and cottonwoods down the creek on our place and the Ramirez place!"

"Herbicide got in the water. The trees may come back, but the way I hear it, Joe 'n' Elena are mad enough to sue him from here to Wednesday."

"Joe's back, then?"

"Came back right after you left. Elena, too, I hear."

"Joe doesn't have lawsuit kind of money."

"True. But Elena's mad, and you know her when she's mad."

"What happened?"

"Oh, Joe saw Assholy out riding around on his horse—guy sits a horse like a sack of straw—and he yells at him, what's he going to do about all Joe's dead trees. And Assholy yells back they weren't trees, they were just weeds, growing along the creek, and Assholy was recovering pasture, and if Joe doesn't like it Joe knows what he can damn well do. Of course, as soon as he said 'recovering pasture,' Joe knew Assholy was an easterner, no point talking to him. That's how they talk back in New England and the Midwest, where they've got trees sprouting up overnight. You remember that hundred-year-old willow, the great big one in the middle of Hi Jewell's hay pasture?''

"The one the cows always lie under after the hay's cut?''

"Assholy killed that, too.''

Shirley put the glasses down with a sigh and subsided onto one of the porch chairs. "Have you met this guy, J.Q.?''

"Assholy? Have I met him? Oh, yeah. You might say.''

"What happened?''

"When I saw 'em killing the snake, I kind of thought—well, you know, the guy's new here, maybe he doesn't know. So I went over to tell him about bull snakes, about they keep the rattlers out, about they kill mice, you know. The whole ecology bit.''

"And?''

"And he puts his finger in my chest and his face about three inches from my face, and he says, 'Boy, you're trespassing on my property, and if I catch you here again, there'll be bloodshed.' ''

"Nice man.''

"Oh, every bit of that.''

"Boy, he called you.''

"That's right. Boy.''

"How old is he?''

"Oh, five-six years younger'n we are, maybe. Fiftyish.''

"No respect for his elders.''

"No respect, period.''

"Where'd you say he was from?''

"East Coast somewhere is all I know.''

"Well, it figures he's from some big city or other. Why didn't he stay there?''

"Some of us are wonderin'. My guess would be, having met him and all, they ran him out.''

"They being?''

16

"Anybody who knew him. Including his former wives and children."

"There were wives and children?"

"Bound to be. That kind of man always has wives and children. You'd think those belligerent nasties would be self-limiting, but they're not. Like rams. The ones who butt heads loudest end up with the ewes. He's bound to have at least two ex-wives who hate him. I mean, I hate him, and I hardly know him. I been trying to figure out for a couple weeks where I'm goin' to hide his body when I kill him."

Shirley stared at J.Q. in amazement. His jaw was clenched, and his nostrils flared. She always thought of J.Q. as a rather unflappable creature, but here he was, madder'n a hailed-on goose.

"Think I'll go see Joe," said Shirley.

"Why don't you wait until daytime," J.Q. suggested in a slightly weary voice. "It's barely six yet. We could maybe have some breakfast first."

She nodded at the idea of breakfast but went on. "And I'll drop in on Mrs. Bostom. Is she really bad, J.Q.?"

"Neb said a month, maybe. She wanted to be at home, so he's keeping her there. The nurse from the hospice comes every day. Neb said she's clearheaded, except the pain gets so bad they give her pills that keep her knocked out."

"Cancer is a rotten way to die. Give me a quick final heart attack every time, J.Q. Something surprising, something that's over quick."

He grinned at her ruefully. "Well, your new neighbor's as good as a deadly disease. He's surprising enough, but I don't think he's going to be over in a hurry."

Over breakfast, Allison announced her intention of riding Beauregard over to the Cavendishes to see if they had a larger pair of boots.

"I've been wearing fives," she explained. "They're getting pretty tight. Mrs. Cavendish told me there's a pair maybe one size bigger in her attic, and if I'd come over Monday, today, she'd look and see. She says from here on I'll have to

17

buy my own, because after Stuffy got up to sevens, she quit outgrowing them and began wearing them out.''

"You've been doing pretty well out of the Cavendishes' castoffs,'' Shirley remarked. "If Martha can't find any in her attic, I guess we can stand you to a pair of boots. Maybe not so fancy as J.Q.'s ostrich ones, but then . . .''

"We ought to raise them,'' said Allison, mouth full of pancakes.

"Don't talk with food in your mouth. Raise what?''

Allison swallowed elaborately before answering. "Ostriches. They've got some at that place on the way to the Cavendishes', that exotic animal farm where the road turns. It's new, Shirley. The people just moved in this spring. I used to ride down their road to get to Crebs.''

"Fifty thousand dollars a breeding pair,'' murmured J.Q. "Ostriches.''

"You're kidding?''

"Would I kid you, lady?''

"What do you mean, used to ride there?'' Shirley asked. "Don't you still ride?''

Allison looked at J.Q. and flushed. "Mr. Assho—Azoli has closed the forest trail through there. Now I have to ride out on the road.''

Shirley took a deep breath. "Well, the Jewells only let us local people use that trail as a courtesy. Neighborliness, you might say. And we let them fish in our beaver ponds. Quid pro quo.''

"What's that mean?''

"You scratch my back and I'll scratch yours,'' said J.Q. "She's saying good neighbors are nice to each other, but with Ass—Azoli, maybe you're better off riding in the road.''

"Much better,'' Shirley said in a firm voice.

"Except he says he's going to put in cattle guards at both ends of his property on Old Mill Road, so I won't be able to ride on the road, either.'' Allison fired this over her shoulder as she left, letting the screen door bang behind her.

By way of explanation, J.Q. said, "Since the Jewell place was north of Old Mill Road and the Stenger place was south and now Azoli owns both, he figures he has the right to put cattle guards at the east and west ends and let his cattle cross between through the neck there.''

"I believe he's mistaken," Shirley said, shaking her head. "I seem to recall that a road constantly used by horses can't be made impassable to horses. I'll talk to Numa Ehrlich and see what legal steps we should take." She looked at the door Allison had gone through. "J.Q., is something wrong with Allison?''

"What do you mean, wrong?''

"Last night . . . I thought I detected . . . I don't know. A kind of carefulness in the way she was talking. As though we weren't close. As though . . .''

"Maybe it's just your being gone for a while. A month can seem forever to a kid.''

"You haven't noticed anything?''

"Well, we've both been a bit upset, but beyond that, can't say I have, no.''

She heaved a sigh. "It's probably nothing. Well, let's see. I want to look around the place, then go see Joe and Mrs. Bostom this morning.''

"You go ahead," said J.Q. "I'll straighten up in here before I go pick up those new gate latches.''

After wandering around the ranch for a while, Shirley got into the Wagoneer and drove to the foot of the driveway, where she paused, trying to decide whether to go straight ahead to the Bostoms or left to the Ramirez place. Curiosity won. She'd stop at the Bostoms after she talked to Joe.

The Ramirez place started just east of the McClintock driveway, extending a mile to the east along Old Mill Road and ending in a ten-acre chunk around the old gravel pit. Little Cawson Creek ran north of those ten acres before entering the Ramirez land, where it made a diagonal gully southwest and ran under Old Mill Road and into the Bostom beaver ponds. There it joined Mill Creek, and from that point on the confluence was called Big Cawson Creek.

Just east of the bridge across Little Cawson, the Ramirez driveway opened across a cattle guard to run a few hundred yards between rail-fenced pastures before approaching the house through a grove of towering firs.

Shirley had always liked the Ramirez house. Though the climate here in the Colorado foothills wasn't right for adobe, Joe's father had achieved a similar effect with earth-colored walls and a red tile roof, which, though it had cost him a mint to put on, had saved him every dime several times over in fire insurance costs. Shirley remembered her father talking to Joe's father about it more than forty years ago. Joe's father had said he would have to clear the trees around the house or put on a tile roof. Shirley's father had said don't be a damn fool, clear the trees, but Ramirez hadn't cleared them. They stood about the place still, somber and dark and cool-feeling, even in the heat of the day. The air was thick with their scent, and the ground beneath them was littered with needles and small, papery cones.

The place seemed deserted. No dog. No cattle in the fields. No horses, either, though the Ramirezes had always had horses when Joe and Elena had lived at home. Smoke rose from the chimney, however, and a car was parked beside the chicken house.

Shirley parked the Wagoneer, got out slowly, and moved around a little, waiting for someone to notice she was there. This failing, she climbed the steps to the porch and knocked on the door. She could hear the knock echoing inside, as though the house were empty. The door opened suddenly, surprisingly, leaving her with her hand still raised.

"Elena?" she said doubtfully. "Is that you?"

Joe was Shirley's age; Elena was five years younger. The woman staring at Shirley looked about seventy, haggard-faced, pouch-eyed, dry-lipped.

"Shirley McClintock?" she said in a rasping voice. "Well, who else would be your size! Shirley! I thought you were out of town."

"I was. I'm back. I thought you were in . . . where? Baltimore, was it?"

"I was. I mean, I am. But I wasn't going to let Joe come

out here and do everything himself, then blame me for it the way he usually does. You remember Take Over Joe.''

"He got that nickname later, I think. We called him Joey." Shirley flushed. Joe had been the do-something-and-think-about-it-later type, but Shirley had called him something kinder when she was ten or eleven. Though secretly.

"Come on in." Elena stood back and beckoned. "Place looks like hell. I look like hell. I've had the flu. I got out of bed to come back for the funeral. The place has had the terminal neglects, I guess. We kept sending Mama money to get things done, cash, because we knew how she was about banks and checks, and when we got here we found every dime we ever sent her, all neatly sorted out in a box in her dresser drawer. She never spent a nickel of it. Lived on pasture rental, I guess, still charging what people charged twenty years ago. Guy that owned the cattle took 'em out Saturday when Joe told him we were tripling the rent. So, let him go cheat the taxpayers by renting BLM land for nothing.''

"I used to see your mama out here, feeding the chickens,'' said Shirley. "She'd invite me in for coffee. Place did look a little down at the mouth, you know, the way it will. J.Q. came over a time or two and fixed something that really needed doing." Like the porch roof. Like the chimney looking to fall down. "You coming back to stay?''

"Me? No. I've got a job I've got to get back to. I've been working ever since the kids grew up and my husband died. You knew 'Fredo died?''

"Your mama told me. . . .''

"Alfredo had been sick a long time; it wasn't a surprise. Well, I've been working twenty years now, building a property management business. Successful, I think you'd say. Surprised hell out of me even though it's just being a housewife on a bigger scale.''

"That's great, Elena. It sounds like you enjoy it.''

"I do most of the time. And when that doesn't keep me busy, I've got volunteer work with LALA to do. 'Fredo got

21

me started in that, and I went on as sort of a memorial to him.''

"Lala?'' Shirley asked, thinking she'd misheard.

"LALA, yes. Latin American Liberation Alliance. Anyhow, I took a vacation from that and business both so I'd be here with Joe to split the place up. At first I thought maybe that guy bought the Jewell place would buy my share of this one, but after what happened with all the trees, I'm not sure either one of us would sell to the bastard.''

Shirley swallowed deeply. "What's your share, Elena?''

"Half. We don't know which half yet. Papa left it to both of us, share and share alike. As long as Mama was alive, we didn't want to split it up. Heck, with our own mother dying when we were so young, Mama was all we ever had. So we've talked some about keeping part of it as kind of a retirement home. Ten years from now we might want it for that. Maybe just the forty acres the house sits on.''

Shirley shook her head. "I'd hate to have Mr. Azoli any closer as a neighbor than he is right now.''

"Well, Shirley, we'd like to keep the place, but . . .''

"I didn't mean that. I just meant, talk to me before you offer it to him. To anybody.''

"You interested in buying, McClintock?'' The voice came from the darkened doorway, not a familiar voice, though the face was familiar enough. Still round, smooth, olive-skinned. He had a mustache now, but the hair was still as dark and thick as she remembered. He was buttoning a flannel shirt and grinning at her.

"Joe! J.Q. said you were home.''

He lumbered across the room and gave her a bear hug, his skin still damp and warm from the shower and smelling of soap. He held her off at arm's length, looking up at her still. He'd gotten thicker but no taller. "You interested in this place?''

"Interested in keeping our new neighbor from destroying anything more. If you're going to sell it.''

Joe's face suffused with an angry red.

"Papa would have a fit,'' said Elena. "The way he loved

22

that creek and all the little animals. We used to sit out there evenings, just watching to see what would come along. Might be raccoons, skunks, maybe a fox. Ermine in the winter.''

"You're not going to let him get away with it?" Shirley asked.

Joe glared angrily, shook his head, didn't answer.

"Are you, Joe? Elena?"

Joe made a gesture, as though readying to hit someone. "I'll tell you what he said to me when I made a formal call to ask about all those dead trees, Shirley. First off, he called me buster. 'Buster,' he said, 'I've been in a lot of fights in my life, and I've won 'em all.' Went on to tell me he had more money than the people he fought with. He said he always makes sure he has more money than the people he fights with. He says I can sue him, but he'll make sure it takes years for it to go anywhere, and meantime I'll have to pay legal costs, which he'll make sure are as high as possible. He says I can't afford to fight him, so I'd better give up now.''

Shirley's mouth dropped open. "He said that? Right out and said it?"

"Right out and said it. He laughed when he said it. I said that was a real fine American attitude, and he said the Pledge of Allegiance ought to be changed from 'liberty and justice for all' to 'lawsuits and lawyers for all,' because the law hasn't anything to do with justice anymore. He says he can buy all the law he needs and only fools think there's any such thing as liberty or justice.''

"He said it was all a game, and the guy with the most money always wins," Elena said in an angry voice. "And he's for sure got more than Joe or I do. We've got our salaries, some savings, our homes, that's all. This land was all Papa had. Joe and I've been paying the taxes while Mama lived here. . . .''

"I can't outbid him." Shirley sighed. "But if you want a fair price . . .''

"We'll see," Joe said wearily, shaking his head. "Elena and me haven't even had a chance to talk yet. We just got here three days ago. Funeral was Friday.''

"I didn't know until after. I could have come home sooner. . . ."

"Nah. Mama didn't even like funerals. She didn't like fuss."

"I'm so sorry about all this," Shirley said. "Damn, Joe, Elena, you'd think we could have something happier to talk about after forty years than this stuff."

Elena shrugged. "Hey, that's what happens. Listen, Shirley, I'm still so tired and half-sick, I'm seeing double. I need a day in bed. How about you and J.Q. come over tomorrow night, Tuesday, okay? We'll have some barbecue, talk about old times."

"I'd like that, but make it at my place. No point you cooking for company when you've been feeling rotten. We've got a freezer full of beef; time we used some of it. I'll get out of your hair. You look like you could use some chicken soup and a nap."

She went back onto the porch, Joe following her closely.

"Shirley, you . . ." His voice was lost in a larger noise.

She shook her head at him, "What, Joe?" There was a screaming in the air, like a jet plane, not far off. Directionless. Irritating.

He came closer, spoke into her ear. "It's that machine of Assholy's. Isn't that what J.Q. calls him?" He laughed. "He starts it up every morning, usually earlier than this. And he goes to sunset. Monday through Sunday."

"His scrub-clearing machine? My God, Joe, don't tell me that goes on seven days a week."

"Seven days a week. Every daylit hour. Either there's only one machine available and he can't speed up the job or he wants it to go on until it drives people crazy. I sat down one day and figured it'll take him two more years at the rate he's goin'. I think it's his way of driving us out, Shirley. I really do!"

"There oughta be a law!"

"There is. Decibel level can't exceed a certain level, and he doesn't exceed it, except now and then, about half the time, when the wind's in the right direction. No law against going night and day, though. Whoever'd think you'd need a law like that? Most people would care something about their neighbors, right? No law against driving your neighbors up the wall. I think he kind of likes it.''

"My God,'' she said again, inadequately.

He leaned closer. "I asked if you knew a good lawyer in town.''

"Pretty good, why?''

"I'd like to . . . I'd like to just talk to somebody. Find out how much of what that bastard said is true. Makes me kind of mad, you know. I was brought up thinking fair was fair, and the law was there to make sure fair was fair.''

"Liberty and justice for all?'' she quoted softly.

"Yeah, damn. Lately . . . lately, I've gotten real cynical about the law. And you ought to hear Elena. She's into this Hispanic thing up to her hips. Bilingual education. Talks about *our* culture all the time. Hell, my culture was right here, like yours. Lately it's like she's more Mexican than the Mexicans, more Puerto Rican than the Puerto Ricans.''

"Well, she told me her husband was into that. I can understand her involvement.''

" 'Fredo was always a militant, very macho about it. More than she was while he was alive, but then, it's like when he died, she had to carry on for him. Well. Anyhow, you got anybody?''

Shirley fished her wallet out of her pocket, burrowed into a zipped pocket, and abstracted a battered card. "Here,'' she said. "Numa Ehrlich. If he doesn't know, he'll tell you who does. We'll talk about it tomorrow.''

"Thanks, Shirley. Good to see you. You haven't changed at all.''

"My hair was not gray when I was eleven or when I was sixteen, Joe Ramirez. I was sort of a brunette.''

"When you were eleven, you were a foot taller'n me and you punched Orville Climpson out when he beat up on me because he said I was a spick. Or was it a dirty Mex?''

She stood there, mouth open once more, remembering. "I did,'' she said at last. "I really did. Bloodied his face for

25

him. Poor Orville. He was probably repeating whatever non-sense he heard at home. What happened to him? Died a long time ago, didn't he? Alcohol, was it?''

Joe shook his head. ''Way I heard the story, Orville was down at the Wild Horse Bar in Columbine and he called some stranger a spick or a greaser or a dumb Indian, and the guy had a gun in his car, so Orville's language got fatally censored. The guy got away. They never caught him, either.''

She nodded thoughtfully. ''Orville used to beat up on people all the time, didn't he? He usually won his fights because he was meaner than the people he picked on. Just like our new . . . well, I guess I won't call him a neighbor.''

Joe grinned ruefully at her as he turned to go back into the house. ''Orville didn't win the last one, Shirley. Guys like that never win the last one.''

Trouble was, the last one never came soon enough for guys like that, Shirley reflected as she drove back down Old Mill Road and turned left into the Bostom place. It wasn't a ranch, had never been worked as a ranch in Shirley's memory as it wasn't big enough to produce a significant crop of anything. The Bostoms had had horses from time to time and maybe a steer for beef and a few chickens, but mostly they'd lived there because they loved the place. Their land was longer than Ramirez's east and west, but it was much narrower north to south, sloping up in a narrow belt from the beaver ponds at the west end to the level top of pine-crowded Indian Bluff at the eastern end. Below the confluence of the two creeks even Bostom's willows were brown, though they looked as though they might recover. The house showed briefly through the foliage, vanished behind a thicker clump, then reappeared, a fairy-tale house, a low brown lost-in-the-woods house, like Hansel and Gretel's. When she came up beside the steps, Neb was standing on the porch, head cocked, waiting to see who had come.

''Good morning, Neb,'' she called as she got out of the car. He shook his head, pointing toward the origin of the screaming sound to indicate he couldn't hear as he stumped down the steps, bent a little but unbowed.

He leaned close enough to come within inches of her ear. "Shirley, girl, we've missed seeing you. Come on in. He must be working up on the top of a hill, the way the sound travels. You can't hear yourself think out here."

They went across the wide porch and into the house, where Shirley put her cheek against Neb's and hugged him. "Neb, I've been gone. And before that you and Oriana were in Florida."

"And before that we were in Arizona," he concluded for her. "Seeing the kids. They said they'd come here, but Ory wanted to go to them. Wanted to see how they lived, she said. See the grandkids and great-grandkids, too. We did. Five grandchildren and nine great-grands. All the grandkids are married but Marilyn's youngest girl." He shut the door and drew her into the living room. Inside, the air was already close, but it was quiet. The sound of the machine came as a distant drone rather than as a shriek. "Can't hear myself think with that thing," he repeated. "You remember our son Mike, don't you?"

"I remember Mike," Shirley said. "He was older than I, but he used to wave at me when he rode by. I remember seeing his picture in the paper when he got on the U.S. Olympic shooting team. But your daughter Marilyn had already left Columbine by the time I got old enough to notice. When did you get back?"

"Well, actually, we got back a little bit before you left, but Ori asked me not to tell anybody. She was real tired. Used up about the last strength she had, but she wanted to make the trip. After that, she just wanted to settle in, you know." He looked through the window, as though there were something out there he wanted to see, tears gathering in his eyes.

"I came to see both of you," Shirley said. "If now's a good time."

"Pretty good. The hospice nurse is with her right now, getting her all cleaned up. She'll have her medicine, then

27

she'll have some good time before she falls asleep. She spends most of the time asleep, except for a little while mid-morning and in the evening.''

He turned and started toward the back of the house. ''You come into the kitchen and have coffee. As soon as the nurse is finished, we'll go back and see her.''

The room Neb called the kitchen was actually a family room cum study cum trophy room stretching across the entire back of the house. Shirley saw it as unchanged from years ago, when she had come here with her parents. The oak and leather furniture was the same. The wagon-wheel chandelier was the same, and the Mexican rugs. The north end of the room held a huge fireplace made of stones Neb and Oriana had collected on their travels, every chunk with its own story. Bookshelves packed full of books on travel and western history and Indian tribes took up the rest of the wall and extended down the adjacent wall under the windows. The paneled space over the long windows showed off the mounted heads of a dozen or so pronghorns, testimony to a much younger Neb's prowess in the Wyoming one-shot antelope hunt.

She turned from her perusal of the heads to find Neb at the stove, fiddling with the old granite pot and a couple of mugs. ''You still take milk and sugar?'' he asked. ''Never did learn to drink coffee like a grown-up, did you?''

''Never did. I remember you and Dad always used to say that.'' She remembered the two of them sitting there for hours, swapping stories while she browsed through the bookshelves, conscious of being seen and not heard. Now she had somewhat the same feeling as she sat at the table with her father's friend, the two of them silently sipping, listening to sounds in the house, barely heard over the muted drone of the scrub cutter to the north.

A woman dressed in slacks and a sweater under a lab coat came quietly into the room, poured a cup for herself, and offered her hand to Shirley.

''Nell Fanger. I'm Mrs. Bostom's nurse.''

"Shirley McClintock. I live across Old Mill Road. The Bostoms have been friends of my folks for a long time."

"Sorry," said Neb, coming to himself. "I should have made introductions, shouldn't I? How is she, Nell?"

"Holding her own, Mr. Bostom. She's up to visitors for a while now."

Neb stood up and beckoned to Shirley. "Let's go see her, then."

They went down the hall and into a room Shirley remembered as a parlor, now a sickroom with a hospital bed set near the closed window and a nearby door half-opened into the downstairs bath. Shirley started to gasp, caught herself, managed to say in a normal voice, "Oriana, it's so good to see you." It wasn't good at all. She was stretched skin and knobby bones, only her eyes looking like the woman Shirley had known.

Neb sat beside the bed and held her hand. Shirley talked of inconsequential things, staying away from the subject of the new landowner at the top of the hill. Oriana sometimes said a few words, mostly about the place.

"Beavers building a new pond down below, Neb says."

"That's right." Neb looked out the window, as though he could see the pond from where he sat. "Last year's kids, maybe, setting up housekeeping."

Long silence.

"Remember springtimes here, the meadowlarks. Remember the meadowlarks, Neb? Oh, didn't I love to hear those meadowlarks."

"Yes, you did, Ori. We both did."

"Hummingbird feeder's right outside the window, where I can watch them." The sick woman turned her head in that direction. The feeder hung there, close to the glass, at the moment unoccupied. "They make such a funny sound, hummers."

Neb got up and went to the window. "Little fella's perched out there on that bare twig at the top of that aspen, right by the creek. See him, Shirley?" He pointed.

Shirley looked, but the tree was a good hundred feet away,

29

and she didn't see the hummer until he took off, a whir of wings and a flash of iridescent red.

"He likes to sit out there on that top twig. Keep an eye on things," Oriana said, her eyes closing. "Mexicans call them *chuparosas*. It means 'flower licker.' That's so funny."

Neb took her hand.

"Like to hear the meadowlarks, Neb. Wish I could."

"I know, honey."

After a time she slept, seeming scarcely to breathe. Neb rose and led Shirley back to the kitchen.

"She's not in any pain," he said. "Had one doctor; man was an idiot. Said he didn't want to give her too much pain-killer, she might get addicted. Asked him how long he thought the addiction might last since she's not going to last more than a few weeks. Stuttered around. I fired him, got another doctor, one the hospice recommended. Idiot."

"They teach them medicine at school, Neb. Not good sense. Some of them never get good sense."

"Too damn little good sense around these days."

She agreed with him.

"Wish that man'd finish up ripping and wrecking," said Neb. "Asked him maybe couldn't he cut down on it, in the early morning especially. Told him about Oriana. He said take her to a hospital if she's that sick but don't bother him with my personal problems."

Shirley swallowed. "Not a nice man, Neb."

He mused, "Man's got a real attitude. Kind of like the words of the old song, you know. It's my misfortune and none of his own."

"Don't think about him."

"I don't. Unless he brings himself forcibly to my attention."

They walked out to Shirley's car.

"Mind if I use your back road over the bluff, Neb?"

"Gate's got a lock on it at the other end. Combination lock. Combination's 168; that's how many years Oriana and I have lived out here between us. She's eighty-three, and I'm eighty-five. Last few years, every birthday we'd change the combination on that lock."

"I didn't know she was raised out here, Neb. I knew you were."

"Oh, sure, Oriana was a sort-of Stenger, a half sister. We was neighbors."

"I never knew that."

"Your daddy never mentioned it?"

"Never did."

"He was sweet on her, you know." Neb laughed, his eyes squeezed shut, tears oozing out. "He was pretty mad when she picked me."

"I never knew that, either. To hear him tell it, my mother was his first love."

"Well, she was his first real love, because he never got anywhere with Oriana." He looked blindly through the browned willows, seeing some other place, some other time. "The two of us were for each other from the first," he said. "Never was anybody else. Never could be."

He turned to go back into the house, waving at her as she went. She started the Wagoneer, turned it, and went down the back road, around behind the house, winding gently through a narrow meadow, then up onto the scrub-fringed sides of Indian Bluff. It was only a jeep trail, half a day's work for a smallish dozer, a road making it possible for Neb and Oriana to get up here for picnics without Oriana having to climb. Neb had told her that when? Years ago. Nothing up here much but rocks and a good view, which was what Shirley had in mind.

At the top, she parked and got out to examine the Azoli holdings. Below her to the northeast, across Old Mill Road, were the ranked metal buildings with their bright metal roofs. Concrete and metal everywhere. Metal cow yards, metal cow sheds, silos, hay barns, equipment barns, metal alleys leading off here and there in geometrical precision. Everything neat and mechanical looking. Evidently the gravel of the roads and drives had been sprayed with permanent defoliant, for not a blade of grass showed except behind fences, where it belonged. No brown-eyed Susans along the fences. No piled heaps of wild autumn clematis on the fences, no ropes of Virginia creeper.

And cows. Big, long-legged fancy cows, bred for long-grass country and about as practical here in the hilly West as tits on a boar. Shirley got out the glasses and took a good look at the cows. Branded. Not just one brand but three. One on either side and some kind of code number on the neck. Hot iron branded. Back in open range days there was a reason for branding, but there was no excuse for it when you were running cattle behind fences. It decreased the value of the hide and hurt the animal. Unless the owner enjoyed hurting the animals. Shirley had known a few who did enjoy it. Real macho, tying up an animal and burning it with a red-hot iron, listening to it bawl in pain. Real macho.

Four hundred yards away, across the old gravel pit, hidden among its cottonwoods, her own fence stretched northward like a ruled line, upward along copses of scrub and intermittent meadows into the dark fur of the national forest. Her eyes were caught by the glimmer of metallic red down in the cottonwood grove. She scanned with the glasses, seeing a huge cottonwood stump and the browned leafiness of surrounding trees and, through the branches, the hindquarter of a red car. Somebody was parked in the gravel pit, down at the end of the paired ruts along the west side of Azoli's fence line. Nobody had taken any gravel out of there for years, though Shirley could remember her father buying a few yards from Hector whenever he wanted to mix concrete or mudproof the driveway. Mostly the road was kept open by teenagers, parking there at night on personal business. Often on Saturday nights there'd be one or two cars down there, lights off, silent, as J.Q. said, except for the heavy breathing. Who would be parked there in the daytime? Even though the grove was far enough from the creek that it had escaped defoliation, Monday morning seemed a little early in the week for parked-car passion.

Of course, Shirley reminded herself, passion was not possessed solely by the young. It could be somebody older, somebody fortyish, say, who'd remembered the place from former times. Some local ranch wife getting it off while she was supposed to be in town shopping.

Or maybe someone merely looking the Martinez place over with an idea of buying it. . . .

Shaking her head, she drove down the east side of the bluff to the road, opened the gate, shut and locked it behind her, and took herself home. She had found out a lot of what she wanted to know, seen a good deal of what she had come to see. She hadn't much liked any of it.

2

After supper Monday evening, J.Q. followed his usual habit of retreating behind the western edition of the *Wall Street Journal*. Allison usurped the phone for an interminable adolescent conversation. Shirley fidgeted.

After about half an hour of seeing her get up and down, up and down, J.Q. put the paper down and remarked, "You feeling like a caged bear? You got a sore paw?"

She came to a halt, for the first time conscious of the mindless movement she'd been going through.

"Place doesn't feel right," she muttered.

He didn't answer. He didn't go back to the paper, either. Instead he filled his pipe and sat back with the bit clenched between his jaws, making no effort to light it.

"You can smoke it if you want to, J.Q."

"Nope. Smoke outside. Windows are all shut, and I'd smoke the place up."

"Open a window."

"Can't. Noise would drive you crazy."

"Well, if you want something to bite on . . ."

"I do. Been wanting something to bite on for about a month now."

"The place doesn't feel right to you, either?"

He shook his head slowly. "First thing I noticed was the small birds. Jays don't seem to care, or crows or magpies, but the small birds are gone."

"It's probably something he did."

"Another thing, I haven't seen a deer on the place in weeks."

"It's that noise."

"Partly that." He sat silently sucking at the cold pipe.

She sighed. "I was thinking. . . ."

"Immutability," he interjected. "Got into the habit of it, I guess."

"Exactly," she confirmed, surprised as she always was when he seemed to read her mind. "You get to thinking things will always be the same. You depend on it."

"Like when you were a kid," he said. "Parents, friends, you thought they'd last forever."

She sat down beside him. "Damn it, J.Q. I know people aren't immortal, but the land ought to be!"

"Ought to be ain't is."

This was a favorite saying of his, one Allison had grown to hate, and Shirley found herself riled by it. No, ought to be wasn't the same as fact, but damn it . . .

"I don't suppose there's anything we can do?" he mused.

Shirley shook her head. "Not really, no. Numa says most laws are written with the supposition that people care about other people's opinions. Men are social animals; most of us care what other people think about us. So, when a man decides he doesn't give a damn about other people, he can make them more than a little miserable without really breaking the law. Numa says Assholy can't shut the road to horse traffic, though he can probably put gates along there that it would take a considerable legal battle to get removed. We have no environmental impact regulations in Ridge County except for developers, and of course Assholy isn't developing, he's just clearing land to plant grass. No law against that."

"So?"

"So. That's really the question. I don't know, J.Q. You've been here all month. You've seen it and heard it day after day. I just got here. I don't know yet."

"Let me know when you figure it out." He buried himself behind his paper once more.

Shirley left him at it and went out into the evening. As she stood on the porch, the machine noise dwindled and died. There was still plenty of light. Maybe there'd been a mechanical breakdown. Maybe he'd blown some major part that would require a week to get fixed. And if so, hooray. Lured by a quiet she had always thought of as intrinsic to the place, she started down the hill along the drive. This was a favorite evening stroll, from the outlet of the duck pond along the stream, listening to the sound of it, watching the water change color in the sunset. Where the soil leveled out near the gate, beaver ponds spread themselves, glimmering in shades of pink and rose with long silvery V's widening behind the half dozen beaver that had come out of their lodges to engage in an evening's recreation. Work and play were all one to a beaver. Shirley's tall silent form was familiar to them, and they took no notice of her.

She watched them puttering at their dams, letting the peace sink in, then went on to the gate, through it, and slantingly across the road to lean on the bridge railing and look down at the Bostom ponds, larger and more complicated than those higher up. There were beaver at work there, too, and a duck family moving busily among the reeds, the half-fledged ducklings plowing the still water behind their parents, answering the soft *wuk-wuk-wuk* with a plaintive peeping.

It was only when she turned to go back that she saw the woman standing on the other side of the road.

"Evening," said Shirley.

"Hi," she responded in a breathy voice. She was thin, blond, rather showily made up around her eyes, forty trying to look like thirty and helped only slightly by being an ectomorph to start with.

"Pleasant night," said Shirley. "Now that the damned noise is shut off for a while."

"Oh," the woman replied with an embarrassed little laugh. "I've told him, you know. I've said he ought to be more thoughtful, but he says it'll be over when it's over."

"Sorry." Shirley hadn't considered the possibility this rather forlorn figure was related to the nemesis. "You're . . . who? Mrs . . . Azoli."

"Rima, yes. You must be Mrs. McClintock. Someone told me you were . . . tall."

"Ms. McClintock," she said absentmindedly. "Talking of that noise, has your husband considered putting more men on the job? I imagine I'm not the only neighbor who would really appreciate his getting it done as quickly as possible."

"I don't think . . . well, it's *his* business. You know. I don't try to . . ."

"What are you?" asked Shirley, suddenly full of impatient rage. "New wife, is that it?"

The woman nodded, astonished.

"Previous wife and children back East somewhere?" Shirley persisted, possessed by a spirit of orneriness.

"Annapolis." She bridled. "How did you know?"

"Well, a man that self-centered usually has some woman paying attendance, which implies either a long time wife or a series of 'em. And someone married to him for very long would be either more positive or more matter-of-fact. You know. You might say, 'Oh, him, that's just his way. He's really very nice.' That's the kind of thing an old wife might say. She'd be used to making excuses for him. Or she could say, 'He does what he damned pleases, and I can't help it.' An old wife might be tired of making excuses. A new wife, faced with an old witch of a neighbor on a tear, might find it more difficult to respond."

"Well." Rima laughed uncomfortably. "Yes. I guess. I'm not that used to him yet."

"I've never met the man, but I'm wondering why any sensible woman would marry him."

The woman flushed again. "That's a rude thing to say!"

Shirley sighed. "You're right. Almost every day I resolve to do better, and then first thing I know, there I am, doing it again. Usually, though, I'm only rude to people who are rude to me first. Usually, that is. And I figure anybody that kills off the local habitat the way your family has, you've been rude first."

"It'll be a showplace when he's finished," she said angrily. "It'll make the rest of the places out here look like slums."

"Oh, it'll be all of that. How to destroy an environment in six easy lessons. How to turn unspoiled nature into an industrial park."

"He's not destroying—"

"How the hell would you know? You're a city girl, aren't you? He's a city person. I'd bet the only way you know the out of doors is . . . sailing. Or is it skiing?" That leathery tan could have come only from long exposure to an unrelenting sun reflected off snow or water.

"I sail, yes. But that doesn't mean . . . we bought books. We read up on ranching. We took some courses. . . ."

Shirley shook her head, angry at herself. This woman had no idea what was going on. Obviously she didn't even know what the word *habitat* meant.

"I'm sorry. Look. You're right. I was rude. Your business is your business, and if your husband is making me furious, that's not your fault. You want to walk up the drive with me and have a drink?"

Rima looked at her watch, a quick, sneaky look, as though the time were somehow shameful. "I . . . I can't. He's . . . he's expecting me back. We have to get up at six, and we go to bed at ten, and he's . . . he's expecting me."

Shirley shrugged, her eyes on the woman's arm. "Another time, maybe."

Rima smiled meaninglessly and turned back the way she had come, walking away cat-footed while Shirley stood looking after her. When the woman had looked at her watch, her sleeve had fallen back to disclose a series of horizontal bruises on the lower arm, the kind that might have been made by strong fingers holding hard enough to do damage. Shaking her head, Shirley returned through the gate, pausing by the tumbled stones of the old mill when she caught sight of a great horned owl silhouetted against the sunset on a twisting branch of scrubby pine. The twilight was very quiet, seeming more so than usual after the constant, daylong noise, and when the owl startled and took off with slow, silent beats of its wide wings, Shirley heard what the owl had heard, the sound of a car back on the road.

She strolled back to the gate and looked northward, arriving at the roadside just in time to see Rima Azoli getting into a dark-colored car that had turned into the old gravel pit road along the north Ramirez fence line. The door slammed, and the car moved northward into the trees. The narrow ruts along the fence line were the only way in or out. Shirley stood at the gate patiently and curiously for some time, but neither the car nor the woman came onto the road again.

When she was halfway back up the drive, the machine noise started up again, howling through the dusk. She could see the lights of the monster along the ridgeline to the north, giant headlights plumbing the twilight, monster eyes glaring at the dark. Unaccountably, she shivered. It wasn't anger this time, but an inexplicable grue. "Goose walked on my grave," she told herself. Her father had sometimes said that to explain sudden feelings of apprehension. Now she muttered it to herself, finding no comfort in the familiar words. Somebody's grave, she thought. Somebody's.

"Mrs. Azoli has at least one local friend," she remarked to J.Q. when she got back to the house.

He looked up, interested, and she told him about the car. "Second time today I've seen a car in there, J.Q. Either that one or another one was there this morning. I saw it from Bostom's place when I was up there spying out the lie of the land."

"I wonder who," he mused.

"Her brother," said Allison from the kitchen doorway.

Shirley raised her eyebrows.

"Honestly. That's who she said." Allison came in and sat

down, bringing with her a plate of cookies and a tall glass of milk. "I was riding Beauregard down there the day before you got home, Shirley. Saturday, right? I was headed home because J.Q. was making fried chicken, and last time I only got white meat because that's all that was left, and we were kind of cantering along pretty fast. . . ."

"Cut to the facts," J.Q. suggested.

"And Beau shied at this car, so I turned him around and around, like you do, and she was standing beside it with this guy, and she was crying. So I told her who I was, being very polite, and asked if something was wrong, and she said no, she was just so happy to see her brother because she hadn't seen him in a long time."

"Ah," said Shirley. "But you got the impression she was maybe not . . ."

"Telling the truth?" Allison asked around a mouthful of cookie. "No. No, I think . . ."

"Swallow first, Allison."

Allison swallowed. "I thought he probably was her brother. He wasn't looking at her like . . . like a boyfriend, you know. Not lovey. Not embarrassed. He looked more like . . ." She thought, reaching for it.

"Grieved?" said J.Q.

"No, more sort of annoyed. More like you look when you have to tell me about math for the fifth or sixth time. When your mouth pinches up."

"Impatient," he suggested with a grin.

"Like that. Yeah. Maybe that's what made me think he was her brother. But I don't think she was telling the truth about why she was crying. She wasn't crying happy. Her face was all wet and swollen, like she couldn't stop."

"Wonder where she came from," Shirley mused. "She says there's a wife and family in Annapolis."

"Easterners!" muttered J.Q. "Damn all easterners."

"We know some nice easterners," Shirley argued. "The Willets, they're from New York City."

"They're not from, they're in. Except for brief visits, the proper place for easterners is in the East," he growled. "Now why would Azoli's wife be meeting her brother down in the gravel pit?''

"Because her husband doesn't like him," said Allison in a matter-of-fact voice. "I'll bet that's it. Or the other way around. So they meet down there to talk over whatever it is. And if Ass—Mr. Azoli asks where she's been, she's just been out for a walk.''

Remembering Rima Azoli's quick peek at her watch, it did make sense. "Some family problem, maybe.''

"Maybe she was married before," Allison went on. "Maybe she had children, you know. Or maybe it's money. Like her parents died, but they cut her off in their will. Or . . .''

"And we have no way of knowing," Shirley said firmly. "And no real business speculating. What we ought to be doing is planning a menu for tomorrow night. Joe and Elena are coming to dinner.''

"You said barbecue," said J.Q. "So let's have barbecue. Sweet corn and au gratin potatoes and coleslaw.''

"And cinnamon rolls," said Allison. "With gooey stuff and nuts.''

"Garlic bread's more in keeping," Shirley objected.

"Yeah, but I like gooey rolls better. The kind you make with the frozen orange juice and butter and brown sugar.''

"Your teeth are going to fall out.''

"I brush!" she cried. "I do exactly what I'm supposed to.''

"Sure you do, honey.'' Shirley hugged her. "If you want to help me make rolls, we'll make rolls. Joe will probably like them, too. As I recall, he had quite a sweet tooth.''

They went into the kitchen together and made up a shopping list, after which Allison went off to bed, followed a little time later by J.Q. At ten o'clock the mechanical howling stopped, moving Shirley to open a window and sit beside it, smelling the night air, pretending to read, actually stewing over what was going on. It was like having a family member in the hospital. It was like when her children had died. Grief and hope and terror all tied up together. This time it was a place she was grieving for, her place. She hadn't known the grief could be so intense, hadn't realized how much of her daily contentment was drawn from the fact of this place, this land, this familiar, much-loved place.

She'd been gone only a month. How could so much have happened in that time?

Even after going to bed she lay awake, stewing about it. What if the Ramirezes sold to Azoli? Then she'd have him right at the foot of the hill, alongside. She couldn't bear it! Sometime along about dawn she had a revelation, one of those bolts from the blue that sometimes split a dark sky, and the resultant relief was enough to let her go off to sleep. When J.Q. and Allison rose in the morning, they decided not to awaken her, and she did not open her eyes until they came back from grocery shopping at almost noon.

Joe and Elena arrived around six. Elena still looked tired and drawn, but a fresh hairdo and a day's rest had dropped about fifteen years from her apparent age.

"Feeling better," she admitted. "The worst is over. I've sort of come to grips with it."

"Better than I have," Joe growled.

"You don't have the flu," his sister objected.

"I wasn't talking about the flu," he said. "I was talking about that damned—"

"We're not going to talk about him this evening," Shirley said firmly. "I drove myself crazy all day yesterday. I refuse to get obsessive about him. I'm going to let the shock subside, then make some rational decisions."

"Hear, hear," said J.Q.

"Tonight I want to catch up on you guys," Shirley went on. "J.Q. and Allison will just have to excuse us if we bore them to death with old times."

"I won't be bored," said J.Q. "Any old sweetheart of Shirley's is an old sweetheart of mine."

Allison actually giggled, making Shirley realize that she'd done very little giggling in the past day or two.

"You two were never sweethearts," said Elena, sounding unaccountably offended. "I mean, Shirley, really!"

"Well, J.Q. may be overstating the matter. I was very sweet on Joe, though. Preadolescence."

"Shirley came to my defense when my family got insulted," Joe agreed. "Her being taller didn't matter much then. Every girl in my class was taller than I was. I was the class shrimp."

"When you were a kid, did they really . . . did they call you names?" Allison asked, her voice suddenly avid.

"Why the interest?" Shirley asked, intently.

"Oh it's just, that's what happened to me. Somebody called me a shrimp," she responded casually.

"If it was a boy, it probably means he likes you," said Joe. "If it was a girl, she may be jealous."

Shirley beckoned at them. "I'm not treating you like company. We're eating in the kitchen. You want a beer first, come on back and help me cook."

"We're having sticky buns," offered Allison. "And I made half of them."

Once gathered in the kitchen, they drank beer and ate largely while Joe laughingly told J.Q. and Allison stories about the old times.

"Remember the time you went hunting with us, Shirley, and Elena scared off all the deer?"

"I did not," Elena objected. "I told you, one of them was a pet."

"What do you mean, a pet?" asked Allison.

"One of them had a collar on," said Elena. "It's against the law now, but people used to find orphan fawns and raise them, make pets of them. Then they'd run off with the wild deer, but they were easy game since they had no fear of people. I always thought that was pretty rotten, shooting somebody's pet deer."

"So she fired over their heads and sent the whole bunch of them running for cover." Joe laughed. "Dad was mad. They were the first deer we'd seen in three days."

"Here?" Allison asked.

43

"Oh, no, honey," said Shirley. "No, we were hunting over on the western slope. Over near Carbondale somewhere, as I recall."

"Some rancher that Dad knew," said Joe. "I can't even remember his name, can you, 'Lena?"

She shook her head. "I know we got enough venison for that whole winter. All three of us got deer, and so did Shirley."

"We made mincemeat out of some of it, I remember."

"Pretty good eating is what I remember," said Joe. "Speaking of eating, do you remember Jack Larue, Shirley?"

"The fat boy."

"Right. Whenever he wasn't eating, he was doing something ornery. Remember the time his mom got some fresh red chilies from somebody down in New Mexico and he put them in the heating duct at school? It was like tear gas!"

"I remember when he put the garter snakes in the girls' bathroom." Shirley laughed. "And do you remember . . ."

"They'll be at it all night," J.Q. said to Allison.

"I don't mind," said Allison. "It's giving me some real good ideas."

Two hours later Shirley cast a glance across the wreckage of the meal and was content. Joe, at least, had a very good appetite. He and J.Q. had reduced the platter of beef ribs to a shattered bone pile. Elena had had several beers but had only picked at her food. Allison was still unwinding rolls inch by sticky inch, though more slowly than at the beginning of the meal.

"Help you clean up," Elena murmured without enthusiasm.

"You will not," said Shirley. "You will sit there and convalesce. Joe will clear, J.Q. will rinse, Allison will quit eating rolls and stack the dishwasher. Meanwhile, I will make coffee and serve dessert. A job for everyone and everyone doing it expeditiously, I always say."

"Shoulda been a drill sergeant," mumbled Joe.

44

"Sometimes wish I had been," she said with a sigh. "Who's for pie?"

"What kind?" asked Allison.

"I have lemon chiffon and apple."

"Some of each."

"Oh, to be young again," murmured Elena. "Allison, you don't know how lucky you are."

Allison gave her a thoughtful look but didn't reply, for which restraint Shirley gave her high marks. "You longing after youth, Elena?"

"No, I wasn't thinking of me. I was thinking of the kids I've been working with in the LALA program back home."

"Some kind of youth program?" asked J.Q.

"Educational program. For Hispanic kids."

"Coddling program for druggies and dropouts," said Joe.

"Joe!" Elena exploded.

"Well, it is."

"You don't know what you're talking about. It's a simple bilingual educational program—"

"For dropouts and druggies. I've seen the kids, 'Lena. You took me on a tour, remember? The ones I saw were teenagers, for God's sake, and they spoke adequate English whenever they felt like it."

"They're stigmatized by their accents. And they really don't understand half of what they hear in English."

"If it's anything to do with cars or motorcycles or anything else that goes *vroom*, they understand it." Joe looked at Shirley and threw up his hands. "Elena spends all her free time lobbying Congress for bilingual education money for LALA programs. Which is spent largely influencing people to lobby Congress for more money."

"That's cynical," his sister said.

"Well, more of it goes into consultants and program supervision and public relations than goes into bilingual teachers, that's for sure."

"That's because we never got enough money to do the job right!"

"I've wondered about that," Shirley said as she cut wedges

45

of pie. "Why is it that Hispanics are the only people in the U.S. who raise this big uproar about bilingual education and culture? I mean, Europeans of all kinds came here and learned English. Asians of all kinds came here and learned English. I'm not implying it's easy, God knows, but they did it. Many of them not only learned English but set up schools for their children to maintain the former language and culture. Why . . ." She turned to put a plate of pie in front of Elena and stopped, horrified at the expression of anger on Elena's face.

"Ouch," murmured Joe. "You've stepped on her corn, Shirley."

"What did I say? I'm sorry, 'Lena. I wasn't throwing rocks. I honestly wanted to know."

"Let me tell her," said Joe, patting his sister on her shoulder. "Shirley, you just made the Joe Ramirez argument. That's what I've said to her over and over. And what she says to me is that Hispanics are different. They're like blacks—"

"African Americans," said Allison.

"They're like African Americans and Native Americans," said Joe. "They did not seek the U.S. on their own behalf. They did not come here of their own free will, seeking the American dream. They were already here and were taken over, like Indians or Mexicans living in the Southwest, or they were brought here against their will like blacks, or they were driven here by cruel fate like Central American refugees."

"I'd say a lot of Europeans and Asians were driven by an even crueler fate," said J.Q.

"That's what I say," said Joe. "But Elena sees it differently."

Elena simmered and glared.

"While I was in Washington," Shirley said, "I attended a cocktail party against my better judgment, and there was an argument about school dropouts and differential literacy rates and so forth. I recall that one of those present, a college president who identified himself as a black, remarked that the real difference was that most of what are now called

46

Hispanics or Latinos are culturally mostly American Indians, that is, native peoples from North, Central, or South America. This man said that neither his own people nor the American Indian races had a tradition of literacy. They were not, so he said, people of the book, as were the people of Europe and Asia and the Mediterranean.''

''Are you saying,'' Elena snarled, ''that Latinos and blacks cannot become literate?''

''I'm obviously not making that point since I was quoting an argument made to me at a cocktail party by a well-educated black,'' said Shirley.

''African American,'' corrected Allison.

Shirley shook her head. ''Well, no. He said he objected to that title unless such labels were used on everyone. In which case I am an Anglo-Celt-American; you, Allison, are a Middle European American; Elena and Joe are Central American Americans. I don't know what J.Q. is.''

''Some days I wonder,'' he answered. ''Scandihoovian American, I suppose. I'm three-quarters Swedish-Norwegian.''

Shirley went on. ''The man at the cocktail party was referring to culture. He was pointing out that most of the African and American Indian cultures—North, Central, and South American—are tribal cultures, and none of them have a culture of literacy. He said he thought this resulted in a present-day culture that valued tribalism more than education.''

''That's despicable,'' said Elena.

Shirley shrugged, looked at Joe. ''I'm not saying it's true. I thought it interesting as a point of view, that's all.''

''There were writing systems in Mesoamerica in pre-Columbian times,'' Elena shouted angrily. ''You know that.''

''Wasn't knowledge of writing confined to a priestly class?''

''You don't know that!''

''You're quite right. I don't.'' Shirley poured coffee and passed it around the table. ''And I'm not emotionally invested in the argument, either, Elena, so don't get mad at me. I just thought it was interesting."

Joe said, "Maybe it would do more good to put books in the kids' houses than to put money into bilingual education. It's a thought. Calm down, Elena. We're not fighting with you, we're just discussing."

Elena took a deep breath, obviously struggling to calm herself. "Shirley, look. Back in Maryland there's this big construction company, A to Z Components. They have half a dozen plants that make structural components for buildings: beams and trusses and panels and I don't know what-all. They hire a lot of Spanish-speaking people at rock-bottom wages, and I mean minimum legal wage, okay? They have to hire them because of the nondiscrimination laws. But all the information put out by the company is in English, including the safety information on the equipment. All the safety training is done in English. And the accident rate for Spanish-speaking people in their plants is more than twice what the Anglo accident rate is. You see what I'm saying?"

"Not really," Shirley replied. "The murder rate among male Hispanics is a lot higher than among most other groups, too. Machismo results in violence quite frequently. Violence involves risk taking; risk taking results in accidents. Are you saying they ought to provide the material in Spanish to people who possibly aren't literate in any language? Or they ought to teach their Spanish-speaking workers to read Spanish and then give them a course in safety? Or they ought to change their culture before hiring them?"

"Damn it! I suppose you're one of those bigots who voted for English to be the official language."

"As a matter of fact, yes, I'm one of those people. Not because I object to people speaking any language they like, but because I don't want to happen here what has happened in Spain with the Basques, in Canada with Quebec, or in Ceylon with the Tamils, or in much of Africa, where inter-tribal conflict is endemic, or in the Baltic states, where peoples are distinguished and separated by the languages they speak."

Joe interrupted angrily. "The thing that really gets me about this whole official language thing is that only the Hispanics are howling about it. You don't see Chinese lobbying against it, or Japanese, or Russian Jews. You don't see Thais or Iranians or Sikhs lobbying for bilingual anything. The fact that there's all this Hispanic outcry makes me wonder if there isn't somebody making one hell of a lot of money out of it."

Elena exploded. "You want my people to give up their culture."

Joe shouted, "Damn it Elena. What do you mean, your culture? We grew up right here, right next door. Our culture is the same as Shirley's culture!"

"I just don't see why we have to be the ones to give up our roots!"

Joe started to reply, but Shirley held up both hands and yelled, "Stop. Whoa. We've gone far enough. Elena's been sick, she's not up to taking us both on, Joe, and ganging up isn't fair. She's really getting angry, and I don't want to win the argument that much. Quit. Enough."

Joe shrugged, simmering. "Sorry, little sister."

Elena growled at him. "Just you wait. We're taking A to Z Components to court, and when we get the settlement, we'll have enough money to carry the battle forward."

"We, who?" asked Shirley in an interested tone.

"The LALA attorneys are bringing a class-action suit against the company, representing all Spanish-speaking people injured on the job. Some of them are just pitiful, Shirley. I could tell you . . ."

"And what I say is—" started Joe.

"That the pie is delicious," said Shirley. "Which, seeing as how I didn't make it, I can say."

"Who made it?" asked Elena.

"J.Q. He makes all the pies around here."

"And most of the salads," said Allison. "But Shirley makes the best cookies and the best gravy."

"So now you know what's important," said Shirley, resolving to stay on neutral subjects for the rest of the evening.

Joe and Elena made noises about leaving about ten o'clock.

49

Shirley sat forward. "Before you go, I want to mention something to you. Think it over. If you're interested, we'll talk more. If you're not, fine, no hard feelings."

"What's all this?" Joe asked, giving her a slightly suspicious look.

"Just an idea I had in the middle of the night. I've got two apartment buildings in D.C. that Martin left me. I quite frankly haven't paid enough attention to them during the last few years. Properly managed, they would be a source of good income. Elena is now into property management, and D.C. is close enough to Baltimore to make her management of the properties sensible. I believe the value of those buildings is probably close to the value of your land here. You've got what left? Around a hundred fifty acres if I remember right. Used to be more, but your dad sold a lot off to my dad when you kids moved away. Now, it could be possible we could make a trade that would be mutually beneficial and save us some of the taxes that might cripple us if each of us tries to sell for cash. I'm not sure about that. I haven't talked to a tax man about it, but I'll do so if you're interested."

Joe and his sister exchanged looks.

"Keep the Ramirez place out of Assholy's hands, huh?" said Joe.

"I don't know, Joe. I guess that's the motivation. If he bought your place, he'd be right outside my front door, so to speak. If it would seal the deal, I'd even agree to leave the house there for you to use during your lifetimes. J.Q. and I don't need any more land, but I've always loved your place."

"Shirley, you just love land!"

"Well, I'm fond of land, yes. That is, undeveloped land," she said soberly. "But this place is special. I grew up here, Joe. Every day of every year I spent away from here, I thought about coming home. Maybe not consciously always, but it was never far from my mind. Never in my life did I think of anyplace but this as home."

"Well," he said after a pause and a long, startled look at her. "That gives us something to talk about tomorrow."

"Let me know if you're interested. If so, we'll explore it. It may not work. No hard feelings if it doesn't."

Elena hugged her. "It's an intriguing thought. I forgive you for being a bigot, Shirley."

"That's all right, Elena. I forgive you for being a knee-jerk liberal."

They both laughed. Joe turned and waved as they left the porch and walked toward their car.

"That suggestion was a surprise," J.Q. murmured as he waved at the departing guests.

"Came to me, like I said. In the middle of the night."

"They're not the only ones who need to think about it," he said soberly. "You need to think about it hard."

"Why, J.Q.? You'd be . . . you'd be against it?"

"Just think about it, love. I've had a bad feeling about things in general lately. I know you're feeling you need to circle the wagons and dig in, but . . . well . . . just take it slow and easy."

Wednesday morning brought a phone call: astonishingly, Rima Azoli.

"You two find somewhere else to be," Shirley told J.Q. and Allison. "Our neighbor lady is coming over for coffee."

"Self-invited?" asked J.Q.

"Not exactly. I shot off my mouth at her last night and apologized by inviting her over for a drink. She said she didn't have time. That was before I saw her and the car down at the gravel pit road. Now she says she wants to talk."

"Will wonders never cease?"

"I have a hunch there's an ulterior motive."

Rima arrived in a little brown truck with a neat logo painted on the doors: Clearview Ranch. Which was certainly apposite, Shirley thought, with the amount of clearing that had gone on over there. Rima wore jeans, fancy boots, and an overstyled western shirt. Dressed for the part, Shirley thought, if not convincingly.

When they were seated at the kitchen table with coffee before them, Rima said, "I wanted to . . . I don't know.

51

Apologize maybe. I told El you were tired of the noise. He . . . he won't do anything about it. I wear earplugs when I'm home.'' She examined her fingers, putting them in her lap with a tiny moue of distaste.

"Ruined your manicure?" Shirley asked in a neutral voice.

"Don't have one. El wants me to work with him, you know, putting in fence and things. I keep breaking my nails."

"Hard to look ladylike around a ranch."

"I suppose. He says he picked me out because I was an outdoor type." She laughed, a shrill sound in the quiet of the kitchen. "I thought I was. His idea of an outdoor type is somebody who works twelve hours a day. Up at six, to work at seven, to bed by nine."

"Why?"

"I don't know. It's like he's . . . obsessed. Not that he didn't always work this way. He worked this way when he was running a company, too."

"Company?"

"Back East. He inherited a big piece of his father's company. His father died a year or so back, and afterward, El ran the company. All the heirs wanted their money, though, his ex-wife and his sisters, mostly, so he sold it. That's where the money came from for this place."

Shirley filled her coffee cup. "Doesn't sound like you're having much fun."

"Oh, sometimes we do. I mean, he bought us some horses. And we're learning to ride. We go out every morning for a ride. That's . . . that's one reason I'm here. He doesn't like those no-trespassing signs you've got on your fence. He wants you to take them down."

Shirley looked at her, dumbfounded. "The place is posted against hunting. It's posted all the way around. It has to be if we want to make a legal case against hunters who might come in."

"He says you don't need to on our side. He'll keep people out."

Shirley shook her head. "Tell him I'm sorry, but no, we'll leave the signs up. I like the wild turkeys, though J.Q. says

52

he hasn't heard even one since your . . . your husband started with the machines. I like the deer, too, though the same thing applies. If your husband hadn't cut down all the scrub, he'd hardly notice the signs, and for legal reasons we'll leave them where they are."

Rima stared into her cup. "I said I'd ask you. That's all."

Shirley poured more coffee for herself. "My foster daughter says she met your brother."

Rima shook her head. "Well, actually, it was my former husband," she said. "I just called him my brother. You know."

"Not to cause talk."

"I wouldn't want El to . . . well, think I was sneaking around. My ex is staying in Columbine for a week or so. He . . . he wants custody of our boys. We've been . . . talking about it." Abruptly she broke into tears and began fumbling in her shirt pocket.

Shirley grabbed a handful of tissues from the box on the windowsill and offered them wordlessly.

"Thanks. I'm sorry. I . . . I didn't mean to . . ."

"That's all right. Lots of people have cried in here, including me."

"El told me . . . he said he'd build a place big enough for me and the boys. He said if I married him, I could have the boys with me. But then . . . then when they came out, he put them in the bunkhouse place, and he said they had to work just like he does, twelve hours a day. And Jimmy . . . Jimmy's my youngest, he's very musical. He . . . he wasn't allowed any time for his music at all. And Bates . . . Bates is a little older, and he just wouldn't take it, so they went back to their dad's place in Cambridge."

"Massachusetts?"

"No, no. In Maryland. Cambridge is where we lived. It's right on Chesapeake Bay, you know, and the boys love to sail. We always used to do a lot of sailing. . . ."

Shirley leaned forward, resting her chin on her hands. "How long ago were you divorced?"

"We were separated for what? Three years now, I guess. But we just got divorced a few months ago."

"After . . . your present husband asked you to marry him."

"Well, yes. Yes, I suppose that's why I went ahead and did it. Paul and I had separated over his drinking. But he joined AA, and I'll give him credit, he's really pulled it together. He used to go on these . . . I don't know what you'd call them."

"Benders?" suggested Shirley. "Sprees?"

"More like wars," she replied flatly. "He used to get drunk and go after people he was mad at. He went after his boss one time. He got fired, of course. That's when we broke up. Not that he couldn't get another job. He did, right away. He's too smart not to. Computers. I don't understand computers at all, but he's some kind of genius. Bates is just like him."

"That's an odd name. Bates."

"Well, he's really William Bates Howard, but he hated being called Billy. Bates was my dad's name."

"So how did you meet your . . . current husband?"

"Oh, we knew him, Paul and I. Knew him and his wife, actually. Clemmy. We used to sail together. We all belonged to the same yacht club. El and I, we'd . . . flirted, I guess you'd say. You know how you do. At dinner at the club, when they had the regatta. You know."

Shirley supposed she did know.

"So, when Clemmy divorced him, he found out where I was living, and he came and asked me to marry him."

"How long after he was divorced?"

"Oh, before he even was. And he got his lawyer to do my divorce, too. We got married the day his was final."

"Why did his wife divorce him?"

"He never said. I've never seen her since. I've seen his kids, of course. They've been here, visiting."

"Did they have to stay in the bunkhouse?" Shirley asked.

"No," she murmured. "No. But then, they're grown up. They're adults. And they only stayed overnight." Her eyes

54

were dry. She wadded up the used tissues and looked vaguely around for somewhere to dispose of them.

"Trash basket's under the sink," said Shirley.

"Thanks. I . . . I guess I was storing that up. It's just . . . I haven't any friends here. I've had nobody to talk to about this except Paul, and he's obviously on his own side, not mine."

"How old are your boys?"

"Thirteen and fifteen."

"Well, that's old enough for young people to know pretty well what they like and don't like."

"They don't like El. Of course, they don't know him very well. And if Paul goes to court, then I go in against him, that'll be El's lawyers, and the boys won't like that. . . ."

"Why don't you suggest to your husband that the boys stay with him for now but leave things legally the way they are—that way you'll leave your options open but won't have to get into any kind of battle that might hurt your children. It sounds like to me you're not really sure they should be with you."

"It's just . . . He's so . . . driven. He can't let anyone alone. It has to be all . . . his way. If I say anything, he says he can divorce me just as quick as he married me."

"Dangerous man," said Shirley.

"Yes. But . . . ."

"But you're in love with him."

Rima shrugged, ran her fingers across her hair, carefully not disturbing it. "Sometimes I'm not sure. I always worked while Paul and I were married. I'm used to having money of my own. It's hard to be dependent on him for everything. You'd understand that."

As far as Shirley was concerned, such an arrangement would not have been hard. It would have been impossible. "You could get a job here."

"He doesn't want me to."

When Rima stood at the door, readying herself to leave, she said hesitatingly, "El doesn't like those signs, Shirley."

"You said that."

"He'll probably take them down himself."

"Then I'll go to the sheriff and charge him with theft."

"It won't do any good, Shirley. I'm telling you."

"Tell him you've told me, Rima. I figure that's what you really came for, wasn't it? He sent you. The rest of the stuff wasn't planned, but he sent you to tell me about the signs."

Rima merely stared at her, saying nothing. After a moment she turned and left. Shirley stood where she was until the little brown truck turned onto Old Mill Road and disappeared behind the trees.

"What do you think?" asked J.Q. from behind her.

"I thought you'd gone to town."

"I got sidetracked out in the barn, fixing that goat manger. So, what do you think?"

"I get this mental picture of a man who inherits from his father a large share in a family business. He runs it, maybe for not very long, and then for some reason sells it. Maybe because people compare him to his father, unfavorably. Or maybe because he's running it into the ground, and the other heirs force a sale. So he decides to do something on his own, something his father never attempted. His wife divorces him, but before the divorce is even final he goes and finds another woman to marry. Not because he loves this other woman, but as though to say to his former wife, 'Hell, I don't need you.' Then he tells the new wife the same thing: 'I don't need you. I can divorce you anytime.' And he goes through life saying the same thing to everyone. To his dead father, to the rest of his family, to the world at large, certainly to his neighbors: 'I do what I like. I don't need anybody.' He's driven by something, or maybe he's one of those guys with energy that simply won't quit. His style is confrontation, anger, hostility. He sounds like trouble to me, J.Q."

"I could have told you that last thing. I can even tell you why. He's about five foot three."

"Napoleon complex, huh?"

"Well, I've known more than one."

"So have I, J.Q. God, he'll hate me, just on general principles."

"I'd suggest you keep all your negotiations through some third party."

"Did you hear the bit about the no-trespassing signs."

"I've already put them back up twice, Shirley."

"That bastard."

"He's all of that."

"I'd like to ride out and look at that fence line."

"We could do that now," he said, giving her a pat. "The horses need exercise."

Shirley put on her boots and, after a moment's hesitation, strapped on a holster and took a handgun from the locked cupboard in her bedroom. They rode east from the house, through the edge of the forested land, around the steep slopes that went up into national forest on the north side, then climbed upslope to a promontory that gave them a view of the entire fence line, even where it ran along clumps of scrub. This was the opposite end of the view she had had from the high bluff on Neb Bostom's place. East lay Azoli's land; north was national forest; south was Ramirez's ten acres around the gravel pit. East of the fence the land was torn and chewed, the ground littered with chunks of wood varying from a few inches to a few feet long.

"He sure didn't leave any cover for bird or beast, did he?"

J.Q. shook his head. "He's also 'cleaning up' his forest."

"What do you mean, 'cleaning up'?"

"Cutting down all the stubs."

She didn't reply. No reply was necessary. Dead and bare trees, stubs, were where woodpeckers made their holes, where owls and other raptors nested, to say nothing of the small birds, such as bluebirds, that moved in when the woodpeckers moved out. The presence of naturally occurring stubs was necessary for certain birds to be able to breed. What could one say about Azoli's act? The man was a destructive idiot, and nothing she could say would change that.

Wordlessly, she focused her glasses on the fence and followed it yard by yard from the place where it left the forest down to the Ramirez line. It seemed to be tight all the way to the gravel pit. Beyond that rose the rocky face of Indian Bluff.

"I used to hunt arrowheads up there," Shirley said, pointing. "Mostly because it was called Indian Bluff. I never found any. Never figured out why it was called that, either."

"Local mythology, probably."

She brought the glasses back down, tracking back up the slope. "Our north boundary fence is a foot or two inside the survey line. Dad always put in all our fences that way. He said if you put them right on the line, somebody's going to fuss about what's on their side of the fence, but if they're totally on your own property, nobody can fuss. I notice Assholy's cleared right to the fence, not to his property line."

J.Q. nodded. "I knew that. So the first time I found the signs down, I put them back up with a little note explaining the matter. Second time I found them down, I just put them back with no comment. That was after my run-in with him. He doesn't steal them, just drops them on the ground in the brush. So all you can charge him with is maybe mischief. Maybe vandalism, I don't know." J.Q. got out his pipe and began to stuff it.

"Is that him?" Shirley asked. A man on horseback was coming down the meadow, a weirdly clad figure in a red cowboy shirt. "What in God's name has he got on?"

"Chaps," said J.Q. "And a cowboy hat. He thinks he's ridin' the range."

"He's cut all his scrub, but he's wearing chaps! Well, git along, little dogies!"

"I told you he's read too many Westerns, seen too many John Wayne movies."

They watched as the rider approached the fence, dismounted, removed his hat, wiped his bald skull with a handkerchief, and then walked eastward, giving the impression of stealth.

"What the hell's he doing?"

The distant figure was leaning across the fence near the edge of a gully, peering in the direction of the gravel pit. After a time he turned back the way he had come, stopping at the fence to quite deliberately remove one of Shirley's signs. Without a second thought, Shirley took the handgun from her hip and fired it three times into the air, the shots coinciding with a lull in the machine noise. The distant figure started, stared toward them, finally seemed to see them on the high point, got back onto his horse without haste, raised his right hand with the middle finger extended, then rode away.

"Did you see what I saw?"

"Umm." J.Q. nodded. "You should have let him alone. Then we'd have both been witnesses. As it is, he can take them down later and then say his man did it without his knowledge. He'll send somebody out here early in the morning. Or at night, when we can't see him. He doesn't want a witness necessarily, but he's a very determined man."

"Maybe we should put one across his bow."

"I don't think it would faze him. I don't think anything short of a bullet through his head would faze him."

They looked at one another, then laughed simultaneously, shamefaced. "You were considering it," Shirley said.

"So were you, lady love!"

As they rode up to the house, a truck turned into the driveway from Old Mill Road. Shirley awaited its arrival while J.Q. led the horses back to the pasture gate, where he unsaddled them and turned them loose. He had time to get both saddles off before the truck arrived, for it crept up the drive at a snail's pace, the driver craning his head this way and that, as though to survey the place. Shirley glanced at J.Q. and shrugged. She didn't recognize the vehicle. He turned his hands palm up. He didn't either.

The man who got out was a stranger to them both, a lean, pale, long-necked individual wearing khaki trousers and a safari jacket with multiple pockets. When he removed his hat, he revealed a freckled scalp and a tonsure of reddish tan hair.

Sandy, thought Shirley. When he was in school, they called him Sandy.

"Horace Rodwinger," he said, offering his hand. "You

must be Ms. McClintock." A large and angular Adam's apple yoyoed up and down his stringy throat as he spoke.

"I am," she admitted. "This is John Quentin, Mr. Rodwinger."

J.Q. came forward, his hand out, to have it shaken solemnly.

"Why I'm here," he said in a petulant voice that strove to be portentous, "is the sheriff suggested I come. Botts Tempe. He says he knows you, Ms. McClintock. Very nice man. Very sympathetic. He suggested I talk to you about this dreadful man—" He punched the air toward the east. "—who is driving us all crazy and who has caused me a considerable financial loss as well."

"I'm sorry," said Shirley. "I don't understand your involvement."

"Hide and Feathers," he said, raising his eyebrows.

"The exotic animal farm." J.Q. nodded. "Allison mentioned it, remember?"

"Ostriches!" said Shirley.

"Ostriches now, yes. The ostrich-hide market is virtually unlimited. Wallets, purses, boots—you name it, we can make it out of ostrich hide. Also, we plan to branch out . . . that is, we plan to *if* we can do something about that person!"

"Trouble?" Shirley asked.

"The noise! The dust! The birds panic, they run into fences, they hurt themselves. I picked this place because it was quiet. My Lord, quiet! It would be quieter in the heart of the city. At least there people try to have some regard for one another."

"Mr. Rodwinger, what did you think we could do about it?"

"Sheriff Tempe said you would have a grasp of the problem. You might know what could be done. I thought, perhaps, a petition. . . ."

J.Q. snorted.

"It doesn't seem at all amusing to me," the visitor said in an offended voice.

"I'm just visualizing Ass—Azoli responding to a petition," said J.Q.

"What J.Q. means is that Mr. Azoli would probably use it for toilet paper," Shirley remarked. "Mr. Azoli doesn't seem to care about public opinion. I have no idea what to do about him."

"How long can this go on!"

"I figure two years or more," said J.Q.

"I'll go bankrupt! The birds won't breed. They won't lay. The young ones are getting hurt!"

"Then sue him for damages," said Shirley. "You've got grounds for a civil suit."

Rodwinger took off his hat, mopped his forehead, put the hat back on. "I thought of that. Do you know how long it takes? Two years, three? Maybe longer? I have to suffer the loss first. Then I have to prove it was his fault. This is monstrous!" His voice trembled with emotion, and his face was white with rage.

Shirley shook her head slowly. "Botts had no business sending you to me. I think he was ducking the issue, and I'm going to call him on it. If a petition would make you feel better, everyone within earshot would no doubt sign it, but that's all it'll do, make some of us feel better."

"I thought all of us . . . together . . ."

"Well, you can certainly talk to some others of us. Have you talked to Martha Cavendish? She's your neighbor."

"I've met Mrs. Cavendish, yes."

"Have you talked to the people at Crepmier School, just across the road from you? Also, you should talk to Joe and Elena Ramirez while they're here, and certainly talk to Neb Bostom. Don't bother Mr. Bostom right now, though. His wife is terminally ill, and he doesn't need any more troubles than he's got."

When Rodwinger left, having made note of the names Shirley had given him, she went into the house to call Botts Tempe, J.Q. trailing after with a bemused expression.

"Botts, what's the big idea siccing this guy on me?"

"Now, Shirley . . ."

"Don't now, Shirley me, Botts Tempe."

"Just get your facts straight before you start yelling, is all. I didn't sic him on you! I told him he should consult with the other neighbors out there before he did anything. He asked who the most knowledgeable person was out there, and I told him you were."

"Oh, hey, thanks a bunch, Botts."

"You don't need to be sarcastic. I thought I'd be doing him and you a favor."

"The only favor anybody out here can appreciate is if this Azoli character drops dead!"

"That bad?"

"Well, Botts, between the destruction of habitat and the noise and the pollution, most of us hate him pretty much."

"I don't guess he cares, huh?"

"Which is the most infuriating thing about him."

"Well . . ."

"Well, Botts. Keep this location in your active file. I've got a bad feeling."

Botts groaned. "You're not planning on . . ."

"I'm not planning on anything. Just keep us in mind is all. It's only a matter of time until something nasty happens. This Rodwinger character was so angry, he was shaking."

She found herself shaking as she hung up. Her jaw as clenched. Her neck was tight. She turned to find J.Q. giving her a sympathetic look.

"Kitchen," he suggested. "Breakfast was a long time ago."

They found Allison already busy putting together a fat sandwich.

"Somebody was shooting," she said anxiously. "I didn't know what to do about it."

"Shirley was," muttered J.Q. "A warning shot. Our neighbor was taking down our signs."

"I heard it." Allison took a large mouthful of ham and cheese. "I was thinking if there'd been more than one shot, I should've saddled Beauregard and ridden out."

62

"Having first called the sheriff, I hope," said Shirley. "Not that he would help much."

Allison nodded. "Oh, yeah, I'd call him. He'd have to come clear away the bodies."

Shirley shuddered theatrically. "Are all young people ghouls these days? Don't talk with your mouth full, Allison."

Allison chewed and swallowed. "I'm not a what-you-said. Hey, kids don't write all that stuff on TV. Grown-ups write it."

"And film it, too," agreed J.Q.

"I give up. Let's have lunch," said Shirley. "I think what we need around here is a little routine. Forget this guy. Forget his noise. Do like his wife does, wear earplugs. Go on about our business."

"We can try," J.Q. agreed, slicing ham as he spoke.

Resolutely, they turned to routine, having to think about it. What should they be doing, would they be doing this time of year? Calves to wean, vaccinate, castrate? A little early for that. Calves to register. Yes. Good time to do that. Shirley put a notebook and pen in the saddlebags, put the saddle back on Zeke, and went out to draw pictures of calves. Every Belted Galloway baby had to have a nice white belt going all the way around his or her middle, and Shirley had to send a drawing of it to the Belted Galloway Society. The cows were somewhere in the big northwest pasture, and she found them at last in a wooded draw as far from the eastern fence as they could get.

When she emerged from the forest several hours later, she decided to look at the east fence line once more to see whether any more of her signs had been removed. Zeke moved through the edge of the forest almost silently, ears forward, noticing everything, ears flicking whenever the machine noise rose to a crescendo.

When they came to the fence line, Shirley turned northward and rode up onto the promontory. The glasses she'd used to get a good look at the calves were still around her neck. She followed the fence line, looking it over post by post. There were half a dozen no-trespassing signs on this stretch, and they all seemed to be in place.

She was about to turn away when a flash of red caught her eye. Something in the grasses, at the far end of the fence, near the Ramirez line. Probably nothing. An oilcan somebody had thrown there. She turned Zeke, rode a few yards, then turned back and looked again. It wasn't visible to the naked eye, only through the glasses.

"Oh, hell," she said to herself, turning Zeke to ride down the hill. She couldn't get there from here. Though scrub had been cleared when the fence had been built originally, and though it was cleared intermittently whenever the wire needed substantial repairs, currently the tangled oak pressed against the line in half a dozen places. She would need to wind her way down to the Ramirez fence and into the corner where she'd seen . . . whatever it was. Zeke seemed to enjoy the prospect, tripping his way through the clearings as though he knew where they were going.

Which is more, thought Shirley, than I do. At the bottom of the slope she headed directly south, down a long clearing at the end of which game trails led off in all directions. She used the cottonwoods around the gravel pit as her guidepost, splashing across the meager flow of Little Cawson Creek to arrive finally at the Ramirez fence and turn eastward along it.

She found nothing in the corner where McClintock, Ramirez, and Azoli land came together. Before her, up the slope, was the cluster of tin-roofed buildings. She rode north along her own fence, peering over it at the chewed land beyond. Nothing. Chunks of wood. Brave new leaves poking up from the mutilated ground. Scrub oak didn't give up easily. All this would have to be repeatedly sprayed with defoliant to keep it down.

She came to the edge of a small gully leading eastward into Little Cawson. Zeke lunged down into it and up the other side while she tried to see what was lying at the bottom of the gully past the fence. Something.

Oh, shit! Someone. Red shirt. Sprawled there with his feet

topward the sedge at the bottom of the gully, his head and torso at the top of the bank. The shirt must have been what she'd seen from up above.

She dismounted and dropped the reins, leaving Zeke tied to the ground. He was well trained. He'd stay there. She tried the fence, but J.Q. had done a good job of tightening it. If she tried to go through it, she'd get hung up. There'd been a gate along here, once. The one Allison had used to get to Cavendish's place. J.Q. had taken it down and spliced new wire across the opening. She had pliers in the saddlebags. There were always pliers in the saddlebags.

Stepping across the cut and trailing wires, she went through onto the chewed ground and stalked toward the gully, vaguely aware of voices up the hill. She found the place, dropped down into the gully, and laid her hand on the man's neck. No pulse. Blood all down the front of him. The body still warm against her hand. Of course in this weather it would stay warm. The blind eyes stared up at her. The mouth sagged as though in surprise. No hat or chaps. Was it the same man as this morning? She stood looking at him for a long moment, trying to judge if he was or wasn't the one who'd given her the finger before riding on up the hill.

With the difference in garb, there was no sure way to tell. He'd been too far away. She wiped her brow and turned to go find the nearest phone.

"Stay right there," said a familiar voice.

She looked up, bemused, to see Botts Tempe standing not fifty feet from her, holding a very businesslike .38 pointed in her direction.

"He's dead," she said. "Shot. What're you doing here?"

"Somebody out here heard shots and called the sheriff's office. I happened to be on my way here when the office got me on the radio. I was on my way pursuant to your warning, McClintock."

"Hell, Botts, I didn't shoot him!"

"Please give me that gun, Shirley."

"I said I didn't shoot him."

His face got red. "You're wearing a gun. Cut out the crap and throw it over here."

Shirley unbuckled the gun and threw it over, meantime using every cussword she knew and making up a few new ones. Botts's nostrils widened at this explosion, then narrowed again as he looked at the cylinder and down the barrel.

"It's been fired," he said ominously.

"I fired it in the air this morning when J.Q. and I saw somebody, this guy maybe, taking down one of my signs."

"Could have been then. Could have been just now," he said.

"I did not shoot him! I don't even know for sure who he is."

Botts gestured for her to go ahead of him as he headed up the hill. He did not put away his gun.

"Who he is, is Mr. El-ay-zar Azoli, and right now you're the best candidate I've got for who killed him. You said it yourself, McClintock. You told me it was only a matter of time."

3

Numa Ehrlich, summoned by Shirley's one permitted phone call, arrived at the sheriff's office expeditiously.

"Shirley, Shirley," he moaned gently, shaking his head on its cranelike neck. "What have you done now?"

"I have done absolutely nothing, Numa. I have spotted something awry from a distance and like a good citizen gone to see what it was, which was a damned corpse."

"More or less your usual type of thing." he said matter-of-factly.

She sighed. It was, more or less. She was what J.Q. defined as an excess finder of bodies. Since nature did not spread things evenly about, he said, some people had to be excess finders, and Shirley was one of them. When he was in the mood for peroration, J.Q. could connect this fact to some law of thermodynamics and go on about it at exhaustive length.

"Of course, if you weren't so . . . intrusively investigative . . ." Numa went on.

"You mean if I didn't stick my damned nose in!"

"The sheriff said you had fired your gun."

"I did, this morning. J.Q. was there at the time. I fired it in the air, Numa. This same guy, or somebody else who's mostly bald, came down the hill over on his side of the fence and started to take down one of my signs. I fired in the air, he stopped, looked around, finally saw us, got back on his horse, made what I'd call a rude gesture, and rode up the hill again. J.Q.'s already had to put the signs back up twice. Azoli's wife told me he didn't want them on the fence. Spoiled his view, I guess. He liked to pretend he owned the world!"

"All of which adds up to motive."

"Hell, Numa. I didn't need that for motive. If ever a man needed killing, this one did, but I didn't do it. I'm not in the habit of going around killing people who bother me. I may think about it. I might even talk about it. But if I actually did it, I wouldn't have time for anything else."

Numa's lips twisted, maybe in amusement, more likely in irritation. "Your problem right now is getting out of here on bail. Though they might let you go on personal recognizance. It's not as though you were an itinerant."

"Hardly," she snorted.

"Can you give me any facts that might assist in this effort?"

"Considering where I found him, I'd say he was probably shot with a rifle," she said. "Anyone close enough to hit him with a handgun would have had to stand right out in the open. There was no good cover close by. As Botts knows, I wasn't carrying a rifle. All my rifles are back at the house, locked up in the gun case."

Numa sighed again, managing to look both patient and long-suffering. "I'll speak to Judge Wilton. He knows you. So far as that goes, however, Botts Tempe knows you and he still brought you in."

"I think he figured he had to, Numa. Wouldn't look good if he didn't. He doesn't really think I shot that guy any more than you do. Before you call the judge, though, call J.Q. Tell him what happened. Ask him to go out and get Zeke."

"Zeke?"

"My horse. I was so shocked, so mad, I forgot him! He'll

probably have sense enough to take himself home, but his reins are trailing, and he might get caught up in something. So ask J.Q. if he'll go get him.''

Shirley was familiar with the so-called women's quarters in the basement of the local jail. She had visited Allison's mother there, so she was not surprised at the lack of space or amenities or even at the smell, which was both antiseptic and unpleasantly musty. She was unpleasantly surprised, however, at the shock of pure terror that surged through her when the steel door clanged shut behind her. When Allison's mother had been in this cell, she had behaved like a hysterical child. For the first time, Shirley thought she really understood why.

She was sitting on the bunk with her eyes shut, head in hands, when Botts Tempe opened the door several hours later.

''Got an order to release you on your own recognizance,'' he grunted. ''Your daddy's old pal, Judge Wilton.''

She stood up, trying not to betray the relief she felt, which, she tried to tell herself, was quite out of keeping with the actual threat to herself. ''Hope you don't mind my leaving,'' she said nastily.

''Hell, no. Takes the blame off me. Anybody accuses me of anything, I can say, nosir, I brought her in and that old fool Judge Wilton let her go. Besides, the doctor got the bullet out.''

''And?''

''And it's a rifle load. No question in his mind. Not that you couldn'ta done it and stashed the rifle somewhere.''

''Well, Botts, if you have any such suspicions, I suggest you go on out to my place and check out my rifles. Check out J.Q.'s armament, too, while you're at it!''

''Already did. Sent a deputy to do that while I was bringin' you in. You coulda had an extra one, not saying you did or didn't, but we checked yours and John Quentin's. He's outside waitin' for you, by the way.''

''Thoughtful of you,'' she said, putting on her jacket. ''Lord, I wish Azoli's mother had had an abortion early.''

"That's not a nice thing to say," he replied primly. "That's very near blasphemous, McClintock."

"Well, hell, Botts. You know me."

"I do. I know you for a godless pagan, McClintock, and I pray for your enlightenment all the time."

"Pagan, maybe. Godless pagan, no. You still goin' to that church?"

His lips tightened, and he gave her a look. "Just because a person or two associated with my church turned out to be murderers doesn't mean the whole church is bad. A few rotten apples doesn't necessarily ruin a barrel full."

"That's all right," she said, patting him on the shoulder. "Your prayin' for me can't do any harm. Might even do me some good; who knows?" Besides, she thought, he'd be more likely to keep it up if he thought it bothered her.

J.Q. was outside in the Wagoneer.

"Numa called me," he said. "Told me he'd got you out."

"They may come get me again," she said bleakly. "Only reason they let me go was it looked like a rifle shot and I wasn't carrying a rifle. 'Course, Botts says I could have shot him and ditched the rifle."

"When the deputy came to the house, I told him they were all there."

"Botts says I could have had an extra nobody knew about. Damn it, Azoli had to have been shot long before I found him! I didn't hear a rifle on the way out there."

"Was that machine working?"

"Yes. Oh, sh—Yes. So I probably wouldn't have heard it!"

"I've been wondering how anybody heard it."

"Whoever it was must have been right next to where it was fired."

"Or be the shooter. Botts didn't tell you who called?"

"No." She shook her head thoughtfully, considering whether it made sense that the caller and the shooter were one and the same. "Botts said he was on his way out there when he got a radio message. He didn't even give me a 'him' or 'her.' "

"I'd say our first order of business should be to find out."

"Why do we have to get involved at all?" she asked in a grumpy voice.

He rubbed the back of his neck, making an angry face. "Way I see it, Shirley, you're still under suspicion, even though they let you go. If you were anybody else, you'd still be in jail, you follow me?"

"Yeah. Well, Botts said as much. Called Judge Wilton an old fool."

Since this was somewhat J.Q.'s own opinion about the judge, he didn't comment. "I hate to say it, but this is one time we need to figure out what really happened." Though he tried to sound unconcerned, he couldn't keep the worry out of his voice or off his face. "Shirley, you know Botts Tempe. He's a good man, but nobody could accuse him of having much imagination. When it comes to anything more complicated than a tavern brawl, he makes heavy going of it."

Shirley stared at him, unbelieving. "You're not saying Botts *really* thinks I did it?"

"I don't know what Botts thinks. I'm not sure. The two of you go round and round. He thinks you're a heretic, and you think he's a little soft in the head, but you've been helpful to each other in the past, and maybe he gives you a little credit for that. Nonetheless, he knows better than almost anybody that ordinarily you make a habit of sticking your nose into things like this. So, if this particular time you don't get involved, he's going to wonder why. The first reason that will pop into his mind is that you really did do it, or perhaps that you're closely involved with whoever did. Believe me, that'll occur to Botts. If it doesn't, there are people in and around Columbine who will point it out to him. There are people in town who aren't crazy about you, Shirley. You know that."

"Oh, well, yes, but . . ."

"No 'yes, but' about it. Sheriffs get elected. They work for county commissioners who also get elected. You've rubbed at least two of them the wrong way in the past. You get a bunch of people using you to get publicity for themselves, talking about privilege and fairness and agitating to put you behind bars no matter who you are, it won't matter what Botts thinks."

"Oh, hell," she muttered. "You always tell me to stay out of stuff."

He went on grimly. "I know I do, usually. This isn't usually. Also, there's the simple matter of having a murderer loose. No matter how much that man needed killing, I don't like the thought of somebody running around out here shooting people."

She nodded. She'd had the same thought. One might not mind much when a villain died until one remembered that oneself or one's kinfolk might be the next victim.

"This time you'd better find out anything you can. It might be somebody you're fond of gets shot next."

"I was just thinking that," she muttered.

He drove silently for a while, not wanting to press the matter further but unable to get it out of his mind. "We waited supper for you," he remarked at last. "Meat loaf. Allison made it."

"She's getting to be a pretty good little cook," Shirley said distractedly. "I was so upset, I wasn't even hungry, but that does sound good."

When they turned into the driveway, the sun was setting behind the hills, turning the sky to shaded satin. Shirley opened the car window.

"The machine isn't working."

"I know. Hasn't been since this afternoon. Quit soon after they found the body, I guess."

"Dare we hope . . ." she breathed.

"Depends on who inherits, I suppose."

"Do you suppose she does?"

"Doubt it. Having met the man, I'd say his eldest son, if he's got one."

"Based on what?"

"Ego. Me first. Next to me my son, fruit of my loins, my immortality, my name, etcetera, etcetera."

72

"Funny," she mused as they parked outside the house.

"Funny what?"

"I never met him. I never saw him until he was dead, but I hated him."

He looked through the windshield at the sunset, seeming to be lost in it. After a long moment he said, "Well, that's the way things are in war. You learn to hate your enemy even though you've never laid eyes on him and oftentimes never do, even after he's dead. The connection between what a man is fighting for and the body of his enemy often seems very remote."

"Was this a war?"

"Oh, my, yes, dear old buzzard. Yes, it was. Maybe still is."

Shirley received several commiserating phone calls during the evening. Cousin Beth had heard it on the evening news and went on at length about it. Old Binky down in Columbine had a long story to tell her about a similar situation in his youth. Rather late in the evening, Neb Bostom called.

"Shirley, somebody told me you'd been arrested."

He sounded troubled and rather feeble, so Shirley put on her heartiest voice.

"Oh, no, no, Neb. It's just I was there when they found the body. Sort of a pro forma thing, you know. It was sweet of you to be concerned, but don't give it a thought. How's Oriana?"

He drew a breath. It rasped. She could hear the pain over the phone.

"I . . . we don't think she's going to last much longer, Shirley. A few days. Mike's here. Got here noon today."

"Is your daughter coming?"

"No. Marilyn's had this bad session with allergies, almost wiped her out this year. She wasn't doing that well when we were there. I told her not to try. Patti came with Mike, though. That's Marilyn's youngest, the unmarried one."

"So you'll have someone with you. If there's anything I can do, Neb."

73

"Nothing. No. I just heard that . . . about that. I was worried about you."

"No need. I'm fine. I'll try and get over to see you tomorrow." She hung up, surprised to find tears brimming.

"What's the matter?" Allison asked in a panicky voice. "You're crying."

"It's just . . . They expect Oriana won't live much longer, Allison. She was . . . she was my mother's friend. She and Neb, they're the last ones of my parents' generation. It just seems so sort of final."

"I'm sorry," Allison said, giving Shirley a hug. "I'm really sorry." She stared into Shirley's face with something more than mere sympathy.

"I know you are, honey. And it isn't that I'm grieving over her. She's had a long life, and she's home with people she loves. It's just . . ."

"Intimations of mortality," J.Q. remarked from behind his paper.

"I guess."

"What does that mean?" Allison asked.

"It means when people die, we become aware of how brief and wonderful life is," he said.

"Well, people are dying around here lately," Allison said in a troubled voice. "Have you figured out who killed Ass— Mr. Azoli yet?"

"I think we'd better be careful to say 'Mr. Azoli' in future," said Shirley. "Out of good manners if not good feeling. No, I haven't figured out anything."

"What time did he get shot? And how was he lying when you found him?" asked J.Q.

"Let's see." She thought about it, recalling the body as she'd found it. "I got there around about four-thirty. The body was still warm, but it would have been. It was over ninety today. He was shot through the head. He must have been standing partway down the bank of the gully or maybe even leaning on one arm as he went down into the gully. If he'd been at the top of it, he'd probably have pitched into it headfirst, or fallen back at the top, depending on where the

74

shot came from. Instead, he fell against the sloping bank, head up, so I'd be inclined to believe he had to have been standing or leaning a little way down the bank, with his upper body and head up where it could be seen. But what was he doing down there?''

"I went over that ground when I stretched the fence. The banks of those gullies are all worn down. Water collects in there, so the grass is high.''

"Yes, there was grass. Sedges, really. Another thing, I didn't see a horse, so either his horse ran off or he was on foot. He wasn't all that far from his own house, but you can't see his buildings from where he was lying. There's a shallow rise between that hides them.''

"Where was the person who shot him?'' asked Allison

"Well, that's really the question, isn't it? He was standing at a low point. He could have been shot from the trees along the creek, or from the trees near the gravel pit, or from up the hill toward his place, providing somebody was at the top of that rise. Then there's always the possibility he caught an accidental shot, a round let off by someone aiming at something else. Depending on which way he was facing at the time, he could have been shot from our property, west or north of him. I don't know, Allison.''

"You really think maybe it was an accident?''

"All I'm saying is it could be. A rifle bullet can be lethal up to . . . to what, J.Q.? I forget.''

"Well over a mile, sometimes. Depending on trajectory. People get killed that way occasionally. A hunter will shoot at a deer, miss, and hit some innocent passerby across the valley.''

The phone rang again, and Shirley got up wearily to answer it. "Somebody has declared this to be McClintock Wednesday,'' she muttered as she picked it up. "Everybody wants to worry over me. McClintock.''

"Shirley. It's Elena. Can you come over here?''

"It's after ten. What's up, Elena?''

"There's some people here. I . . . Joe says we should have somebody here with a clear head.''

75

Shirley laughed explosively. "Lord, Elena, you've got the wrong girl! I'm under suspicion of murder. Didn't you know?"

"Of course I knew," Elena said impatiently. "But you didn't do it. I know that. You shoot off your mouth a lot, Shirley, but you're not actually evil. I really need you."

"Oh, hell. . . ." She hung up and stood hunched, hands in her pockets. "Elena says she needs a clear head. You both want to come along? Maybe among the three of us . . ."

"I guess," said Allison, not looking thrilled at the idea.

"Yeah, I guess," J.Q. responded more slowly. "Just to keep you out of trouble."

They drove slowly down the dark drive, stopping as the headlights caught the delicate figure of a doe with a half-grown fawn trailing her.

"First one I've seen in weeks," whispered J.Q.

"No machine this afternoon," Allison replied, just as softly.

Shirley switched off the headlights and rolled slowly forward as the graceful animals leapt into the darkness.

The Ramirez windows shed light on several cars pulled up near the porch. When the Wagoneer pulled up beside them, Joe opened the front door and came out to welcome them.

"Glad you could come." he said, hugging Shirley. "Hi, J.Q. Who's this?"

"Allison, my foster daughter," Shirley explained. "Elena said she needed a level head, and we thought maybe we had one of those among the three of us."

"Well, they need one, all right. Elena's in there with three LALA people—"

"Local?" she interrupted, surprised.

"Oh, yes. LALA's got chapters all over. The bunch here around Denver seems to be mostly into sanctuary and smuggling in aliens and all that stuff."

"Smuggling in aliens?" asked J.Q.

"Refugees. People running away from down there, Central America, anywhere. So long as they're Latino. Hispanic. Whatever. They hide them from immigration, you know."

76

"So what's the big trouble?" asked Shirley.

"Wait," he said. "You'll find out." He opened the door and ushered them in.

Elena rose from among the group gathered around the empty fireplace. "Shirley. You brought J.Q. This must be Allison. I'm not sure this is exactly the place for . . ."

"Allison'll be fine, Elena. Let her sit over in the corner there. She knows about kids being seen and not heard."

"I didn't mean . . ."

"Never mind. Now, what is all this?"

Elena gestured toward one of her guests, a gaunt, shock-headed man in a clerical collar. "This is Father Cisneros, Shirley, J.Q. Father is vice chairman of the Denver LALA."

"Father." Shirley nodded.

Elena put her hand on the shoulder of the woman next to the priest and squeezed her affectionately. "Henrietta Labolis is executive secretary of the alliance." Henrietta was heavyset, with dark, gray-flecked hair pulled back into an enormous smooth bun at her neck. "And this is Olivar Desfuentes, chairman of the political action committee."

Shirley nodded impatiently. "I ask again, Elena, why the summons?"

"Join us, please," said the priest. His voice was younger than his face, which had lines netting his eyes and bracketing his mouth. "Ms. McClintock. Mr. Jaikew."

"John Quentin," he said, seating himself. "People call me J.Q."

Elena seated herself, folding her hands in her lap. "Shirley, you remember the other day I told you about the construction firm in Maryland. The one LALA was planning to sue for discrimination and the injuries and all."

"A to Z Construction, wasn't it?" Shirley nodded

"A to Z Components. What I didn't know then, what we found out today, Azoli was head of the company."

"Azoli?" Shirley asked incredulously.

"He didn't run it for long," said Henrietta. "He was CEO for a short time after his father died, that's all. It had been his father's company."

"Most of the members of the Azoli family owned stock in it," Desfuentes said in a heavily accented voice. He was a bulky, pockmarked, and mustached forty, with deep-set eyes. "The main stockholder was A.Z. Azoli—"

"Allesandro Zacharias Azoli," interrupted Elena.

"But you must have known," Shirley said. "When we talked the other night, you must have known they were related."

"I knew he had the same last name," said Elena. "That's all. Honestly, Shirley. I didn't draw any connection except to think maybe they were distant cousins or something. We were suing the company in Maryland; why would I connect it with a rancher in Colorado? We were going to name the board of directors in the suit, and we knew there were people named Azoli on the board, but we always talked about the A to Z case, not the Azoli case. We'd never met any of them."

The priest interrupted. "Besides, the name we knew was Allesandro, not Eleazar. Our attorneys had intended to name Allesandro Azoli as majority stockholder, along with his sisters, his brother, his wife, his children—all of whom owned stock in the company. When Allesandro died, his shares were split up among the family."

"And his position as executive officer went to his eldest son," said Desfuentes.

Henrietta Labolis interjected, "But the important thing is, Azoli isn't associated with the company anymore because it's been sold! The Baltimore lawyers found that out late yesterday. They faxed the information to all LALA chapters this morning."

"Why was the company sold?" asked J.Q.

"Father Cisneros and I called up and asked them that question. There are rumors the family didn't much care for the way Eleazar was running things. He didn't have a majority of stock, so he didn't have anything like his father's clout. Whatever the reason was, they rounded up over fifty percent of the stock and forced a sale. Evidently the negotiations started right after the old man died; the sale took place some time ago, and yesterday they finally got around to announcing it publicly.''

Father Cisneros took up the story. "The lawyers believe the negotiations were kept quiet so the buyers wouldn't know about the pending LALA suit.''

Elena cried, "They certainly did keep it quiet. I met regularly with the LALA chapter in Baltimore, and I didn't know about it until Henrietta called me this morning.''

"That's when you made the connection with your new neighbor,'' said Shirley.

"Yes.''

"I presume this changes your plans for a civil suit,'' Shirley remarked.

Elena threw up her hands. "I have no idea what LALA can do now! Can a privately held company be sued after it's sold to someone else? Evidently the man who made all the decisions is dead, and so's the man who took over from him. Who could make restitution? The former stockholders?''

"Is that what you asked me to come here for? To give you worthless legal advice in response to rhetorical questions?''

"No, it isn't,'' Joe said angrily. "What it's about, Shirley, is this: it's been suggested by some of the local LALA people that Azoli's death can be used to publicize their grievances.''

Shirley shook her head in bafflement. "I don't get it.''

Joe grimaced. "They want to do newspaper interviews. TV interviews. They want to speculate that he may have been killed because of the way he treated Hispanics.''

"Are you crazy?'' she exploded. "That's the kind of thing terrorist gangs do, claim responsibility for any act of senseless violence just to get their names in the papers! And did it ever occur to you somebody might take you seriously?''

Desfuentes looked at the priest, and both of them at Henrietta Labolis.

"We have alibis,'' she said hesitatingly. "We can prove *we* didn't do it.''

"Can you prove your families didn't? How about your friends? Or people who are acquaintances or hangers-on? You realize since LALA's a national organization, the FBI would probably get involved. You might find yourself charged with conspiracy. Have you any idea what an FBI investigation might do to you? You're acting like damned fools."

"I told you," Joe snarled at his sister.

Shirley echoed the snarl. "I have said from time to time that being a damned fool is a right undoubtedly protected by the Constitution of the U.S., but this goes beyond mere stupidity." She turned on the priest. "Did someone in LALA kill him?"

"Of course not!" he snapped.

"Does LALA normally advocate killing people in order to make a political point? Is murder worth it if it gets the Hispanic cause mentioned by the media? What are you going to say in these interviews: 'Oh, personally we abhor violence, but we can understand the frustrations which caused the person to shoot Eleazar Azoli? Which is just what terrorist sympathizers always say when somebody throws a bomb into the abortion clinic or kills a bunch of people in an airport. Do you want people to see you in that light?"

"I said no! We weren't going to do anything but tell the media he might have been killed because of the way he treated our people."

"Who was your martyr going to be? Hmm? Was one of you going to be the suspect? Hauled up before the world only to be proved innocent, was that it?"

Henrietta flushed. "We hadn't thought that far ahead."

Shirley fumed. "In my opinion, which you've asked for, drawing any attention to LALA in this connection would be suicidal for the organization. As well as for some of you personally."

"It would take the pressure off you," said J.Q.

Joe looked up alertly. "What?"

"Nothing," she said, glancing at Allison, who had become very pale and quiet in her corner.

"They don't really think you did it, do they, Shirley?" Joe asked. "Come on!"

"I have no idea what they think!" She rubbed her forehead. "Is the local LALA group pretty militant?"

Elena exchanged glances with Father Cisneros. "Some members or . . . associates of it are."

"I don't suppose it had occurred to you armchair strategists that some member or members of your group might actually have done it."

Shocked silence. From the corner, Allison's voice piped: "Did any of them know about Azoli being here?"

And silence again.

Father Cisneros wiped his mouth with a handkerchief and grimaced uncomfortably. "The thought never crossed my mind."

"Thus speaketh the unworldly," muttered Shirley. "Well, you're at liberty to do what you like. J.Q.'s right. What might be bad for you will probably be good for me."

"I think we'd better talk with the members," murmured Elena.

"But we did," Henrietta cried. "I talked to over half of them on the phone this evening."

"It's the half you didn't talk to that has me worried," Elena said. "Shirley's right. We haven't considered that one or more of our people might actually have done this thing. Who was in office when you got the fax from the lawyers? Who was there when you and Father talked to them?"

"I don't see that that's relevant!" Henrietta exclaimed, suddenly paling.

"It's quite relevant," said Desfuentes. "Who was there?"

"My secretary. Jaime Montano and two other members of the fiesta committee. . . ." Her voice trailed off, and she evaded Desfuentes's eyes.

"Who else?" he demanded.

"My son."

"Antonio? Or Bonifacio?"

"Bony." She looked pleadingly at Father Cisneros, who turned away abruptly.

"Oh, fine. That's just great," said Desfuentes.

"What?" asked J.Q. "What's great?"

Father Cisneros shrugged, saying softly, "Bonifacio has gained a reputation as a hothead."

"Bonifacio Labolis is a flaming anarchist," muttered Desfuentes. "An incipient revolutionary. Or so he says."

"Which illustrates what I meant," Shirley said in a mild voice. "I think you can see now where calling attention to yourselves might lead." She got to her feet. "Joe, you'll forgive us if we run on home. All three of us have had a long day."

J.Q. and Allison preceded them as Joe took her by the arm and accompanied her to the car. "This whole LALA thing is nuts," he mumbled. "I don't know how Elena got mixed up with this, I really don't. She was always sensible, you know, even as a kid, but she's gone way off on this tangent."

"Do you know about Henrietta's son? Bony, did they call him?"

"Just what Elena's told me in passing. Even though Henny's a lot younger, she and Elena go way back, like you and I do. Elena used to baby-sit Henny when she was a kid, got to be sort of the second mama, you know. They always stayed in touch. Elena tells me Henny got married right after graduation, always worked, even when her husband was around, because he couldn't hold a job. You know the scenario. Henny took night courses and worked; he drank and chased women and talked macho. After about six or seven years he ran off and left her with two boys and a girl to support. Her oldest son seems to have picked his dad as a role model. Nothing is his fault. You know the routine. 'I steal stuff, but I never had no daddy. I sell drugs, but it's because I'm poor. I dropped out of school, but it was my ma's fault; she was so busy working, she couldn't help me with homework.' "

"I've heard the story from the professional apologists," Shirley said, suddenly depressed. "From the ones who make their livings assisting problem families."

"Well, the family's no problem except for him. He makes excuses for himself, and Henrietta makes excuses for him, so Elena does, too, except when she's feeling honest. Meantime, from what I hear, Henrietta's daughter and the younger son do well in school, stay out of trouble, and plan to go to college. You figure it out."

"Joe, can't you talk some sense into Elena? There's causes and causes, but this sounds . . ."

"I know. I've told her. You won't say anything about this to the sheriff, will you?"

"Of course not. Not unless I get hauled in again and it looks like I'm really under suspicion. I'm no martyr, Joe. Don't expect it of me."

"I wouldn't expect it, but I wish I knew. . . ."

"Whether any of the LALA people were involved in it?"

"Right. It could be dangerous for Elena if they are."

"Ask around. When you go back in there, tell the good father and the others they'd better find out all they can, just for their own protection. If someone associated with LALA was involved, Elena had better disassociate herself."

"She wouldn't be that sensible. She'd probably want to stay here and raise money for the defense instead!"

Shirley shrugged. "She's a grown woman, Joe. Hell, she's a grandma. You're not going to change her now."

He turned wordlessly back to the house as Shirley got into the Wagoneer next to J.Q.

"That was strange!" said Allison from the backseat.

"That was ridiculous," muttered Shirley. "Can you imagine! What were they thinking of?"

"Not thinking," remarked J.Q. "Just reacting, defining everything that happens in the world in terms of their own pet cause."

"I don't understand what you just said," Allison complained.

"I said some people see everything from their own point of view. Let's suppose you're a . . . a feminist. Somebody declares war against your country, and you say it wouldn't have happened if women were running things. Or somebody asks who's going to win the Super Bowl, and the other person responds that no women are playing, so she's not interested."

"Right," muttered Shirley.

He gave her a sidelong glance, his mouth quirking. "Or someone remarks it's a beautiful sunset, and the other one asks how he can admire a sunset when there are women in bondage in Arab countries.''

Shirley grunted.

"You mean, Elena didn't think about the murder being a murder at all. She just thought she could use it to help LALA,'' said Allison.

"Well, maybe not Elena, but somebody thought exactly that,'' J.Q. answered. "There are people who believe that any publicity is good publicity. Unfortunately.''

"Do you think one of them really did do it?'' Allison asked.

"I might think so if the timing weren't so tight,'' said Shirley. "They find out his morning that this Azoli is the bad Azoli, or at least he's the son of the bad Azoli, so somebody shoots him by midafternoon? I mean, that's really moving, isn't it?''

"Well.'' Allison gave it judicious consideration. "She said her son was hotheaded. And that's what hotheaded people do, isn't it? Just do things and think about them later?''

"She's got you there, Shirley.''

"Indeed. Allison, you're showing perspicacity.''

"Is that like perseverance?''

"Even better,'' said Shirley. "Not nearly as dull.''

As they turned into the McClintock driveway, Shirley saw headlights emerging from the Ramirez place and turning east. "Someone else is leaving hastily,'' she commented. "I've got a feeling about that.''

"Which is?'' J.Q. asked.

"I'm guessing that Father Cisneros jumped the gun.''

"Jumped the gun how?''

"He had a very funny expression on his face when Henrietta spoke about her son being a hothead. That combination of surprise and embarrassment one gets when one realizes one has done something foolish.''

"You think he told somebody?'' Allison asked.

"I think it's very possible he told somebody without considering the consequences, either this morning, after he knew Azoli was a local resident, or this afternoon, when he heard

84

about the murder. He said, you'll recall, that it hadn't occurred to him any of the LALA people might actually be involved. I'd give you three to one he's zooming back to town to see if he can cut off the word before it spreads, and I'll bet whoever he told falls into the category of militant.''

"You didn't say anything to Joe."

"Well, no point, really. He's upset enough about Elena. If I'm wrong, it would only worry him more."

"You think Elena might actually be a suspect?"

"She used to be a pretty good shot, J.Q. And she always had a reputation for getting fired up. As Allison says, she was known for doing things and thinking about them later." She yawned widely. "Lord, I'm tired. Finding bodies just takes it out of you."

"I'd think sitting in jail takes it out of you."

"That, too," she said, managing with difficulty to keep her voice from shaking. When J.Q. had said "jail," some deep part of her had shuddered as though struck by cold. Now she felt a queasiness, almost a nausea.

They drew up before the house and got out into the quiet of late evening, with stars spangling the sky and a soughing of wind soft in the trees up the hill.

"This is the way it ought to be," said J.Q.

"It's the way it always was," Shirley said bitterly, her arms folded tight across her belly to hold herself in. "Before that bastard came."

J.Q. found Shirley on the porch drinking coffee at about seven in the morning.

"You're up early for a Thursday," he commented.

"I'm up early for any day. Trying to figure out what I'm going to do next." Actually, she had been awake since two in the morning. She'd wakened then, heart thudding like a drum, full of nighttime terrors, keeping herself from screaming only with difficulty. She recalled the dream as full of accusation and confinement, and it had taken a quarter of an hour for her to calm herself.

"What's the matter, love?" he asked, examining her closely.

"I'm terrified," she said, turning away from him to hide her face. "No real reason to be. I didn't kill him, but I'm terrified. I haven't felt like this since young Marty disappeared. This is how I felt all those weeks of waiting before we finally accepted that he was dead." She heard the tremor in her voice with disbelief.

"You've had no chance to relax since you got back. You're tired."

"I'm tired, yes."

"We'll find out who did it."

"It's not just . . . ." Without willing it, her head turned to the left, where the riven acres began across the distant fence, where the stream trickled between its denuded banks. "It's like rape," she whispered. "I feel . . . what is it the victims always say? I feel violated, J.Q. He's dead, but I want to resurrect him so I can kill him again. Look what he's done!"

She turned away, brushing at her face with her hands.

"Shhh," he said, putting his arms around her.

They rocked to and fro in the early sunlight.

At last she drew away, shaking her head. "In the middle of the night I woke up with the idea I ought to find Rima Azoli's ex-husband, the man Allison met."

"I suppose you have a reason."

"It seemed logical when I thought of it. Somebody out here called the sheriff's office saying they heard shots. How many people are there within a mile of here? The Bostoms and their son and granddaughter. Maybe the nurse from the hospice, if she happened to be at Bostom's place at the time. Then there's the Ramirezes, the Azolis and their hired men, and you, me, Allison. Plus whoever's been hanging out down in the gravel pit. Well, so start eliminating from that list. It wasn't you or me or Allison. It wasn't Joe or Elena. I doubt very much that Neb or his son is paying any attention to anything but Oriana; besides, from their place you couldn't hear shots over the noise of that machine. So, that brings us to the hospice nurse maybe coming or going, or to the Azoli household or somebody in the gravel pit. Rima told Allison the person she'd been meeting was her brother. She told me it was her husband. I think I ought to talk to him."

"If she'll tell you where he's staying."

"If he's driving out here to talk to her every day, he's probably staying in Columbine, and there's only what? Three motels?"

"One dirty pillow joint, two clean hostels, one of which is fairly comfortable. The Lazy N. I think it's a Best Western. Do you know her ex's name?"

"Paul Howard. If I can find out where he's staying, I may catch him before he leaves for the day."

She went inside to the phone, leaving J.Q. to stand at the porch rail and marvel at the quiet. He was still there when she emerged ten minutes later, the car keys jingling in her hand.

"Right the first time. I found him at the Lazy N. We're going to have breakfast."

"On what basis?"

"On the basis that Rima told me about him, that I'm suspected of this killing and need all the information I can get to clear myself."

"How did he sound?"

"Half-asleep. I think I woke him."

"You're incorrigible. Blatantly devious, even." He said it in his usual bantering tone, but he was still watching her more closely than usual.

"Right. I'll be back when I get back, J.Q."

The day was already warm, though a film of cloud lay high against the sun. As she drove out the gate, the trees shivered in an abrupt gust of wind, a momentary coolness that swept on down the stream and was gone. In the afternoon such gusts could pile onto one another, making a squall line ahead of the thunderheads that swept across the valley, spilling rain in trailing gray clouds.

She turned southeast on County 64, sliding a little on the gravel as she made the corner, dazzled by the reflection in her rearview mirror of the sun on the tin roofs behind her.

Only a man who cared nothing for his neighbors would put on roofs like that. Glass-walled high rises in the city threw that same kind of light: harsh, glittering, hard on the eyes and the soul. Inimical to life.

It took her half an hour to get into Columbine, not hurrying. Paul Howard had not been really awake when she had spoken to him. She hoped he'd be awake when she arrived at the motel but was somewhat disappointed in this desire by the sight of the widely yawning person awaiting her beneath the office portico. He had an engagingly lumpy face, with crinkled eyes under floppy grayish hair. As she approached, a three-cornered grin split his luxuriant, still-golden beard.

She pulled up and reached across the open passenger door. "Paul Howard?"

"Yeah." He yawned again. "I think. You must be McClintock."

"There's a Village Inn that way." She pointed. "You want to have breakfast?"

"Coffee," he agreed. "Maybe food after I've had coffee. I can't wake up out here."

"Probably the altitude," Shirley told him as he shut the door and settled back into the seat. "People come from the coast, they find they're sleepy for weeks, sometimes months. Not as much oxygen here."

"Could be that," he agreed. "Could be this whole mess. Rima's up to her neck, you know."

"No. I didn't know. Is she a suspect?"

"I imagine she is. That fat little sheriff sure bored in on her yesterday afternoon. He got to me last night."

"Was she the one who heard the shots?"

"We both did. She's the one who called after I dropped her off, but we both heard them. They went off right near us."

"Where were you?"

"Where we'd been holding our little conferences for the past week. Down those ruts west of where she lived. Lives. Only place she could get to without him knowing."

"She didn't have a car?"

"Not anymore she didn't have a car. She had a car before they were married. He told her to sell it, it was getting old, he'd buy her another one. Just like he told her he'd make a place for the boys. She told me what you suggested about the boys. I told her you were smarter than she was."

"I'll bet she loved that," Shirley commented as she parked next to the Village Inn. "He wasn't treating her very well, either, you know."

"Well, he knocked her around a little. You know, I never did that, even when I was dead drunk. Never hit her once. Now I almost wish I had, so she'd have made excuses for me the way she did for him." He got out, yawned, stretched, and followed Shirley inside. "Of course, I wasn't a rich man's son and he was. That was probably the difference." When they had been seated and provided with coffee, he cradled his cup against his lower lip and said, "Even though he did have money, it hasn't been easy on her. She's started smoking again, and she hasn't done that since she quit ten years ago. What are you interested in all this for?"

"I'm fishing," she admitted. "I want to know about the shots you heard."

"Well, we were down there in the trees. We've been meeting down there to talk things over whenever she figured she could get away for an hour or two. Every day we kind of get things sorted out, and every night she changes her mind. Well, it was too hot to sit in the car, so we were perched on an old stump down there. Rima kept getting up and down, brushing at herself. She's deathly afraid of ticks. Every time a blade of grass tickles her leg or arm, she's sure she's got a tick. She told me what you had suggested to her, about leaving things the way they are legally but letting the boys stay with me. That's what they want. I've promised them both I'm sticking with AA. That's all they care about, for me to stay sober."

"How did she feel about my suggestion?"

"She couldn't make up her mind." He drank deeply and reached for the menu. "What's good here?"

"Breakfast is breakfast. I'm having one of their skillet things: hash browns, eggs, sausage."

"Sounds all right." He folded the menu and yawned once more while Shirley beckoned the waitress over and gave her the order.

"Rima?" she prompted when the waitress had filled their cups and gone. "How did she feel?"

"She misses the boys. Hell, I know she does. She was a good mother, better than I was a father. But this bastard she married, he was bad news. Rima told me she was doing the best for the boys, guaranteeing their lives. She thought he'd send them to college, you know."

"You think he wouldn't have?"

"I think he only did what he wanted to do. He did some things to make himself feel big, and he did some to get himself what he wanted. He wanted Rima, so he promised her stuff. She married him, he didn't need to be nice anymore. Hell, he doesn't want my boys. He's got grown kids of his own. His son called Rima this morning. Said he was flying out today, she should prepare a room for him. She said he might want to stay in town, and he told her no, the ranch was now his, and he wanted to look it over. She called me up in hysterics."

"Did she think she'd inherit it?"

"Well, you know, he got her to work twelve hours a day on the place by convincing her they were building the place together. Naturally, she'd think she had a share in it."

"Did he ever actually say he was leaving her the place?"

"I don't know. She didn't say."

Shirley thought about this, making mental notes. "So you and she were down in the gravel pit, sitting on a stump, talking about the boys."

"Right. She was crying. She never has a handkerchief, so I'd given her mine and she was sitting there getting mascara all over it, the way she always did, and these shots happened!"

"Happened?"

"I mean, like they hit us. Loud. Like the gun had gone off right next to us."

"What time was it?"

"I didn't look at my watch until a little later, when I dropped Rima off. It was four-thirty then."

"How much time had passed?"

"Oh, ten minutes, maybe."

"You said shots? Plural?"

"It sounded like shots. A bunch. The sheriff said it might have been echoes. I suppose it could have been. Kind of a *banga-banga.*"

"If it was echoes, it was off something close, is that what you're saying? No time between the report and the echo?"

"I suppose. Don't ask me. I'm no expert."

"Not a sportsman?"

"With guns? Not a chance. Never in the military. My sport was always sailing, our sport was. Rima and the boys and I used to do a lot of that. Back before I got to be a souse."

"Why did you?" she asked curiously. "Get to be a souse, I mean."

He made a face at her as the waitress approached with their orders.

When they were alone again, Shirley said, "None of my business, right?"

"No. I don't mind telling you. I figure I owe you for what you said to Rima. The truth of it is, I don't know. I was working hard. The job was tough; I was under a lot of pressure, I started having two or three when I got home, just to relax. Then a few with lunch. Then lunch just sort of faded into evening, and the weekends disappeared. I never decided to, you know."

"But Rima left you."

"Well, no. What happened was, she moved me out. I don't blame her. She worked full time. And she had a house and the boys to take care of. I was no help. I was sure no role model for the boys, and she knew it."

"So you joined AA."

"Not at first. At first I blamed her, the way you do. After a while, though, I lost my job, things started falling out from under me. That's when I started with AA."

"And you were planning to get back together?"

"I think we would have, if it hadn't been for him. Azoli. What happened with him was his wife got a block of stock when her father-in-law died last spring. I guess the old man liked her. Hell, I knew her and I liked her. She was a real good person. Anyhow, once she had money of her own, I guess she figured she didn't need to be married to Azoli anymore. She'd got tired of being . . . I don't know, hit, maybe. Or just yelled at or put down or whatever. I knew him before, remember. Rima and I . . . we were around them as a couple, and he could be a nasty son of a bitch. So she divorced him. First thing he did was find somebody to marry, that's all. He didn't care much who. Anybody to show his wife he didn't give a damn what she did."

"I don't suppose she cared if he married again."

"According to Rima, his kids did. They thought his doing it so soon was kind of an insult to their mother. Which it was."

"So his kids were pissed off at him? How many kids? How old?"

"He's got three. His son Charles would be twenty-seven, twenty-eight by now. His daughter Nancy's a few years younger. And his youngest would be about twenty-two. I don't remember the younger boy's name. I'm not sure we ever met him. Charles and Nancy are both married."

"And his kids inherit everything?"

"Well, what else can you figure from what Charles said to Rima? He told her the place was his, he was coming out to look it over."

"What's she going to do?"

"Well, naturally . . . I hope we'll get back together."

"Would you say you had a motive?"

"For killing him?" He laid down his fork. "Well, sure. Probably. But I didn't. I've never shot a gun in my life."

"Where are your sons now?"

"Home. I got a woman to come in and fix dinner, stay there nights. Rima and I split the money from our house when we were divorced. I put my share into a little place right down on Chesapeake Bay. The boys have their boats there. It's home, like I say."

"What did Rima do with her share?"

"Her lawyer told her to put it into something that would give her income. So far as I know, that's what she did."

"So she's not destitute?"

He shrugged as he scooped up a last forkful of potatoes. "You'll have to ask her. I've stayed away from that subject. It's a sore point with her."

"A sore point?"

"Right. Married to me, she had a job of her own, her own income. The boys were grown up enough to look after themselves a lot of the time, and she was pretty independent. So she divorces me, marries this rich guy, and she's worse off than she was with me. It's a sore point."

Shirley dropped him off, stopped at the Safeway to pick up a short list of groceries, then drove home in a thoughtful mood. When she came to the ruts leading down into the gravel pit, she turned in. She couldn't see the big stump from the road. After running straight along the fence for a hundred yards, the ruts bent to the left. The place where the car had stood was unmistakable. Recent tire tracks led through the grove and stopped against a weedy bank. Nearby was the huge stump, the area nearby littered with lipstick-stained cigarette ends and the silver glint of chewing gum wrappers. Paul Howard had popped gum in his mouth on the way back to his motel. Rima, so he had said, had started smoking again. The litter was sufficient to account for more than a few lengthy conferences.

If someone had fired from nearby, there might be other litter. Something someone had dropped. Maybe even . . .

Surely Botts and his men would have searched the area.

But maybe not. She wasn't dressed for searching at the moment, but that could be quickly remedied. She backed the car out of the trees, swung it onto the road, and went home.

"Get anything useful?" J.Q. demanded as soon as she entered the house.

"Maybe. You got time to help me for an hour, maybe?"

He gave her a questioning glance, and she explained what she had in mind.

"Botts's men have probably been all over it."

"Well, maybe. Maybe not. He's not as good a looker as we are, J.Q. Besides, I cut the fence over there yesterday, and we need to fix that. Allison can go with us."

"Allison's gone over to Crebs to play volleyball."

"Well, leave her a note. You get the fencing tools while I change clothes."

A quarter of an hour later they parked where the other car had parked, sat on the stump where Rima and Paul had sat, and tried to figure out where someone might have shot from. They were only thirty feet from the dilapidated fence that separated the gravel pit from a ten-acre, south-protruding tongue of McClintock land. Across that ten acres, Little Cawson Creek ran in a shallow wooded cut from right to left, down from Azoli land into Ramirez land. The gully where Azoli had been found was upstream, a little inside the Azoli fence, to the left of the stream and invisible to them from where they sat.

"The shot could have come from anywhere. Even with the leaves turned all brown, the trees along the stream would have hidden him."

"Or her," said Shirley.

"Or her. And there are green trees around us here, with more up and down the creek. Like hunting a needle in a haystack. Well, it won't hurt to poke around a little. You want me to fix our fence?"

"No, you look around the gravel pit here. I'll do the fence, then look where the stream goes through our place." The question of what Azoli had been doing in the gully had been bothering her, and the excuse of fixing the trailing wires of the boundary fence would give her an excuse for a brief reconnaissance.

She splashed across the creek, frowning at the browned

willows and dropping her tools by the trailing fence wires before she went on upstream to the place where the gully led off to the left. Crushed and trampled grasses marked where the body had lain: Azoli's, her own boot marks, those of the sheriff and his men. From her crouched position she could see nothing that would have brought Azoli into the gully. When she stood up and stepped to her left, she caught a glimpse of the sign at the gully bottom. It was half-buried in tall grasses, green and white enamel on light metal: ''MCCLINTOCK'S. NO HUNTING. NO TRESPASSING.'' She had the signs made a hundred at a time and went around the perimeter every fall, replacing the shot-up or rusted ones. This one had new, unrusted bullet holes in it. Two. Right through the ''Nos,'' she observed.

Taking the sign with her, she went back and fixed the fence, pulling the trailing ends taut with the stretcher, poking the cut wire into metal sleeves and squeezing them tight with a patented tool she always felt guilty about using. Splicing fence this way was easy and quick, but it wasn't the way she'd been taught to mend fence. Her father would have been scandalized. Every time she used the splicing tool, she imagined him looking over her shoulder, shaking his head.

After taking the tools and sign back to the car, she moved along the stream, looking for a place with a clear view of the place where the body had been found. There were several stretches along the bank with a clear view of the gully, but none of them were hidden from the stump where Paul and Rima had supposedly been sitting.

J.Q. came strolling back toward the car, carrying his hat in both hands. She called, ''If the shot came from here, Rima and Paul had to have seen who did it! Anyplace with a view of the gully can be seen from this stump!''

''There's no clear shot between here and the road,'' said J.Q. ''My poking around was a waste of time, except for these.'' He emptied his hat onto the car seat: a pile of brilliantly lavender mushrooms.

''*Lepista nuda,*'' cried Shirley. ''Where'd you find them?''

''When I walked back toward the road, right along the

ruts." He divided the pile into two. "I'm surprised I didn't see them when we drove in. This bunch is a little dry: it came up yesterday or the day before, but these big ones here are fresh. What do you say to mushrooms on toast for lunch?"

Shirley stroked the mushrooms, some of them almost five inches across, their velvety surfaces like kidskin. The striking color shaded from pale grayed violet on the cap to deep purple at the edge, next to the gills, identifying them unmistakably. No other fungus had that color, that conformation.

Shirley smiled, remembering. "You know where I first learned about these, J.Q.? Neb and Oriana Bostom took me and my brother mushrooming when I was about ten. Dad and Mother had never paid any attention to mushrooms except to tell me to leave them alone. The first thing we found that day was *Agaricus campestris* in the horse pasture. I'll never forget how I felt when Neb turned one over and showed me the pink gills. There was this sense of astonishment. Then, coming back to the house, we found a big bunch of *Lepista*, and that was even more surprising. I'd never thought of mushrooms as being those fancy colors, that pale pink and gorgeous violet, never thought of them as somehow related to me. Part of my world. I remember Neb's being all excited when we found them." She stroked them again. "Why don't we take these over to Neb and Mike. They might enjoy them."

"All right by me," he said, gripping her shoulder with one big hand.

They backed out, stopping long enough for J.Q. to point out where the fungus had grown so they could keep it in mind for future forays: just past the slight bend that hid the stump.

When they pulled up near the Bostom house, Shirley nodded toward the long-faced man who came out onto the porch. "That's Mike. Lord, he looks a lot like Neb, doesn't he? Like Neb used to look, anyhow."

J.Q. got out and offered his hand; Shirley followed. Neb came out onto the porch, and they murmured together. Oriana was sinking, Neb said. The nurse was there.

"We found these," said Shirley, offering the fresh mushrooms. "It made me think of you and Oriana, Neb. You probably don't remember, but you and she took me mushrooming one day, the first day I ever saw these. I was only about ten."

"I remember taking you more than once," he said. "You had good eyes! Mike, look at that. Remember how your mother used to make these on scrambled eggs? She said they were the one kind she could never resist."

"Most delicious in the world," Mike said. "That's what she used to say. Whenever I started off on some expedition into the woods, she'd tell me to watch for purple. Where'd you find them?"

Shirley said, "We were fixing our north fence, where I cut it. They were down near there."

"You still having sign trouble there?" Neb asked J.Q.

J.Q. tilted his hand to and fro. "Not since yesterday."

Shirley gave him a curious look, then turned back to the old man. "We won't stay, Neb. We just wanted you to have these. Wanted you to know we were thinking about you."

Neb shook his head. "You keep them, honey. It'd be a pity to waste them, and Patti, Marilyn's daughter, she's doing all the cooking. I can tell you right now, she won't fix these."

"You're sure, Neb? Mike?"

"Dad's right," said Mike. "Patti's suspicious of anything that doesn't come in a box ready for the microwave. At breakfast this morning she wouldn't even cook eggs from Dad's chickens because there's a rooster. She said 'fertile eggs' in the same tone of voice she'd say 'strychnine.' "

"She's vegetarian?"

"No." Mike laughed silently. "Just peculiar."

Neb went back into the house, while Mike walked with them back to the car. "Poor Dad. He's taking this awfully hard. I don't think he'll last a year without Mom. I really don't. He hardly leaves her side. When I got here, I made him take a little walk, just to get out of the house. I think it's the first time he's been away from her in a week. He's pale as a ghost."

"Is there anything I can do, Mike?"

"No. There really isn't, Shirley. Patti's taking care of Dad and me. After I picked her up at the airport, we stopped and bought enough groceries to last a good while. I've got a rental car, so we can get around okay. The nurse comes every day. It's just . . . waiting."

She gave him a hug, which seemed to surprise him.

On their way home she said, "How did Neb know we were having sign trouble?"

"That time I ran into him in town while you were gone. I was pretty annoyed because I'd spent the afternoon putting them back up for the second time, and I told him about it."

Allison returned in time to admire the purple mushrooms before Shirley sliced, sautéed, and served them, talking the while to J.Q. about well-remembered forays in the past.

"If you guys hunt mushrooms all the time, how come I never saw these purple ones before?" Allison wanted to know.

"We don't find them often," Shirley told her. "They aren't really plentiful here on the ranch. There's one place along the road up in the pines, toward our back fence, where we try to remember to look for them in late July or August. And three or four times, I've found some down along the west fence line."

"You mean they come up in the same place every year?"

Shirley nodded. "The mushroom plant, what you might think of as the roots, is underground. It may be quite large, yards and yards around, maybe, and it stays there, year after year. Then, when conditions are right, it sends up what are called fruiting bodies, and that's what we're eating."

"Like what kind of conditions are right?"

"Oh, the right moisture, the right temperature. Also, a lot of mushrooms have relationships with other plants. They need something that other plants produce, and they won't fruit unless they have it. You can look year after year, and there's nothing. But if things are just right, then suddenly there's a whole crop springing up overnight."

J.Q. said, "When we find a place where a choice mushroom grows, we check it out from time to time to see if there's a harvest.''

"They taste like ordinary mushrooms to me," Allison said doubtfully. "Is it worth all that trouble? They don't even stay purple when they're cooked. They're just ordinary mushroom color. Sort of brownish.''

"Well, they don't taste ordinary to me," said Shirley, much offended. "And since my taste buds don't distinguish among colors, I don't care whether they stay purple or not.''

"Next time we'll feed you peanut butter and jelly," J.Q. threatened, amused, "and save the special stuff for Shirley and me.''

Allison flounced slightly. Though she'd been living with Shirley for almost a year now, since right after her eleventh birthday, she was still finding out what Shirley and J.Q. thought important. Both of them attached considerable significance to things Allison's parents had never noticed. Like wild mushrooms. Or how birds or animals acted. Or how certain kinds of food or wine tasted, or the way the wind smelled.

Allison's mother had been more interested in clothes, and hair, and makeup. She'd enjoyed long giggly conversations on the phone with her friends. Allison's father had talked abut money mostly, and neither of them had talked to Allison very much. Considering what had happened to them, Allison sometimes wondered if it was right, her liking where she was living now better than she'd liked living with them.

That particular thought had bothered her ever since she'd moved in with Shirley and J.Q. Since school had let out this spring, it had become even more so. She didn't like thinking about that.

"Did you find out anything new this morning?" she asked, trying to get her mind off the subject.

"Not really. This afternoon I'm going to call Botts," Shirley announced around a mouthful of mushrooms. "I want to know when Azoli was shot.''

"But you know, don't you? Didn't Paul Howard say he heard the shot at around four-thirty?''

"If we believe what he said, it was four-fifteen or -twenty. That'd be about right. He and Rima heard it, then they talked about it for a while, then got in the car, backed up, drove up the hill to the Azoli driveway, she got out of the car, then he looked at his watch and it said four-thirty. So the shot they heard was ten minutes earlier, maybe."

"Closer to five, unless they spent a lot of time talking about it."

Shirley shrugged. "At this point we have only his word for that. I'd kind of like to know if that was actually when he was shot. They didn't see him get hit, you know. They just heard the shot. It might not have been the shot that killed him."

"And you didn't hear it?"

"I didn't hear it. I suppose I must have started down the hill about that same time. I got there maybe twenty to five."

"And he was down when you saw him from up the hill. You didn't see him fall."

"Well, I saw something red and it didn't move, put it that way. I assume he was already down and what I saw was the red shirt."

"What was he doing there? Down in the gully?"

"He may have been going to pick up a sign, one of my no-trespassing signs. I went there and looked around this morning. One of my signs was in the bottom of the gully. It had two new bullet holes in it."

"That isn't unusual," J.Q. muttered.

"Except what it was doing there. You said Azoli dropped ours on our side of the fence."

"The two times I put them back, he did."

"So, where did the one come from down in the gully?"

"Maybe he decided to take them back with him so J.Q. couldn't put them up anymore," offered Allison. "And he dropped one of them."

"Possible," Shirley said. "Were there bullet holes in any of them when you put them back up?"

"Not that I remember."

"So, we've got a sign in a strange place with two strange—

that is, unexplainable—bullet holes in it.'' Shirley stretched. ''Interesting. I'm still going to call Botts.''

Botts Tempe, when reached by phone, declined to discuss the matter.

''You're a suspect, McClintock! I'm not going to tell you what we know.''

''Oh, shit, Sheriff. You know I didn't kill him! All I'm interested in is finding out who did. The man was already down when I saw him from the edge of the woods. I just want to know how long he'd been dead when you guys got there.''

''I'm not saying anything. I go blabbing to you and then have to arrest you later, it'll make me look bad.''

''Tough guy,'' she commented when she hung up.

''Does he think you did it?'' asked Allison.

''He does not. He knows better. But he's getting a high pretending he does.'' Shirley spoke firmly, concealing the trepidation she felt. There had been a certain hostility in Botts's voice.

''He didn't tell you anything?'' asked J.Q.

''He did not.''

''Who do you think did it, Shirley?'' Allison asked.

''Well, if we ask who had motive and opportunity, my two main suspects would probably be Rima Azoli or Paul Howard or maybe both. If they did it, they almost had to do it together. I have only Paul Howard's word that they were sitting together on a comfortable stump when they heard the shots. Meantime, I have Rima's story that Paul used to get very belligerent when he drank, and despite all the talk about AA, maybe he'd been drinking yesterday.''

''Who else?''

''Well, there's the LALA contingent. The most worrisome person from that bunch seems to be a kid named Bonifacio Labolis. From the way Father Cisneros acted, though, I have a hunch there are some others we might be worried about, if we knew who they were.''

''Are you including Elena in that bunch?'' asked J.Q.

''No. Elena is a separate suspect. And Joe has his own

separate motives. Hate, mostly. Of course, that motive applies to me, too. Then there's the guy from the ostrich farm.''

"Mr. Rodwinger," said Allison.

"Horace," muttered J.Q.

"I have no idea if he's capable of it or not, but maybe we can find out. I think I'll drive over there this afternoon.'' She glanced at the other two. "Either of you want to go?"

"Not me." J.Q. frowned at her. "Somebody has to fix that panel in the goat pen before all the bucks get out again."

Allison said, "Jeffrey's mom is taking him and his sister and two other kids to Celebrity to swim, and she said I could come along."

"I didn't know you could swim."

"I can't. But a lot of kids go who can't swim. You can come down the chutes even if you can't swim."

"Swimming lessons," Shirley said firmly. "Where do we get the kid swimming lessons, J.Q.?"

"Send her to camp," he said. "Either that or wait until she's a little older and buy her a membership at Palace Pines Country Club."

"That's going a bit far," said Shirley, gulping at the thought. Palace Pines was notable for exclusivity, the kind maintained by monstrous membership fees. "Despite my having always regretted that I don't know how to swim, I don't think I'd go to that extent."

"It's not as though we had a lot of water to contend with around here," said J.Q.

"It's just something everyone ought to be able to do. Like being able to type. Or drive a car."

"Do I have a say here?" Allison asked, her tone a little shrill. "Like, is what I think important?"

Shirley flushed. "Sorry, Allison. Of course it is."

"I'll learn on my own when I get to junior high. They take busloads of kids to the Lakewood Y twice a week for classes. It's after school, and it's only five dollars a class."

Shirley rubbed her nose and grinned. "I should quit worrying about you. You have it all figured out."

"Ms. Minging does. She's got a whole list of stuff on the

bulletin board, stuff we're supposed to think about. Including traveling to other countries to improve foreign languages.''

''Anytime soon?'' J.Q. asked mildly.

''I guess next summer will be soon enough. That's after I have a year of Spanish.'' She looked plaintively at Shirley. ''May I have money for Celebrity this afternoon?''

''Your allowance won't cover?''

''I didn't get any this week. You've both been . . . doing other stuff. You've been preoccupied.''

''Lord, she sounds more like you every day, J.Q.'' Shirley went to get her wallet.

4

THE OSTRICH FARM lay north of the Cavendish place, down a long straight driveway edged on both sides by the remnants of old windbreaks of juniper, Russian olive, and lilac that formed impenetrable tangles in some places and left twiggy gaps of dead or dying trees in others. Such belts of hardy, drought-resistant trees and shrubs were found throughout the arid and windswept western plains, right up to the foothills. They were recommended by county conservation departments, which provided the infant trees by the dozens and hundreds to ranch and farm owners. When properly planted, watered, and grown, they provided protection for people and stock against winter's blizzards and the thunderhead squalls of summer, against both hail and drying wind. The existence of the windbreaks certainly illustrated the difference between East and West, Shirley thought as she peered through the occasional holes at the northeast corner of Azoli's land. Westerners revered trees. Easterners, at least Azoli-like easterners, seemed to regard them as weeds to be grubbed out as they had been on the slopes west of her, as chewed and brown as the land along her own fences. In the East, trees would grow again in a decade or so. Here, it would take a century.

When she came to the end of the access road and turned onto a graveled drive leading toward the buildings, she got her first clear view of the monster machine that had been chewing the scrub into chips. It squatted halfway up the nearest hill to the west, a dirty yellow horror with caterpillar treads and an oil-streaked fuel wagon attached behind. A battered pickup truck was parked nearby, and two men moved slowly around the monster like worker termites tending the obscene bulk of their queen.

The road swung to the right. On either side tall chain-link fences made a labyrinth of empty pens, many of them with small stablelike shelters along the back. While the pens and shelters were obviously new, the house was not. New shingles speckled the weathered roof, and against peeling gray clapboard the raw wood of new porch steps and railings made a vehement statement of reconstruction.

She turned the Wagoneer and parked it facing away from the house just as Horace Rodwinger and a pimply, stringy-haired person emerged from a nearby outbuilding, the boy carrying a shotgun slanted carelessly in her direction.

Shirley sat tight, rolled down the window, and called, "It's Shirley McClintock, Mr. Rodwinger."

"Who? Oh. Oh, yes. Well. Welcome." He mumbled something to the boy, who gave her one of those gaping, sneering looks much cultivated by dissident youth before he carried his armament back into the shed.

"Were you expecting invaders?" she asked as he came toward her.

"What?" He seemed confused.

"Your friend with the gun. I asked if you were expecting trouble."

"Am I expecting trouble! You would not *believe* the trouble I expect," he fumed. "That . . . that man's son was here this morning. Would you believe that? That man's son came here on his way from the airport, called me names, threatened me, told me if I brought any kind of suit against them

105

for damages, they would countersue, they would tie me up in court, they would cost me thousands! Can you believe the gall!''

"This was . . .'' What had Paul Howard said Azoli's son's name was? "Charles? Charles Azoli.''

"C.K. Azoli. That's what he said. 'I'm C.K. Azoli, and you have me to deal with now.' The nerve!''

"How did he get the idea you were going to sue him?''

"Well, because I told Eleazar Azoli so.''

"When did you do that?''

"When I left your place yesterday. As I was passing his driveway, he came skidding out in that truck of his, almost ran into me, yelled at me, made a gesture, you know, and I was so *angry*! I rolled down my window and just told him my partners and I were suing him for damages!''

"That would have been when? About half past noon?''

"I suppose. Thereabouts. He laughed at me. Told me to sue away, he got fat on lawsuits. Told me all my birds could die of terror for all he cared. Told me he was moving the machine up on my fence line to give me a taste of what it really sounded like up close. And he did!''

"The machine came up here yesterday?''

"Oh, it did indeed! Not that it hadn't been here before.''

"What time did it arrive?''

"Late. Late in the afternoon. They didn't use it. It just came crunching up the hill like some *awful* enormous locust, and then they parked it and went away.''

"Late in the afternoon is when?''

"Suppertime. Five-thirty. Six. I was in the house.''

"So after you spoke to him at noon, he had plenty of time to speak to the men running the machine.''

"Well, of course he did. And I was waiting this morning for it to start up, just *gritting* my teeth, sure I was going to lose the birds, when his *son* arrived!''

"You didn't know Azoli was dead?''

"Not until then, I didn't! I hadn't heard about it. I had such a headache last night, I went to bed, didn't even listen to the news, if one could call that news! It was no news to me! If ever a man just *begged* to be slaughtered, it was that man.''

''So when the son showed up, he already knew you'd threatened his father with a lawsuit, and he told you his father was dead.''

''That's right. I wasn't surprised, but I was shocked. Shocked!''

He looked shocked. As he spoke, his hands trembled, and he repeatedly wiped his mouth where flecks of saliva showed at the corners.

''That's when I told Mervin to load the shotgun. We have it to use against coyotes, you know. Not that they're any threat to the grown birds, but they might try to make off with a chick.''

''That's Mervin in the shed over there?''

''Mervin. My stepson. And what Marthine thinks about it all, I don't know.''

''Marthine?'' Shirley didn't believe she'd heard correctly.

''My wife. She put up almost half the money for this place. We thought it would be a good thing for Mervin, too. Having a nice out-of-door place for him to work. She wanted to get him out of the city. He wasn't going about with nice people at all. So *awful*, these days, cities. Bad for young people. Well, bad for everyone!''

''And raising ostriches was your idea?''

''Well, not really, no. I'd had some experience with poultry. My parents ran a hatchery when I was a child, so I'm *familiar* with the field. You know, diseases and feeding and all that. Really, Marthine had the idea. She read about it in a magazine. *New Entrepreneurs*, it's called.''

''She read about ostriches.''

''Ostriches, and later some other kinds of animals: different kinds of goats, like Kashmir goats, you know, or those kinds with the curly coats, Persian lamb.''

''I guess I'm trying to figure why you started with ostriches.''

''Well, that's where the immediate return is. Marthine had enough money to buy a pair. And I had some money from

107

Mama, so I used mine to build the pens and the buildings. And a friend of Marthine's invested in us, enough to lease this land for ten years. It wasn't expensive. The people don't want to sell, but they do want someone on it, to keep it agricultural, you know. For taxes.''

Shirley gazed through the links of the nearest fence into the face of a very tall and supercilious bird with amazing eyelashes. "All this for one pair?''

"Well, they've already hatched a *dozen* chicks, and they grow quite fast. And so far, thank the Lord, none of them have died, not that some of them won't if that dreadful noise goes on. So, in a manner of speaking, we already have a six hundred percent return on our investment. And, of course, we don't need all that many male birds, assuming they're about half and half, which is usual. We'll trade a couple of our males for unrelated ones. There's an ostrich newsletter that advertises trade. And that will still leave us a few to use for feathers and hides.''

He sighed deeply. "We were doing so very well. We were *quite* pleased about everything until . . . Well! And now I suppose that extremely nasty young man will just pick up where his father left off, won't he? He'll start ripping and tearing, just like his father did.''

"I shouldn't be surprised,'' said Shirley. "It's interesting that Mr. Azoli talked to his son yesterday after talking to you. Azoli—the dead one—might have said something to his son that would be a clue as to who killed him.''

"Ms. McClintock, believe me when I tell you everything that man said was a clue as to who wanted to kill him. He just literally *begged* to be murdered. I'll tell you the absolute truth, if I'd had any experience at *all* in shooting people, I'd have shot him myself. I really would.''

The screen door banged from the house, and a woman came out, yelling, "Who is it, Horry?''

"It's the McClintock ranch, Marthine. You know, I told you.''

Shirley was accustomed to being thought of as large, but

this was the first time she recalled being accused of being a ranch all by herself.

"Howdy," said the woman as she approached. "I'm Marthine." She offered a huge, red hand, which Shirley took with some trepidation, only to find it firm and gentle on her own. The woman herself resembled the duchess in *Alice*, an enormous jaw and pugnacious lower lip below piggy little eyes, the whole belied by a smile of extraordinary sweetness. "Poor old Horry here, he's in a state. Two Azolis in two days is two too many for anybody. Suppose you feel the same."

"I haven't met the younger one yet," Shirley said diffidently. "I guess I can be thankful for that."

"Let's thank God for small mercies," Marthine agreed. "You want to come in have some ice tea? I just made some fresh. Horry here had a little problem once on a time, so we don't hold with hard liquor, but I always say nothing beats ice tea on a hot afternoon."

Horry looked at his boots, lower lip out, like a scolded child.

"Horry, you show her the birds while I straighten up the front room; give me ten minutes, you hear?" And she went back the way she had come, leaving Horry to glance at Shirley from beneath his scanty lashes.

"I'd like to see the baby birds," she said pleasantly, trying to be gentle. Poor Horry probably had had enough of being overwhelmed by females. He led the way to the pens, and within minutes she was crouched among a dozen fluffy babies, feeding them grain from an extended palm, the little beaks hitting her hand with repeated soft blows.

"You don't leave them with their parents?" she asked.

"Well, not with that noise," he said plaintively. "Hero— that's the male. Hecate's the female. Marthine named them. Well, Hero was simply *racing* back and forth, throwing himself up against the fence, and we were afraid he'd hurt the little ones, so we brought them in here. They're precocious, of course, so they really don't need parents except to protect them from predators. Not as long as they have plenty of food and water."

Their precocity was not in doubt. Certainly the young ones needed no help in eating. The mixed grain they were offered disappeared in moments, and the chicks scurried off, moving all together, back and forth, like a school of fuzzy fish.

"Their necks aren't as long as I thought they'd be," said Shirley.

"No. They come out of the egg rather short-necked," he agreed. "So do other long-necked birds, by the way. Peacocks, for example. When they're first hatched, they all look like baby chicks. I think it must be a matter of mechanics. It would be hard to fold a long neck up inside the egg and still give the baby room to peck its way out. Maybe I mean leverage. Whatever. But their necks will grow longer *very* quickly."

"My foster daughter would love to see them," said Shirley. "Would you mind if she rode over some time?"

"Not if she comes alone, no. I'm sure she'd be well behaved. I think the woman at the school is going to bring all the children over this fall, at least she asked if we'd mind. So much better to bring them all at *once*, with a responsible adult, rather than have them sneaking in, maybe scaring the birds."

He stood up and led the way back to the house. Inside, Shirley was shown into the scrupulously neat though sparsely furnished living room and given a tall glass of icy tea along with a plate of lemon cookies.

"Aren't the little birds cunning?" asked Marthine. "I do love watching them. And I just hate it when they get frightened. Poor babies. All they know how to do is run, and of course when they're in pens, they can't get away, so they just run and run and run until they drop."

"At least the machine isn't functioning today," Shirley said. "And maybe it won't in the future. Unless the new Azoli intends to continue in the same vein as the old one."

"You know," Marthine said thoughtfully, "I have not been able to figure out what Azoli thought he was doing. I know for a fact he paid over three thousand an acre for that land. Now, that's development land prices, not cattle ranch prices.

He could have had better grassland out near Elizabeth for around five hundred dollars an acre, so buying here doesn't make economic sense for a cattle rancher. Also, the number of acres he'll gain clearing the scrub won't yield commensurate dollars for beef. He could sell cattle off that place for decades and not pay off his initial investment."

Shirley's jaw dropped. Whatever she might have expected from the woman, it would not have been this cogent, and from her own point of view correct, analysis of the economic aspects of Azoli's behavior.

"What do *you* think he was doing?" Marthine demanded.

Shirley sat back thoughtfully. "I don't know, Marthine. I thought maybe he had some kind of tax fiddle going. Maybe he actually expected to develop the land—ten or fifteen years from now, when the market for development land comes back, assuming it ever does—but for now he wanted to maintain an agricultural tax status."

"I've thought of that," said Marthine. "I suppose it's possible."

"Marthine is very *smart* about things like that," said Horace, munching on his third cookie. "She used to work for a tax accountant."

Marthine smiled sweetly at him, and he blushed.

Shirley had a fleeting thought about strange bedfellows.

"Do you have children?" she asked Marthine. "I met Mervin."

"Poor Mervin," she said, shaking her head. "Mervin takes after his father, my first husband. Sneaky. Born sneaky and died sneaky. Not a good influence. We have high hopes though, don't we, Horry? Country air can work wonders." She sipped at her tea, making a little moue, then went on with her former subject as though there had been no deviation.

"So, if he's not doing it for beef, what's he doing it for? It doesn't make sense as development, either. I know for a fact the roads and bridges he put in aren't up to county code, so even though he's spent a mint on them, he can't use them if he subdivides. And people who move out here, even into

111

developments, still want the feeling of country: wildness, birds, animals, fish. You know. They'll want forest and deer and wildflowers, not acres of nothing but grass."

"Marthine thinks it's ignorance," offered Horace.

"Sheer ignorance," she agreed. "The only country the man ever saw was in golf courses, so that's what he wanted to make it look like. He wouldn't know a great blue heron if one flew up his ass."

Horace choked.

"Sorry, Horry," said his wife. "I got carried away." She turned to Shirley confidingly. "Horry doesn't like dirty talk from women. Well, not from anyone, actually. His mama was very ladylike. Horry lived with her right up until she died last year."

"Marthine reminds me of Mama a *lot*," said Horry, taking another cookie. "Except when she forgets herself a little."

Shirley put her glass to her lips and kept it there while her surge of amusement subsided.

"Mama always said a lady mustn't forget herself," Horace went on. "Since most everybody else was *all* too ready to do it for her."

Shirley looked away hastily, only to see Marthine's left eye—the one away from Horace—drop shut in an unmistakable wink.

Horace went on. "When I heard that man taking Mama's name in vain, I tell you, I got very angry. I was just *livid*."

"Your mama's name?" Shirley asked, lost.

Marthine answered. "The son, when he was here this morning. He called Horry a son-of-a-you-know," said Marthine.

"I think the phrase is merely an elaborate way of insulting the man addressed," Shirley commented to Horry. "Not actually a reference to anyone's mother."

"I don't care," said Horace. "As far as I am concerned, he insulted Mama. Shooting is simply too good for a man like that."

"I guess I'm going to have to meet him," Shirley replied,

with a feeling of slight nausea at the pit of her stomach. Every time she thought of Azoli, dead or alive, she felt a sickening rage. As though . . . as though she were considering confrontation with a rapist. One who had attacked her personally. She did not want to think of the father. She did not want to meet the son.

"I understand you were arrested," said Marthine.

Shirley came back to herself with a start. "I guess that's what happened, yes."

"I just wanted you to know, Horry and I do not for one moment believe you had anything to do with his death. I am a very good judge of character. I think you would love to have done him in but would have been prevented from doing so by a very good upbringing in clean, moral surroundings." Marthine nodded to herself, a satisfied expression on her face saying more clearly than words that she was filing this opinion against future need.

Shirley, searching vainly for a reply, could come up with nothing but a gargled "Thank you."

"Now," Marthine continued. "Horry and I have to clean the pens before evening. Clean pens mean healthy birds, isn't that so, Horry? Besides, Mervin needs to be kept busy. I know you'll excuse us."

Shirley rose, saw herself out, and went bemusedly to her car, already rehearsing what she was going to tell J.Q. He would not believe either Horry or Marthine, no matter if she swore on a stack of Bibles. He would have to meet them for himself.

When she left the driveway, she glanced at her watch: three-thirty. She was immediately across County 64 from the Crepmier School, and since Ms. Minging's car was parked beside it, Shirley drove in and hammered on the locked door until Ms. Minging herself came to let her in.

"Your usual forceful self, I see, Shirley," she said reprovingly. "With only a little more effort, you could undoubtedly have broken the door down." Ms. Minging turned and led the way back down the hall to the room that served in part as her office, where she gestured politely toward an armchair, inviting her guest to sit.

"I'm feeling a little frustrated and pent up," Shirley admitted. "Sorry if I sounded like an invasion."

"Rumor hath it that you are in trouble with Botts Tempe," said Ms. Minging.

"Xanthippe, I swear to God I have not done anything even slightly evil."

If Ms. Minging was startled by Shirley's use of her seldom used given name, she did not show it. "Shirley, so far as I can remember, you have never done things that were evil. Ill advised, certainly. Presumptuous, often. Arrogant, in some cases. But not evil."

"Well, in this particular case I wasn't even arrogant or presumptuous. I just caught sight of the man's red shirt and rode down to see what was what. There I was, bending over the body, when Botts showed up."

Ms. Minging fixed Shirley with a falcon's eye and said firmly, "More or less the way I heard the story from Allison. She's very worried about you, you know."

"Allison told you?"

"She called me yesterday, while you were in jail. She was frantic, Shirley. If you will recall her mother . . ."

Shirley nodded slowly. Of course Shirley's being in jail would have made Allison frantic. She had been frantic when her own mother had been in jail, suspected of killing her husband, Allison's father. "J.Q. and I tried to be reassuring," she said weakly.

"She knows you're being reassuring. But you were reassuring about her mother, and her mother ended up dead. She fears you aren't telling her the truth because you think it may frighten her. When she called me yesterday, she made a date to see me this morning, hoping I might give her a more unbiased view."

"I thought she was over here playing volleyball. Oh, damn, Xanthippe."

"Is she right about the threat to you? Are you troubled?"

"I'm scared," Shirley blurted, surprising herself. "I've

never been suspected of anything like this. It's a terrible feeling. Like being . . . chained up, impotent. Unable to act. I
get the same feeling from being suspected that I do when I
see what that man did to the land. Sort of a choked feeling.
Frustration. Suppressed rage. Inability to do anything to set
things right. You know me, Xanthippe. I've always been a
meddler, always had to push in and fix things. Now I can't.
I wake up in the night with heartburn, almost unable to
breathe.''

"I should imagine it would feel like that. Well, I'd be
frightened also, in your place. However, from everything I
hear, there should be no lack of suspects.''

"I've met several.''

"Who? Just for my information.'' She sat back with a look
of pleasant inquiry, the same look she used when eliciting
adolescent troubles from the willing or unwilling.

Shirley settled back into the saggy old chair. "Well, let's
see. There's Mrs. Azoli, Rima. There's her ex-husband, Paul
Howard. They alibi one another, but certainly each of them
has a motive. There's our local ostrich farmers, Horace and
Marthine Rodwinger, whom I have just met.''

"Not Horry?'' Ms. Minging asked with twinkling eyes.
"Surely not dear Horry.''

"No, more likely Marthine. She has a certain indomita-
bility. And then there's her son, Mervin. I received only a
sneer and a vaguely threatening gesture with a shotgun from
Mervin, so I can't say whether he might be capable or not.''

"Who else?''

"Well, there are my neighbors and old friends, Elena and
Joe Ramirez.'' Shirley expatiated briefly on the subject of
Elena and LALA. "And LALA leads us to Father Cisneros
and Olivar Desfuentes and to a woman named Henrietta Labolis and her son Bonifacio, who is said to be a budding
terrorist.''

"That sounds like enough.''

"Perhaps, but it's not all. There's also C.K. Azoli, a son
by his former marriage. He showed up at the ostrich farm

115

this morning, uttering threatening noises and making an Azoli of himself.''

"The former wife and children live on the East Coast, I understand.''

"I understand the same. But I don't know where any of them were yesterday, including C.K. Azoli. I was told he called Rima last night and told her to prepare a room for him, but he could have been calling from Denver for all I know.''

"All those, and you're still frightened?''

Shirley shook her head. "I was the only one standing over the body. And except for Joe and Elena, I may be the only one intimately familiar with a rifle.''

"You mentioned several men, any of whom might have served in the military. Military men are familiar with rifles.''

"True. Though Paul Howard said he wasn't.'' Shirley sighed.

"And what do you intend to do? Find out who really did it, I hope?''

"J.Q. suggests that's a good idea. He doesn't repose much confidence in Botts Tempe for anything that isn't perfectly straightforward, and nothing about this case seems very straightforward. Since I have a countywide reputation as a meddler, J.Q. says if I don't look into it, my failure to do so might be attributed to my having guilty knowledge. As to what I can do—I'm not sure. Talk with the people I've just mentioned, I guess. Azoli's son. Henrietta Labolis's son.'' She stood up and stretched. "So, I'd better get at it.'' She gave the other woman a searching look. "Meantime, what can I do for Allison?''

Ms. Minging's expression became slightly troubled. "I'm worried about Allison. Something's bothering her. Something more than she said. She's worried about you, yes, but there's something else going on. I've seen her several times while you were away, and each time I was conscious of this . . . preoccupation. I couldn't get at it. So far as what you can do, I'd suggest you be honest. Tell her you're frightened but that you've been frightened before. Tell her being frightened for oneself and for others is part of life."

"She's a tough little thing." Shirley sat back down.

"Perhaps not as tough as we've thought. She is a good little thing, though. I've enjoyed her, Shirley McClintock. I'll miss her next year when she goes on to junior high."

"She said something about a summer trip."

"The sixth grade will have Spanish this coming year. I've located a good teacher to come in three times a week for conversational southwestern Spanish, and I thought a trip to New Mexico next summer would be an excellent reward for those who do well. There are places down there where Spanish is the predominant local language. If the students have an opportunity to speak Spanish at all, it's more likely to be southwestern than it is Castilian, so why not get a little exposure. As a matter of fact, I wondered if you and J.Q. might not enjoy the trip. I'll need two or three helpers."

"Livestock," said Shirley, turning up her hands. "It's hard for both of us to leave at the same time. We usually cover for each other." As J.Q. had done during her recent trip to Washington. As she did during J.Q.'s infrequent trips East to visit with his children and grandchildren.

"Assuming always that we can find someone to take care of the livestock, of course," Ms. Minging agreed sweetly, giving the impression she had already arranged for a cow, goat, and chicken sitter.

Shirley struggled out of the comfortable old chair. "Thanks for the help. I wish Allison weren't involved. She doesn't need any more family upsets. I've tried to keep her from learning the details surrounding her mother's murder. I figured maybe, when she was older . . ."

"I don't know, Shirley. Sometimes things like that can't be kept quiet. But I know definitely she's going to be upset about you. Accept that. You can't keep her from it, and it's better to acknowledge it than cover it up. You also might try to find out, gently, what's bothering her."

Shirley left, obscurely comforted by Xanthippe Minging's bland assumption that she, Shirley, would be around next summer to accompany the kids to New Mexico and as obscurely dismayed at what she had said about Allison.

Shirley would mention it to J.Q. Perhaps together they could figure something out. Right now, however, it was time to get home and get some supper started while she cogitated about what she would do next.

J.Q. came in with his hat full of eggs to find her staring into the freezer.

"Were you planning on taking something out of there, or are you just overheated?" he asked, setting the eggs one by one into a bowl by the sink.

"Supper," she muttered. "I forgot what I was doing."

"Obviously. If you'd sniffed the air, if you'd looked on the stove, you'd have seen that I made a pot of menudo for supper. Allison isn't crazy about it, but she can have a hamburger."

"Great," she said without enthusiasm.

"You like menudo," he said, surprised.

"I'm crazy about menudo, your menudo. It's better than anyone else's menudo in the whole world. What I was really doing standing here was trying to figure out what to do next about the other thing."

"We've had this conversation before."

"Right."

"I usually suggest that you flop around stirring up mud until something leaps out of the pool and runs off in a great hurry. At which point you chase after it, baying."

"I remember words to that effect. I don't remember your saying 'flop' or 'baying,' but words to that effect."

"Sit down. I'll give you some soup."

She sat and was rewarded with a large bowl of soup and several flour tortillas, hot out of the microwave.

"Ms. Minging says Allison is upset over this whole thing," she said plaintively.

"Well, of course she is. You knew that."

"I was telling myself we were keeping her out of it."

"If we're in it, she can't be out of it. She's fond of us, you know. It's not as though we're mere acquaintances. The best thing we can do for Allison is figure out who did this thing."

"It's not just this thing Allison's upset about, either. Ms. Minging says—"

Outside in the driveway, Dog set up a monotonous barking, her challenging bark: "Stranger, stranger."

J.Q. went to the door. "Azoli ranch truck," he called in a low voice. "Man driving."

"The son," she said with conviction.

"What son?"

"Azoli's son, Charles. He showed up at the ostrich farm this morning. Threatened Horace Rodwinger. I suppose he's come to do the same for me." She patted her mouth with a napkin, hitched up her trousers, and joined J.Q. at the door. A thirtyish man with more forehead than hair was strutting up the front steps, paying no attention to Dog, who kept snapping at his heels.

"You McClintock?" he demanded when he had stopped a pace outside the screen door.

"That's right," Shirley drawled, looking up and down his five foot six.

"You the bitch that shot my father?"

J.Q.'s grip on her arm tightened.

"You must be carbon-copy Azoli," Shirley said levelly. "No, if any bitch shot your father, it was probably your mother. I understand she had a motive."

His jaw dropped. "My mother's never been near this place! Sheriff said you were his best suspect, and what I want to know is why you aren't in jail." He cocked his head, narrowed his eyes, inserted his thumbs into his belt, and stood spraddle-legged, aggression in every line of his body.

Cock rooster, thought Shirley. Just like his daddy.

"You're trespassing," she said flatly.

"I go where I damned please," he snarled. "According to my father, this is a historic access road, and I'll use it when I see fit."

"Access to what?" blurted J.Q.

"To this side of the Azoli ranch."

119

Shirley took a deep breath. "If your father said that, he was as stupid about the law as he was about everything else he did. We used to be friends with the Jewells. We let them ride through our property, and they let us ride through theirs. We were not friends with your father. We are not friends with you. You have no permission to use any road on or over my property. If you try to do so, I'll have you arrested."

His face turned red. "My father was not stupid! What right have you got to call him stupid?"

"When I see a man spending a lot of money he'll never get back, I consider it—"

"What do you mean?" he cried. "Never get back?"

Something in his tone made her glance at him sharply. His cocky expression had changed to something more wary.

"Your father spent a great deal of money doing things to the land over there," she said flatly. "Things other ranchers, people who make their living by ranching, haven't felt it necessary to do. He spent money which is unlikely to be recovered either through ranch operations or through eventual sale for development. I'd call it ego money."

"He was clearing . . ."

"In the East one clears land. Out here, in the West, one does everything possible to conserve woodlands. When one clears scrub, one is careful where one does it. Your father has been clear-cutting everything, including hilltops and rocky hillsides. Such ground doesn't produce good grass or anything else. Such ground does tend to erode without cover. When it erodes, it takes the grass with it. He was also spraying extensively with weed killer. Weed killer kills everything but grass, including the nutritious forbs that cattle find attractive. In addition, he's destroyed the wildlife habitat on his place, and people who buy mountain development land like to have wildlife about. Natural streams, trees, copses. As one of our neighbors has commented, your father has made the place look like a damned golf course or an industrial park, and he's probably spent upwards of a million dollars dollars doing it. What did you think he was doing?"

He blurted, "He said, investing . . . our money."

"Your money?"

"The foundation money. For us . . . for . . ." Abruptly, he turned on his heel and left, almost running down the steps, pulling the truck into a tight turn that sprayed gravel in all directions.

"I don't think he meant to say that," said J.Q.

"No, he certainly didn't," she said thoughtfully.

"Where'd you come up with that money bit?"

"Actually, I didn't. Horace Rodwinger's wife did. She gave me quite a good thumbnail analysis of what Azoli was doing wrong from a profit or investment point of view. I'd been so angry at him, I hadn't considered the money angle. But even she had no idea Azoli was using someone else's money. I can't imagine . . ."

"Think a minute," said J.Q. "What was it they said the other night at Joe and Elena's? About A.Z. Azoli's money being left to various members of the family? Is it possible daddy left a chunk of stock in his son's control as a family foundation, income to go to his grandchildren? That would avoid the tax you get charged when you skip a generation in a will, wouldn't it?"

"It's possible. And the children expected a return, maybe? Maybe even counted on it, made plans based on it. That would explain the sudden retreat of C.K. Azoli, wouldn't it?" She shook her head slowly. "Maybe."

"Maybe?"

"This visit of his was kind of pat, wasn't it? His strutting up here and challenging me? Why? What was that all about?"

"Maybe he just wanted a look at you, Shirley. You are sort of . . . monumental."

"I've had enough size remarks today, J.Q."

"Sorry."

"Horace Rodwinger introduced me as the McClintock ranch."

J.Q.'s face remained suspiciously calm, and she glared at him, daring him.

"I didn't say a word," he asserted.

"You were thinking."

"It's still a free country. However, you're right. His visit was a little pat."

"As though he might be trying to make a point?" she asked.

"About what?"

"Well, I don't think it was to make the point he didn't know daddy was throwing around foundation money like a drunken sailor."

"Which would have been a motive?"

"Right. A motive for sonny. Or whoever else was supposed to benefit from the foundation."

"A foundation which is entirely conjectural on our part. For which we have no evidence whatsoever."

"True."

"Your soup's getting cold."

"I'll put it in the microwave." She mused. "The visit itself was suspicious. Come to think of it, his visit to Rodwinger's place, earlier today, was also pretty strange. Here he comes in like a house afire, throwing threats this way and that. As though to make the point he'd just arrived. Which he wouldn't need to do if he had, actually, just arrived. Do you suppose it's possible he got here yesterday? Or even earlier? Whenever he got here, he probably arrived by air. We need someone to ask the airlines."

"Who might that be?"

"Well, if I weren't Botts's main suspect, I'd ask him. Since I am his main suspect, there's only one person I can think of: our friend in Lakewood." She was referring to Lieutenant Inigo Castigar of the Lakewood police, a darkly handsome Latin who bought a steer each year from Shirley and occasionally brought his ash-blond daughters and wife to the ranch for a day wandering in the woods or fishing in the beaver ponds.

"He and Marcia and the girls have been out a couple of times since you last asked him for anything," J.Q. said. "He might grant you a favor."

She dialed from memory, hearing the ringing go on and

on before the answering machine cut in. She left her name and number.

"You called him at home?"

"Well, yes. It's going to be a personal favor."

"To help keep you out of jail is a personal favor?"

"Well, what else would you call it? A community service?" She took the steaming soup from the microwave and sat down at the table once more. "I'll make a list, J.Q. It always helps to make a list."

She had just dipped her spoon in the bowl when the phone rang. J.Q. answered it, then handed it to her wordlessly.

"McClintock."

"Ms. McClintock. It's Rima Azoli. I don't know how to ask you . . . I . . . Can I come over there? Please?"

Shirley gestured to J.Q., shrugging. He put his head near hers, listening.

"What is it, Rima?" Shirley asked.

"Charles just got back here. He's in a rage! I . . . I haven't anywhere to go! I haven't any money. I don't even have a car! I can't reach Paul. . . ."

"You're saying you're being thrown out?"

"Charles! It's Charles!"

"Listen, Rima. J.Q. will come over and get you. Okay?"

"Thank you. I . . . Thank you."

Shirley hung up. "Well?"

"It seems you've volunteered my services."

"I thought maybe I could finish my soup while you were fetching her."

"What do you think has happened?"

"She says Charles is in a rage. It would only be a guess, but I'd think he's told her to get out."

"Can he do that? Legally?"

"Who knows? I don't. She probably doesn't know, either. He may be threatening her, giving her no chance to find out."

J.Q. shook his head at her and went out to get the car while Shirley calmly continued eating her soup. It might be the only chance she would have to eat anything for a while,

123

and J.Q.'s menudo was the best menudo in the world, full of chewy bits and rich with posole and ristra chilies, ancho chilies, and garlic and oregano. She hated watery menudo.

She had wiped up the last of the soup with her final tortilla when J.Q. returned. Shirley heard Rima expostulating and J.Q.'s voice in calm return. Then they came in, J.Q. carrying a small suitcase.

"I told him . . . I don't mean to stay . . . it's just, I have to figure out where, what I'm going to do," the woman babbled.

"Sit down," said Shirley, pushing a chair from beneath the table with one booted foot. "Have some soup."

"No, I, that is . . . what I needed . . ."

"Have . . . some . . . soup," Shirley repeated, as though she were talking to someone more than slightly deaf. "You can't do anything until you calm down. You're jittering around like a drop of water in a skillet. For God's sake, woman, sit!"

The last word, uttered in a slightly muffled shout, got Rima's attention, and she sat. J.Q. half filled a bowl and set it before her.

"I'm not really hungry," she said. "It's not . . ."

"Eat," said Shirley. "When was the last meal you had?"

"I . . . I don't remember. Yesterday, I think. I had coffee. . . ."

"Sure. Probably eight or ten cups the way you're shaking. Now sit there and eat that soup."

The woman focused on the bowl in front of her. "What?" she asked suspiciously. "What is it?"

"Philadelphia pepper pot," said J.Q. firmly, glaring at Shirley.

"Oh." Rima dipped her spoon, tasted, swallowed. "It's very . . . very flavorful."

"It is indeed," said Shirley. "Now, suppose I tell you what's happened and you correct me if I go wrong. Your husband's son arrived when? This morning?"

"At the ranch. Yes. This morning."

"Don't put the spoon down. Keep eating. He told you the

124

ranch had been bought with . . . ah . . . family money. That is, money which would now go to your husband's children.''

"And his sister's children, too," said Rima. "All the grandchildren. That's what Charles said.''

"When the business was sold, all this money was left in your husband's hands to manage, right?''

Rima nodded, the spoon tilting perilously.

"Eat," Shirley commanded. "He told his children and his sister and so forth that he was investing the money. So, when he died, his son came out to take over, right?''

"That's what he said. And I told him my money was in it, too, but I don't have any papers! El never gave me any papers! He said I didn't need them!''

"Your money?''

"All of it! Every cent I had!''

"That's the money you got from your divorce settlement, when you and Paul broke up and sold your house?''

"Yes. We sold it for two hundred thousand, and we each got half. We bought it cheaply, years ago. It was a very good buy, and we'd put a lot of work into it. And El said I had to put it back into a residence, to avoid taxes, you know, so he took it and put it into the house!''

"The house you were living in? Over there on the ranch?''

"But he didn't give me a note or anything! And now Charles says I don't have anything coming!''

"Charles is behaving like his father's son, in short. Well. It seems to me, Rima, you need a lawyer more than anything.''

"I don't have any money to pay a lawyer!" she cried, putting her spoon down and burrowing in her pocket for a tissue to wipe her wet cheeks.

"J.Q., hand her a tissue from the box over there. Go ahead and cry, but don't stop eating. I'll ask Numa Ehrlich; he's my attorney. He'll know someone young and hungry and nasty-minded who'll represent you on some kind of contingency basis.''

"But if I use it up paying lawyers, I won't have anything. It was all I had. I don't even have a car anymore.''

Shirley nodded thoughtfully. "Where's Paul?"

"I don't know. I've been calling his motel over and over. He isn't there."

"When he turns up, will he provide a home base for you?"

"He was only going to stay one more day. He has to get back to work."

"I suppose you're glad, now, that your sons were with him."

"Oh, Lord. I suppose. Yes. This has all turned out to be such . . . such a mess." Her voice rose in an agonized howl.

"Are you grieving over your husband, Rima?"

"I haven't had time," the woman wailed. "Nobody gives me any time to do anything!"

Shirley patted her hand and sat quietly while Rima wept, wiped her eyes, then wept again. Her husband had died only the day before. Presumably she had loved him, or had convinced herself she did. Certainly she had worked like a slavey, putting all of herself and her resources at the man's bidding.

Gradually Rima grew calmer. When she seemed to have recovered herself, J.Q. asked, "Who do you think killed him? Presumably not Shirley, or you wouldn't be here."

She shook her head. "I don't think Shirley did it. The sheriff asked me that yesterday, did I think she did it. I told him no. I told him Shirley didn't like what El was doing, but she wouldn't kill him. Charles thinks she did, though. Or says he does. He thought so before he came over here, and more now. When he came back from here, he was raving! But then, he would. El was like that, too. He didn't like women bigger than he was. He always got angry at any woman he couldn't order around. Well, I fell for him, and much good it did me!"

"So who do you think?" J.Q. persisted.

"I don't know. Maybe Charles did it. Maybe that man down by the road. He had words with El. Or maybe it was an accident. People do get shot by accident."

"That man down by the road?" Shirley asked. "You mean Joe Ramirez."

"Yes. He told El he'd kill him." She wiped her eyes again.

"To tell the truth, though, there was scarcely a day somebody or other didn't tell El they'd kill him. El just sort of attracted hate."

Shirley could agree with that.

"Rima, what do you know about your husband's business? Before he sold the family business, I mean."

"Well, when Paul and I first knew him and Clemmy, El worked for his father. He was vice president in charge of operations. He always said he really ran things. His father just occupied a chair."

"Did he ever mention the company being sued?"

"You mean that discrimination thing?"

"Possibly. Was there a discrimination thing?"

"He mentioned it to me once. Some group was going to sue him because the company policies weren't printed in Spanish, something like that."

"What did he say about it?"

"He said they weren't printed in Russian, either. Or Thai, or Vietnamese. He said he had employees from all those places, and he couldn't conduct classes in English for everyone."

"He could have, of course," said J.Q. "It would have been a nice idea, in fact."

Rima shook her head. "I don't know that much about it. I do know he was angry because that's one of the things that got his family all turned against his managing the company."

"His family. You mean his children?"

"His children, and his ex-wife, and his sister and her children. And his mother, too, and his father's sister. They all inherited from El's father. And El was supposed to run the company. But the relatives were pissed at El, because he and Clemmy were divorced and they all liked Clemmy. And they knew about this suit, and El told me they were jealous of him anyhow, so they voted to sell the company."

"What about the foundation?" J.Q. asked.

"What foundation?" She looked at him blankly.

"Was some of El's father's stock left in the form of a family foundation? To benefit the heirs?"

"Oh, you mean the ranch. Well, yes. The foundation owns the ranch. Everything is in the name of Eleazar Azoli, for the Azoli Family Foundation. That was how the money was invested. The income got shared by all the family."

"What if there hadn't been any income?"

Rima thought about it. "There'd have to be some, wouldn't there? From selling cattle?"

"Rima, I'd be surprised if there's even one percent return on the money your husband put into that place. Maybe four or five years from now there will be more, but not anytime soon."

"I don't understand that."

"Well, think it out. He paid three thousand an acre for two thousand acres. He's probably put a million into clearing it, and fencing it, and moving buildings around. He's got what? Fifty or a hundred head of cattle? Expensive cattle, by the way, that take a lot of hay to grow, not cattle that are good on sparse pasture. Next year, that'll increase by fifty percent, and so on, but this first year, he'll have maybe fifty steers to sell. What do you think you get for fifty steers? Say a dollar a pound, which is high, and twelve hundred pounds per animal. That's sixty thousand. Invested in any good bank—granted, finding a good bank these days isn't easy— that same amount of money would have brought in at least eight percent, say half a million. Net.

"Here in the West, we figure five acres to the cow. It's not like back East, where you've got rain bringing belly-high grass up all summer long. The capacity of that ranch is about four hundred head. Say he had got up to capacity and marketed two hundred fat steers and around a hundred eighty purebred heifers a year, allowing ten percent for replacement. That would bring in almost half million, but it would be gross, not net, and his expenses have to run at least thirty percent, more nearly forty percent. So, as an investment, it sucks."

Rima stared at the wall, her mouth open. "That's what he meant," she murmured at last.

"Meant what?"

"When he said he'd get all the juice out of it. He said he'd squeeze all the juice out and give them the rest."

"The juice being?" asked J.Q.

Rima didn't answer.

"Did he think of the juice as the having of it?" Shirley speculated. "Was it getting to live here and ride his horse around his lordly acres, being king of the country, ripping and tearing and making the world over in his image? Putting on his chaps and his hat and yippie-ki-yi-ing around? Maybe that was enough for him, but there wouldn't be any income for anyone else. At least, not for a number of years."

"He was getting even," Rima said. "They shouldn't have forced him to sell the company."

"I can't imagine his father leaving him the authority to spend the money just any old way he liked," said Shirley.

"The old man wouldn't have thought of it like that," J.Q. interjected. "What was willed to the foundation was stock in a profitable company. The old man wouldn't have expected the family to force a sale. He would never have expected his son would have to make decisions about investing the money. It was already invested."

"That's right," said Rima. "He thought El would go on running the company, making a profit, and everybody would do fine."

"Which explains Charles's haste, confusion, anger, whatever, when I said what I said," Shirley murmured. "He came out here to protect an investment, and he's just found out the investment isn't what he thought it was." She tapped the table reflectively. "Rima, you said the lawsuit was one reason his family forced the sale, What was the other reason?"

"Oh, it was Clemmy. They all liked Clemmy. And they took her side in the divorce. And it made El mad, so he threatened them, you know. . . ."

" 'If you know what's good for you, you'll stay on my good side' kind of thing?"

"Something like that. There were fights. Anyhow, they were all convinced he'd ruin the business, just to be nasty. They wanted their money. And they got their money, the part each of them inherited personally. What El had was the foundation money, plus his own personal share of the business."

"And what money you had."

She grimaced. "Well, yes, he had that, too."

Shirley patted her shoulder. "Tell you what. There's a guest house out back. I had company staying there not long ago, so it should still be reasonably clean. There's no problem if you'd like to use it for a while. You go on out there, wash your face, maybe take a nap. There's a phone out there; you can keep trying to reach Paul. Meantime, I'll call my lawyer and see if I can get him to recommend someone to represent you."

"I'm being so much trouble," she mumbled, the tears starting up again. "There should be a funeral. I don't even know what to do about a funeral."

"Well, I rather imagine his children will want his body shipped back East, and if I were you, I'd let them do it. You don't need the grief, Rima."

Rima's soup bowl was almost empty. A little color had come into her face.

"Come on," Shirley said, offering her hand. J.Q. brought the small suitcase, and they went together out to the old bunkhouse that Shirley now used as a guest house. When they returned to the house, they found Allison in the kitchen making a peanut butter and jelly sandwich.

"I see we've got company," Allison said, licking her fingers. "I guess she doesn't think Shirley did it, huh, J.Q.? Or she wouldn't be here."

"She might think I'd done it and still have come here," Shirley replied. "She didn't have much choice."

"That's not true," J.Q. asserted, with a sidelong warning look at Shirley. "Rima does not believe Shirley had anything to do with her husband's death." He raised his eyebrows at Shirley, inviting her participation in honesty.

Shirley sighed. "J.Q.'s right, honey. Most people who know me don't think I had anything to do with it. People who don't know me are different. I can't pretend that doesn't

130

bother me, because it does. The best thing we can do is find out who did it right away."

"Are you scared?" Allison asked, eyes very round.

"Sometimes," Shirley admitted. "Every now and then I'm scared silly. My stomach knots up; I start to sweat; it feels like my heart is racing. But there's no point howling about it. That won't help."

"We have to persevere," said Allison. "That's what J.Q. says when he teaches me math. No matter how one feels, one must persevere." She hugged Shirley, giving her a rather sticky kiss on the cheek. "So what can I do? I helped that other time, didn't I? So this time, what can I do?"

"Honey, believe me, I'm not even sure what I can do next. Talk to Bonifacio Labolis, I guess. And his mama. Which means driving into town. I thought since I've had supper, I'd do that now."

"Are you going to call first?" asked J.Q.

"Didn't think I would," she answered. "I don't want to warn them that I'm coming. Not them or Father Cisneros, because I want to talk to him, too."

Shirley stuck her head into the guest house, intending to tell Rima Azoli that she was leaving for a few hours. She found the woman huddled on the couch, deep in sleep, her mouth slightly open, mascara smeared in runnels down both cheeks. The phone stood beside the couch, stretched to the limit of its cord. Evidently Rima had tried to reach Paul before crying herself to sleep. There was no point in disturbing her.

She did disturb Elena, however, when she knocked on the Ramirez door.

"Were you asleep?" she asked, noting Elena's bleary eyes and untidy hair.

"Relapse," Elena yawned. "Feels like the flu came back again. Not really. Just tired. Joe and I sat up until late last night, talking over your offer. No decision yet."

"Well, let me know when you decide. What I want right now is your friend Henrietta's address."

131

"Why? You think she's involved?"

"I doubt it. Some of her friends or relatives might be, though. Come on, Elena. I need to talk to her."

"Only if you'll promise not to be . . . awful to her."

"I'm not usually awful to anyone."

"I mean about LALA."

"I won't even mention LALA. Well, I won't mention it more than necessary. I won't throw bricks at it."

"Kind of you," Elena said heavily. "She lives in Wheatridge, 4603 Idyll."

"And Father Cisneros?"

"What do you want to talk to Father about?"

"I want to ask him if he mentioned Azoli to anyone prior to the meeting we had the other night."

"What makes you think he did?"

Shirley shrugged. "I just want to ask him, is all."

"He's at Our Lady of Perpetual Comfort."

"Which is where?"

Elena gave her the address, a few blocks from Henrietta's house. Shirley got in the car and left, stopping at the end of the drive to wave at Mike Bostom, who was driving by.

She got out and went over to him. "Mike, I've been thinking about you and Neb. Would your Mom know me if I came to visit?"

"I don't believe so, Shirley," he said in a weary voice. "Dad and I were with her about ten this morning. We had all the windows open. She wanted to smell the air, she said. The meadowlarks were singing. Her face kind of lit up, and she whispered something to Dad, and then in a minute or two she went to sleep. The nurse says she may not ever wake up again. She's out of it. No pain. No nothing. But poor Dad, he's suffering so."

"I could come over. . . ."

"Wait. When it's over, that's when he'll need friends."

Shirley reached through the car window to squeeze his shoulder. "No matter how much you think you're used to the idea that someone is dying, when the time comes, you aren't. I remember when my first husband died, it was like that. I'm on my way to town, Mike. Is there anything I can pick up for you?''

"Oh, Shirley, would you? I got all the way there and back, and I forgot to mail this letter." He handed an envelope through the window. "I'm not thinking."

"I'll drop it into a box for you." She waited until he turned into Bostom driveway, then swung left along the gravel to the county road. The Azoli place was quiet as she went past. She saw no one moving about, heard nothing as she went by. Almost like a cease-fire. If only it would last.

It was about six, late enough that the evening rush hour was over. Traffic was light on the way down from the foothills. Even with a brief stop to drop off the envelope Mike had given her, it took only a little over half an hour to reach the Labolis address, a 1920s bungalow set on a narrow lot behind a paint-peeling picket fence. It was full daylight, but lamplight shone through the living room windows onto the sheltered porch. Shirley knew the house, knew houses like it. The small rooms had dark varnished floors, double-hung windows that stuck when one tried to open them, cramped closets, a bathroom floored with tiny hexagonal tiles, the grout joints between them grayed by generations of feet. Living room and dining room were divided by an archway, perhaps with bookcases on either side. The kitchen would have painted cabinets and fourteen coats of paint, the latest of which was probably white. Possibly there'd be a geranium on the windowsill, bright curtains, red or yellow, and a red or yellow Formica-topped table. The linoleum would be cracked in the corners, or maybe brand-new. When she and Marty had been first married, they had lived in a house exactly like this one, even to the paint flaking from the fence.

She pressed the doorbell, heard nothing, opened the screen, and knocked. Inside, a door opened; the sound of music thumped faintly behind steps approaching. A small window in the door opened, and a pasty face peered at her through the ornamental grill.

"Yeah?"

"Is Henrietta Labolis at home?" Shirley asked.

"She's not here."

"Do you expect her?"

"Yeah. She'll be here."

"Could I wait for her?"

"Don't give a shit," said the face, shutting the tiny window. Footsteps receded.

Shirley, staring at the locked door, told herself she had just met Bonifacio. She fished out a notebook, wrote a note, checked the mailbox to see if there was mail inside, and, finding there was, inserted the note. She would see Father Cisneros first. Our Lady of Perpetual Comfort was only a few minutes away.

The rectory sat at the rear of the church, facing the cross street. Shirley knocked, was admitted by a housekeeper, so identified by a full-length apron, and was shown into a front parlor almost as sparsely furnished as the Rodwinger house had been.

"You won't keep him, will you?" the housekeeper asked, anxiously. "I've just about got his supper ready."

"Five minutes," said Shirley. "Is that too long?"

"Should be about right," she said over a shoulder as she slid out of the room. "I'll get him."

The room was of about the same vintage as the Labolis house, quiet and clean, with cream-painted walls and shiny, almost black varnished woodwork. It smelled of furniture polish. The rug was threadbare, the walls plentifully furnished with saints, either anguished or anguishing. From somewhere toward the back of the house came a murmur of voices, the muted ringing of a phone. Shirley barely had a chance to seat herself on an uncompromisingly uncomfortable straight chair before Father Cisneros himself came through the door.

"Ms. McClintock." He sat down in the next chair. "I hardly expected to see you again soon. I didn't get the impression you were very sympathetic to our aims. . . ."

Shirley grinned at him. "What I'm sympathetic to is finding out who killed Eleazar Azoli so I can get on with my life. And the best way to do that is ask people questions. I've got only one for you. Yesterday, after Henrietta told you about Azoli living here in Colorado, did you tell someone else?"

He flushed. "Why do you think I told anyone?"

"A hunch."

"Even if I did, it had nothing to do with his death."

"I don't buy that, Father. Not as certainty. You would not have told anyone who was not interested. Anyone interested in Azoli being here in Colorado would have had to have a reason for that interest, and that reason could only have been inimical to Azoli himself. I don't for one moment believe you told some unconcerned individual. You'd have had no reason to."

"As a matter of fact, I called a friend of mine in Washington."

"D.C.?"

"Yes. He's a lobbyist for Latino causes. He'd been provided with some unofficial information by the LALA attorneys."

"Concerning?"

"A to Z Components had some government contracts."

"And LALA hoped to adversely affect those contracts?"

"Well, it was a weapon we might have used. Our lobbyist had mentioned the upcoming suit to a few congressmen."

"So you called your lobbyist to be sure he knew Azoli was no longer connected with the construction firm?"

He nodded.

"Father, level with me. You were worried last night when you headed back for town. Why?"

He threw up his hands. "He isn't really 'our' lobbyist. He lobbies for Latino causes, including some . . . some . . ."

"Radical ones?"

"Well, more militant ones, put it that way."

"You wanted to warn him not to say anything to them."

"He already had."

"Ah. You wouldn't care to tell me when, or how?"

He shrugged. "I can understand your concern. I don't think it will help you, but he'd called the head of Eggen, here in Denver."

"Of what?"

"Sorry. Of the EGN."

"Which is?"

"El Gente Nuevo."

" The new . . . what? The new people?"

"Well, it's what some of our southwestern people call themselves. It implies a Spanish-Indian-Mexican amalgam. The man here is Trank Valencia."

"Trank?"

"Tranquiliano, I believe."

"Is he the kind of person who might. . . ?"

"Absolutely not. His name fits him. He's almost impossible to get riled up."

"Ah. You wouldn't know if Mr. Valencia called anyone else here locally, would you?"

He shook his head, started to speak, was interrupted by the arrival of the housekeeper. "Father!" she said, giving Shirley a reproachful glance. "Your supper!"

"I won't keep you from your meal," Shirley said. "But when you've finished, will you call Mr. Valencia and find out? All I want to know is, did he call anyone here in Colorado at any time before four-thirty, our time?"

"Surely you don't think . . ."

"Look, Father. I didn't kill Eleazar Azoli. I have no idea who did. I don't know if LALA or this EGN is involved. I do know the more red herrings I have to drag across the sheriff's trail, the better. Whether I think it's likely or not, it will help. If you don't mind."

He shrugged, agreed, and left Shirley to find her own way out as he followed his housekeeper toward the back of the house. The hallway smelled wonderfully of roast lamb, making Shirley wish she'd eaten a bit more of J.Q.'s menudo.

Henrietta's house, when Shirley returned there and found her quarry at home, smelled of nothing much. Certainly not of roasted meat. Henrietta herself, looking tired and grumpy, had a glass in her hand when she came to the door.

"Gin and tonic," she said, raising the glass. "You want one?"

"A weak one," Shirley agreed. "You got my note?"

"Got your note. Had words with Bony. Not that it's unusual to have words with Bony. Did he really tell you he didn't give a shit?"

"I mentioned it in the note because I felt it probably mattered to you as a professional. The next person at your front door might be important to you."

"Do you have children?" Henrietta asked, leading the way back to the kitchen.

"I lost both my son and my daughter," said Shirley, feeling the familiar choking sensation that those words always summoned up. Marty. Sal. My son. My daughter.

"Oh, I am sorry."

"It was a long time ago."

"Both at once?"

"No. No, my daughter was killed by a drunk driver. And my son the anthropologist went on an expedition and never returned. She was twelve. He was twenty-one." She kept her face and voice expressionless.

"A little older than Bony. Bony's twenty."

"Young for a militant."

Henrietta handed her a tall glass and seated herself at the kitchen table, which stood before an open window looking out onto the backyard. "Let's sit here. The living room is stuffy." She swallowed a good inch of her own drink, setting it down with a deeply heaved breath. "He is young. But then, militancy comes easy to the young. And to the thoughtless. It's great to have a cause because it excuses everything, doesn't it? Bony finds it easier to excuse his failings than to confront them, let's put it that way. We are about at the point of no return."

"Meaning?" Shirley looked at her quizzically.

"Meaning I can't countenance some of the stuff that goes on. I've said he either stops or he leaves here. If I can't influence his life-style, I'm not going to go on supporting it."

"Is that what's called tough love?"

"I suppose. I'd call it coming to the end of my tether. I

just can't go on watching, worrying. He runs with this crowd, all more or less like him, sneery, indolent, don't read, don't think, aside from their 'cause,' nothing in their heads but rock music, drugs, sex, and making big money without any effort whatsoever. Maybe that's overstating. He may not be that bad.''

"Small favors," murmured Shirley.

"At least he's never been in jail. His best friend, Marmot Marquez—can you believe a nickname like that?—seems to have spent most of his youth in juvenile hall and has been in jail twice since he turned eighteen a couple of years ago. Violent crimes both times. Marmot, thank the Lord, has recently departed.''

"He was also a militant?"

"Well, so to speak. Both he and Bony were hangers-on of this new people bunch. They lent him a certain legitimacy.''

"El Gente Nuevo?"

"Who told you about that?"

"Father Cisneros mentioned it. What's their program?"

"They have job training and literacy programs, but so far as Marmot and Bony were concerned, the program was to blame the Anglo world for everything. If they can't read, it's the Anglos' fault. If they can't keep a job, it's the Anglos' fault. Never mind they don't show up to work, or show up drunk or stoned half the time, that's the Anglos' fault too. And any of us older Latinos who have decent jobs must be Tió Tomáses.''

"Do they do anything positive?"

"Well, they talk a lot about gaining 'respect.' The crimes Marquez was convicted for had something to do with his getting even with people who didn't show respect. Mostly they just strut around and paint nasty graffiti and maybe make bomb threats, stuff like that. At least I heard Marquez's bunch did that.''

"Are you saying he belonged to a gang?"

"Not really a gang. Not like the black gangs, at least. The black gangs are into drugs pretty much. Well, come to that, maybe Marmot's bunch is a gang. I have no proof. What I do have is another son and a daughter who are proud to be Hispanic, who speak good English and pretty good Spanish. They get good grades in school. I'm not going to let them be pulled down to Bony's level."

Shirley regarded her thoughtfully. "El Gente Nuevo must have some more or less responsible persons in charge, right? Father Cisneros mentioned Tranquiliano somebody. Why did he put up with Bony and Marmot?"

"Tranquiliano wouldn't put up with either of them. But part of the program is working with people who've maybe been in prison, getting them jobs, maybe putting them to work in the program. Mostly, they're respectable. They have jobs and live in houses and have wives and families." She made a face. "They've become the kind of people their grandkids will revolt against."

Shirley laughed. "You're a cynic."

"More and more as time goes on. Even though I work more closely with Latin American causes than Elena does, I'm not nearly as militant as she is. She's a believer, a philosophical believer. Because of her husband, I think. Something working there, something sentimental or guilty, as though she's doing it for him. She makes excuses for everything the locos do, but me, I've seen how they hurt people, and that I don't like. Elena's never bumped hard against the reality, that's all."

"You think this . . . Marmot could have killed Azoli?"

The woman flushed deeply. "Don't ask me, Shirley. I didn't like the kid, but maybe that was just because of the way he influenced Bony. Sometimes two people who might be relatively harmless on their own turn lethal when you mix them. Or am I being melodramatic?"

Shirley considered this. "No. I think that can happen. Group members can egg each other on."

"Bony and Marmot certainly did that. I think either of them alone might have tended to be big talk but no action. But put the two of them together and they got up to really stupid, destructive stuff. I guess what I'm saying is, maybe

Marmot could have killed him. Maybe Bony could have. But more likely it would have taken the two of them together, which didn't happen because Marmot—thank the good Lord—moved away."

"Moved away?"

"He got picked up on a criminal trespass charge and got probation from some sympathetic judge—soulmate to Elena, no doubt—and his family decided to remove him from further temptation." She leaned back in her chair and yawned, somewhat cheered by the conversation or the drink or both. "You want to stay to supper? I'm beginning to be hungry."

Shirley shook her head. "Thanks, but no. I ate before I left the house. What I do need to do, Henrietta, is eliminate Bony as a possibility. You can understand that."

The woman frowned. "You can hardly expect me . . ."

"I haven't mentioned his name to the sheriff. I will, if it seems useful, unless I know for an absolute fact he wasn't involved. I'm no martyr! I told Elena and Joe the same. I'm not a romance heroine who goes around tight-lipped, protecting my friends while people snug the noose around my neck."

The woman shook the glass in her hand, making the ice rattle, swirled it, shook it again with a wry grin. "Right, you're no romance heroine. All you need to know is where he was yesterday afternoon, right?"

"Where he can prove he was yesterday afternoon. I won't take his word for it, or yours. I'd have lied for my kids, anytime."

Henrietta grimaced. "Yeah. Well, mother love and all that aside, I'd like to know where he was, too. I'll see what I can find out. One thing I'm sure of, Bony had no motive to kill Azoli. He didn't even know about Azoli."

Shirley, departing with friendly words, thought of reminding Henrietta that her son could have known about Azoli. He'd been present when the lawyer had called, and he might have found out through the local EGN. Let it alone. Wait until Henny found out whatever Henny was going to find out.

"I'll call you," Henrietta promised. "When I find out."

"Please," Shirley murmured, heading for her car. It was time to go home. Thursday had gone on quite long enough.

5

When Shirley arrived home, she found a strange car in the driveway. Since the color was that of the car she'd seen in the gravel pit, she assumed Rima had reached her ex and summoned him to provide emotional support.

"Rima's former husband?" she asked J.Q. when she came in, thrusting a thumb in the direction of the car outside.

"I suppose," he mumbled from behind his paper. "Dog barked when he drove in. I looked out, and Rima was waiting in the drive, and they both went into the guest house. I don't know who else it might be."

Shirley sat down with a groan.

"What?" he asked in a concerned voice.

Why had she groaned? "I don't hurt anywhere," she said after thinking about it. "It must just be that the idea of talking to the two of them makes me weary. I want to find out more about this shot they heard, see if they agree about where they were, what it sounded like, but . . ."

"What did he say this morning?"

"He said it sounded like it was on top of them. Immediately reverberations, *banga-banga*."

J.Q. peered over his paper. "But they didn't see the shooter?"

"Said not. Of course, they could be lying."

"Something doesn't fit, that's sure. Any shooter with a view of Azoli would have been in view of Rima and Paul. The trees are sparse. They wouldn't hide anyone."

"That's true only if the shot they heard was the shot that killed Azoli. We have no proof it was."

He put the paper down and gave her a thoughtful look. "You really think somebody was down there letting off red-herring shots?"

"Well, look at it, J.Q. How many ways can we interpret what they say? Either the shot they heard was the shot that killed him or it wasn't! If it wasn't, then Rima and Paul could be right about the shot's coming from nearby, possibly from among the trees along the road. It could have been a random shot, not aimed at anything. If it was the shot that killed him, however, then the two of them could be lying about not seeing the shooter. The biggest reason for lying, of course, would be if one or both of them did it."

"Maybe they were lying about *where* they were," said a small voice from the kitchen door. "Maybe they didn't see the person because they were somewhere else."

"A point requiring clarification, Holmes," said J.Q. with a bow in Allison's direction.

"Right, Sherlock." Shirley made a bow of her own. "Come on in, Allison. I was just about to tell J.Q. about my meetings with the LALA people." She sat down and rocked back on the chair legs as she filled them in on her meetings with Father Cisneros, Henrietta, and Henrietta's most unpleasant son.

"What was that name you said?" Allison asked. "Bony's friend?"

"Marmot Marquez," Shirley repeated. "Who has, supposedly and to general thanksgiving, moved away."

"He's moved here, is where he's moved to," said Allison. "He's over at the ostrich farm."

"How do you know that?" Shirley asked, astonished.

143

"Oh, I was going over to Crebs, and this sort of stringy-haired guy was leaning up against the mailbox across the road. He had a gun, like he'd been hunting, and he said hi, so I said hi, and he said something about Beauregard being a good-looking horse, and who was I. So I said who I was, and he told me he was Marmot Marquez."

"Young? Kind of pimply?" Shirley asked disbelievingly. "Mervin? Marthine's son Mervin is Marmot Marquez?"

"Doesn't it fit?" asked J.Q.

"Oh, it fits, I suppose. Marthine and Horace said they'd removed Mervin from the bad company he'd been keeping in the city. They had high hopes that they'd changed his life. One thing for sure, they didn't know they had a perfect terrorist's target in Azoli."

"He didn't look much like a terrorist," said Allison in a doubtful voice. "But he was carrying a rifle."

"Don't terrorists look pretty scruffy?" Shirley asked. "I thought he looked the type. Are you sure it was a rifle? Not a shotgun."

"He had a rifle," Allison asserted. "J.Q. taught me the difference."

"Isn't that interesting?" said J.Q. "What's Marthine? I mean ethnically?"

"Anglo. Well, European. Dutch maybe. Or German. She has that energetic death-to-all-dirt look. Mervin must get his personality from his father, Marthine's first husband. She described him as being sneaky. Lived sneaky, died sneaky is what she said."

"That could explain the nickname," said J.Q. "If Mervin is also sneaky. Marmots are, more or less."

Shirley had always thought of marmots as skinny animals wearing the fur of larger creatures, like spindly youths dressed in raccoon coats. She relished their boneless sprawl, which could turn in an instant to vanishment. "Marmots aren't any sneakier than any other rodent," she objected.

J.Q. mused, "But other rodents wouldn't do. Mouse Marquez? Rat Marquez? No sonority to that."

"Prairie Dog Marquez," offered Allison. "Chipmunk Marquez?"

Shirley waved them down. "Come on, guys. Be serious. If this kid thought Azoli was an enemy of his people, could he have done something about it?"

"How would he have found out about Azoli in the first place?" J.Q. asked.

"He had two sources of information. Henrietta said her son Bony was in Henrietta's office when the call came through from Washington, and Father Cisneros says he called a lobbyist in Washington who works for EGN, which is an activist Hispanic group, and that person called their local office, which, it turns out, is not foreign territory to either Bony or Marmot."

"But didn't Henrietta say Bony and Marmot were harmless?"

"She said she thought they were probably fairly harmless apart, but they may not have been apart. Bony could have driven up here to join his friend. Or maybe someone else from EGN went off on a tangent of his own. Whoever it was didn't need to be from Ridge County, God knows. My round trip down to the city this afternoon took only about half an hour each way. We're not exactly on the back side of the moon."

"When Henrietta finds out what her son was doing yesterday afternoon, she'll tell you, won't she?"

"I imagine she'll tell me if I ask. I don't know how we find out what Mervin was doing, however."

"The same way. Ask. From what you say about Marthine, she probably keeps pretty close tabs on him."

Shirley yawned. "My curiosity is at odds with my need to curl up and sleep for about ten hours. I'm too weary to talk to Marthine. Or anybody. I want a bite of something and then bed."

"You don't sound too tired," said Allison. "You sound better. Not so jumpy."

"It's simple exhaustion. No jumps left." She concluded

145

this statement with another enormous and uncontrollable yawn.

"Go on in and have your shower," said J.Q. "Allison can bring you another bowl of menudo."

"That awful soup!" Allison made a face. "Yech. Pigs' feet and cows' stomachs."

"I like it," Shirley murmured as she wandered off to her bedroom. "Pigs' feet and all." The sound of Allison's voice raised behind her made her think, not for the first time, how lucky she was to have the child. And how determined she was to keep her happy.

Allison brought the soup along with a bowl of raw vegetables. "J.Q. says you need these for vitamins," she told Shirley severely. "Can I sit here and talk to you while you eat?"

"Of course you can," Shirley responded, wondering if this might be a good time for a heart-to-heart. Maybe she could find out what was bothering the child.

"I used to keep my mom company sometimes at night before she went to sleep," Allison murmured.

"I used to do the same thing with my mother when I was your age. That's when I used to find out all the family gossip. I'd sit on the foot of the bed, and she'd tell me all about my naughty uncle or my weird cousins. Around here, I'm afraid we all fall into bed without much ceremony."

"J.Q. says it's because we work hard," the girl murmured, examining her hands intently. "Are you and J.Q. ever going to get married?" The words came out in a rush, as though she were afraid they might not come at all.

Shirley caught her breath. She stopped chewing and made herself start breathing again, searching for an answer that would satisfy both Allison and herself. "It's not something we've worried much about, Allison. To my mind, marriage is a religious or legal matter. You know how J.Q. and I feel about most religious things—formal ones, at least—and at our age, I don't think legal contracts are necessary. It's not as though we were a young couple starting a family."

"I'm your family."

"You certainly are. But you're our family regardless. You know you can depend on either or both of us as long as we're alive. Do you think you'd feel any differently toward either me or J.Q. if we were married? Does it make a real difference to you?"

Silence. Shirley spooned soup into her mouth, chewed, and swallowed, watching the child's face, seeing her mouth move as she tried words and discarded them. Was this what had been troubling her?

After a time Allison said, "I guess what's really important is whether it would make a difference to you."

"Well, you've got to keep in mind I was married twice. Both my husbands died. I treasure J.Q.'s company very much. I'm a rational, sensible person, and yet I can't get it out of my head that my marrying J.Q. might . . . might endanger him somehow."

"That's silly," Allison snorted.

"Right. So's this business of my being an excess body finder. Nonetheless, I do find them. So . . . I humor myself. I think J.Q. and I are pretty good as we are."

"Does he think so?"

"Well, J.Q. was married, too. He and his wife got a divorce a long time ago, after their kids were grown up, when they found they no longer shared any of the same enjoyments. That happens to people sometimes."

"Maybe people shouldn't get married at all!"

Shirley leaned back into the pillows and considered the question. "I suppose my views are unorthodox, but I've always felt the main reason for marriage is to make provision for mutual care and sustenance—including care and sustenance of children. I've always thought it would be nice if any group of people were allowed to 'get married,' whether it was a same-sex couple or a dozen unrelated people. A contract like that could take the place of the extended family that many people don't have. And if a whole group of people could contract a marriage, then it wouldn't be so tragic if one member of it got sick or died or ran off! The way things are, too many people get hurt when a marriage breaks up.

147

After divorce, men, as a group, have a higher standard of living while their children have a lower. Women still make only about sixty percent of what men do for the same work. Men are still paid 'breadwinner' wages, though it's as often the women who do the breadwinning.''

''Would you make people stay married?''

''Under the current system? No. You can't force people to live together. No, what I'd do is I'd put a thirty percent surcharge on the income tax of all nonchaste single and divorced men and use the proceeds to support all the children of single or divorced women.''

''What's nonchaste?''

''Men who have sex with women.'' She laughed. ''All men but those in prisons or monasteries. Presumably, all nonchaste men are the fathers of all fatherless children!''

''The men wouldn't like that much.''

''I think you can safely say that. Right.''

''Besides, some women just don't care how many babies they have, so it wouldn't be fair.''

''True.'' She shook her head sadly, noting almost absently that Allison looked shaken.

''Is she giving you the responsibility lecture?'' J.Q. asked from the doorway.

''I don't know how she got started,'' Allison answered tremulously, looking away. ''All I did was ask her why . . . why something.''

Shirley handed her empty bowl to J.Q. ''Sorry, J.Q. I got sidetracked. Allison asked me why you and I didn't get married, and I . . . told her.''

J.Q. blinked slowly. ''Oh, you did, did you?''

''I believe so. From my own point of view, of course. You are at liberty to offer your own explanations.''

''I think I've heard enough about it,'' Allison said in a high, disturbed voice as she left the room in some haste. ''I think you're probably fine the way you are.''

''Well!'' J.Q. exclaimed, looking after her. ''I think the kid is severely overdosed on polemic, Shirley, my dear. Did you bewilder her with vehemence and long words?''

"Oh, J.Q., you're right. It was something I said. I got carried away, and I said something that upset her, and whatever's been bothering her, I've probably made it worse!"

"It's all right, love. We'll fix it when we figure out what it is. Poor kid. Do you ever wish you were a kid again?"

"A kid? Her age? No. Things are too tough for kids these days. I'd like to be forty-five, maybe. I'd like to have stayed about forty-five."

"I'm with Allison in one respect." He patted her shoulder as he turned to leave. "I think you're probably fine the way you are."

Friday morning brought an early phone call that Shirley, her head under the pillow, told herself she did not hear. The silence that followed was more disturbing than the ringing had been, however, and she found herself irrevocably awake. Twenty minutes later she stalked into the kitchen to find J.Q. pouring coffee and Rima poised outside the screen door, one hand extended like a beggar seeking alms.

"I don't want to intrude," she called when she saw Shirley come into the kitchen.

Shirley opened the door and ushered her in. "You ready for breakfast?"

"Paul just got here a few minutes ago. We'll have breakfast in town. I just stopped to say thank you."

"Nonsense. Bring him in."

"Oh, Shirley, that's an imposition."

"It probably is, but I need to talk to the two of you about that shot you heard, so we might as well do it over breakfast. I've got some homemade rolls in the freezer. Eggs are no problem. We've got more eggs than we know what to do with."

"Well, if you're sure it's no trouble. . . ." She twinkled a TV interviewee smile and went busily out the door and back down the path to the guest house.

"Isn't she the little busy bee. He got here a few minutes ago, my foot," muttered J.Q. "He's been here all night. I looked out at four this morning; the car was still there."

"Now, now, J.Q.," she murmured as she took the rolls from the freezer and put them in the microwave. "As Allison made clear last night, we are not good persons to comment on whether others are living in sin."

"I don't care how Rima lives. It's her little social fibs about it that make me itchy. Don't make any breakfast for Allison."

"She's off breakfast?"

"She's gone. She had a bowl of cereal a few minutes ago and rode over to Cavendish's. Mrs. Cavendish bought a new gelding, and Stuffy wants to show it off."

"Is that what the seven o'clock phone call was?"

"That was it. Besides, I think Allison needs a break from us. We're codgers, Shirley. Opinionated as all get out."

"Me and my big mouth!" Shirley sighed.

"Well, you did go on and on last night. McClintock on the soapbox."

Shirley's forehead furrowed. "God. It's been so long since I was a mother, J.Q. I started out last night wanting to find out what was bothering Allison, and before I knew it, there I was, on the lecture circuit! I'm doing it all wrong! But I want her to think about responsibility. And I want her to be wary, too. There's lots of dangers out there for kids her age, boys and girls both. It's an age when a lot of kids get into trouble through too much unquestioning trust."

J.Q.'s reply, if any, was cut off by Rima calling gaily from the doorway, "Here we are!" She came in with a charmingly social smile, leading her companion by the hand, as though arriving at a cocktail party. Paul himself looked merely tired, grumpy, and in need of coffee.

J.Q. remained ostentatiously dug in behind his paper. Shirley kept a straight face as she filled the cups, put the heated rolls on the table, and then busied herself with the omelet pan.

"Ranch eggs," Paul murmured after his first bite. "They taste nothing like store eggs."

"I agree with you," Shirley remarked. "Fresh eggs are one of the small enjoyments I count on in my old age."

"And for which we pay a heavy price," muttered J.Q. "In time, shotgun shells, and chicken feed."

"True," Shirley agreed. "The coyotes are as fond of chicken as we are of the eggs. But whenever I eat them, I convince myself it's worth it. Nice of you both to share the harvest."

"I wish I felt we merited the hospitality," Paul muttered. "I feel like I'm here under false pretenses."

"You're here mostly for the reason I gave Rima: because I need to find out from the two of you more about that shot you heard. I'd like to know exactly where you were sitting when you heard the shot and how long you'd been there."

"What difference does it make?" Rima cried.

"It means a lot to me, Rima. You heard a shot, but you didn't see where it hit. The shot you heard might not have been the one that killed your husband. My neck's on the block, and I need to know. Where, and how long?"

Paul patted his ex-wife's hand as he said, "Well, we'd been there almost an hour, right, Rimmy? I got there about three, three-fifteen. Rima showed up after ten or fifteen minutes. I didn't look at my watch, so I'm guessing. She came walking down the road. I saw her in my rearview mirror, so I got out of the car. We both wandered over and sat on that big flat-topped stump."

"Facing which way?" asked J.Q.

"Facing? Well, back toward the car, I guess. Back toward the road. And we talked."

"For a long time?"

"Well." He shrugged, looked at his ex-wife, shrugged again. "It didn't seem too long, but I suppose it could have been an hour."

"How many cigarettes did you smoke, Rima?"

"Not many . . . oh, two, I think. Maybe three. That'd be about an hour's worth."

"And then?"

Rima said, "And then we heard the shot. I mean, we both jumped out of our skins. It sounded like it happened right next to us."

151

"Then what did you do?"

"We looked around. We jumped up and looked around, all around, to see if we could see where it came from." Rima put down her fork. "We didn't see anyone, honestly, Shirley. We really *didn't*."

"Yeah, well, that's the interesting thing," Shirley drawled. "J.Q. and I walked all along the stream, all along the edge of the woods where the gravel pit is, and there simply isn't anyplace nearby where someone could have seen your husband without being seen from that stump."

"You may not have noticed, but it's like a theater," J.Q. explained. "The stump is on an open, flat place, separated by gravelly open ground from the creek to the north. The slopes up to the east and west are open. The trees along the creek are sparse on our side of the fence and nonexistent on the Azoli side. There is no cover."

"Well, whoever it was was probably back in the trees!" cried Rima. "Toward the road."

"If he or she was back in the trees, he or she couldn't see the gully where your husband was. Honestly. Go take a look for yourself."

"Maybe the person was up the hill, north of us."

"Then you'd have heard the shot as coming from that direction, not from right next to you."

"So, what are you trying to say?" asked Rima.

That you may be lying to us, twit, thought Shirley.

She said, "I'm questioning whether the shot you heard was actually the shot that killed your husband. The way the land lies indicates it wasn't. If you were there for an hour or more, he must have been shot an hour earlier. The autopsy may confirm that."

"Do you know what the autopsy findings are?" demanded Paul.

Shirley laughed shortly. "Far's I know, they haven't done an autopsy yet. If they have, nobody's made me privy to the results."

"Well, I was in that gravel pit for at least an hour, and I heard only one shot," Paul asserted firmly.

"Have you done any shooting yourself?" asked J.Q. "So's you could judge distance, for example? Or direction?"

"Not guilty," Howard said, turning up his hands. "Aside from trying to win a stuffed animal at a shooting gallery at a county fair or two, I don't think I've ever fired a gun."

"How'd you do winning the prize?" J.Q. asked.

"Zilch. The girl I was trying to impress went off with somebody else."

"I never went to a county fair with you," said Rima.

"I had a life before I met you, pet," he said. His smile sagged at the ends, showing teeth. "Just as I'm likely to have a life after, unless you make up your mind pretty soon. El Azoli is now dead, Rima. Let's get on home and forget he ever happened!"

"I don't think the sheriff will quite let you do that," Shirley remarked, refilling their coffee cups. "Even though I'm suspect number one, you're still witnesses, so to speak."

"I didn't mean today." Paul turned to Shirley. "I know we can't leave right away. But Rima says she wants to hang around, even after all this is settled, so she can get her money back. I say, hell, hire a lawyer and let him do that. Let's get on with our lives."

"That hundred thousand was a good part of my life," Rima cried angrily. "Sixteen or so years of it."

"I thought the boys were a good part of your life," he said in a sober voice. "I thought I was. . . ."

"I'm sorry," said Shirley. "But my kitchen isn't the time or place for you two to have an intimate discussion of your marital difficulties. You're welcome to use the guest house as long as necessary to get your lives resolved, but right now we're talking about something else."

"I just don't see why El's kids should get everything he had and everything I had, too," she cried, eyes filling with tears. "It's rotten."

Paul shouted at her, "I told you, we'll get a lawyer to fight that battle. You can't do anything. Come on, Rimsky-Corsetoff."

Rima blushed red. Shirley pretended she neither heard nor

153

saw. J.Q. snorted. Paul pulled Rima to her feet and, over her protests, led her out the back door.

"Rimsky-Corsetoff?" asked J.Q.

Shirley said stiffly, "Even I have on occasion been the recipient of honeyed words and silly names."

"Such as?"

She blushed. "None of your damned business. I merely mention it as a caution. I wouldn't be too amused if I were you. You, too, could be called something silly."

"Surely not. Not dignified me."

Shirley sniffed. "Do you *believe* those two?"

"Do I believe what? That they are suited to one another? That they did indeed spend an hour on the old stump going over old, old ground? That they heard a shot?"

"All the above."

"Yeah. More or less."

"Which leaves me nowhere," she said angrily.

"If they're telling the truth, then the shot that killed Azoli had to be fired before they got there. And that should let you out."

She shook her head. "If I had a witness to the fact I was out in the west pasture all afternoon, drawing pictures of calves, it would let me out. But nobody saw me there that I know of. A low-flying hawk, maybe. I can't prove when I finished up over there and rode over to the east fence line."

"Well, let's say at the least it will obfuscate the issue."

"Botts is so obfuscated right now, a little more won't faze him." She bit her lip, astonished to find herself shaking.

"It will at least put him off your tracks," he insisted, getting up to put his arms around her. "Come on, old dear. It'll give us breathing space."

She took a shuddering breath. "I know. I'm being silly. It's just that we haven't found out anything useful. . . ."

"That's not it," he murmured. "That's not what's got you shaking. What is it, Shirley? What's going on with you?"

"I hated him," she whispered in return. "I hated him, J.Q. I've disliked people before, but never like this. Every time I think about him, I hate him. He spoiled my place! He

154

spoiled my lovely place. He raped it and ruined it. Whenever I think of him dead, I feel guilt bubbling up like lava, because I wanted him dead so badly! And then when Botts thinks I did it, I want to say yes, yes, I wanted him dead!''

"Shhh." He held her tightly against him, patting her broad back with a leathery hand. "You wouldn't have done it. You'd have thought about it. You'd have talked to me about it. We'd have plotted how we could do it, a dozen different highly original methods of homicide. Finally, we'd have made a black joke of it, and that would have been the end of it. You wouldn't have killed him. We wouldn't have."

She took another deep breath. "Maybe. I'm not as sure as you are."

"You underrate yourself. A new thing, for you. Come on, now. Best thing to do is find out who really did it and stop terrifying yourself with guilt feelings."

She clenched her jaw, pressing her hands at the sides of her head. He was right, of course. J.Q. was almost always right. Certainly always sensible. There was no excuse for her behaving this way. "Who do I go after now?" she asked him. "Marmot Marquez? Bony? Azoli's son? Who?"

"A first step might be to verify what Rima and Paul told us about their meeting in the gravel pit. Could they possibly have been seen by anyone?"

"Mike Bostom, maybe. Or old Neb. But I will not bother them at a time like this."

"All right, don't. You can talk to Joe and Elena. They might have seen Paul and Rima at one time or another. Or some visitor to the Ramirez house might have seen them, perhaps someone who came to pay a condolence call after the funeral, before you got back. Whether it was on that day or some other day, maybe you can get some independent verification on their pattern, how often they met and for how long."

"I have to see Elena anyhow. I didn't give her any data on the Washington buildings the other night, and I'm sure she'll want to see the income and expense figures at least. While I'm there, I'll ask her and Joe."

She straightened up, telling herself sternly to behave, to get on with it, start by phoning Elena, which she did, receiving an invitation to come on over. As she was getting into the car, Paul Howard hailed her from the guest house door and came trotting out.

"Shirley, are you going into town?"

"I'm going down to Ramirez's right now. I may go to town later. Why?"

"I was going to let Rima have my car. She wants to go over and pick up her things. She needs a vehicle to bring her suitcases back in, but she doesn't think I'd better go over there."

Shirley rubbed her forehead, conquering irritation. Damn people! "Why don't you drop her off on your way to town, and I'll pick her up when I'm through at Elena and Joe's, in an hour or so."

"It'll take her that long to pack."

"She's moving out, is she?"

"Well, it's that or stay and fight Charles. His attitude surprises me, quite frankly. I always used to think he liked us, me and Rima; liked us as people, not just friends of his folks. I thought he was a pretty good kid. Now he's turned into Mr. Hyde. He really resents Rima, and he's made it pretty clear he wants her to go."

"She'd be smart to get out of there anyhow. Too many furies raging around."

"I can tell her you'll pick her up?"

"Yes. Tell her to be patient. I'll get there eventually."

Mike and Neb Bostom were walking slowly toward her along the roadside as Shirley left the driveway, Mike carrying a small sheaf of wildflowers, bright against his khaki shirt. He waved at her with his free hand, and she rolled to a stop.

"How's Oriana this morning?" she asked, wishing there were some ritual phrase she could have uttered. Something that was comforting without requiring a response. Something Indian, maybe. Some Navajo phrase about walking in beauty. Though, come to think of it, that wouldn't do for someone

156

with a dying relative. The Navajo were afraid of death. Would it be kinder not to mention her at all?

Mike shook his head. "She's just the same, Shirley."

"I see you've been flower gathering."

Mike said, "I talked Dad into coming out with me while the nurse is there." He shifted the flowers and leaned into the open window. "Where are you headed?"

Without thinking, she said, "Over to Ramirez's. I'm trying to put together enough information to get myself off the sheriff's suspect list."

"You're really worried about that," said Mike, sounding surprised.

"Lord, yes," she blurted, surprising herself in turn.

Neb had been looking away toward the hills, obviously in some other world, but now he turned toward her, an expression of concern on his face. "You don't think anyone believes you did it, do you, Shirley?"

"What I think won't help me much, Neb. Not unless Botts Tempe can find another suspect. I'm going over to ask Joe and Elena if they've ever seen Mrs. Azoli and her ex-husband in the old gravel pit. Evidently the two of them have been holding family conferences down there for a week or more."

Neb nodded slowly. "So that's who that was. A kind of blondy-gray-haired fellow with a beard? I saw him—that is, them."

"When did you see them, Neb?"

Neb scratched his head. "Oh, when was it? They were sitting on a stump down there, talking. That is, he was talking, she was crying mostly."

"That must have been when I sent you out for a walk," said Mike. "You haven't been getting out of the house enough."

"I suppose that's when it must have been."

Shirley nodded. "The fact you saw them may help, Neb. There's a timing anomaly that J.Q. and I haven't figured out yet, but it'll probably untangle eventually. Where'd you find the mariposa lilies?" She pointed toward the flowers in Mike's hands. "I haven't seen any yet this year."

"Old eagle-eye here found them. Spied them in that yucca flat down at the foot of the bluff."

"Oriana likes them," Neb said in a rough voice. "Always said they were her favorite."

"We'd better get back to her," his son said softly. "Come on, Dad."

The two went slowly down into their own driveway as Shirley crossed the bridge to the Ramirez drive. When she drove up to the house, Elena and Joe were sitting side by side on the front porch, leaning well back in their wicker chairs, eyes closed.

Elena opened one eye as Shirley approached. "Coffee's hot," she said as Shirley seated herself beside them. "If you want it iced, you'll have to do it yourself. I'm too tired to get up."

"Hot's okay," Shirley murmured. "Dad always said hot coffee kept you cooler on a hot day. How come you're so tired?"

"Joe kept me up all night, arguing."

Joe merely grunted, whether in agreement or dissent, Shirley couldn't tell.

"First it was about your offer on your property. And then it was about whether LALA is a bunch of nihilist nuts. And then it was about whether I was Mama's favorite or he was."

"It seemed important last night." Joe yawned. "Turns out we both thought the other one was the favorite. I never knew that."

"I think that's the standard opinion for siblings," Shirley offered. "If there's only two of them, that is. Maybe it works the same way for three. Four or more, I think you'd have different dynamics."

"You had a brother, didn't you?"

"An older brother, yes. You remember Sean. I was always jealous of Sean. Then, after he died, I really missed him." Shirley poured a cup of coffee from the thermos on the table, sugared it heavily, and sipped at it. "Did you two come to any conclusion about the offer I made, or did you just fight about it?"

"Well, we ended up with the idea now that Azoli's dead, you might not want to make the trade."

Shirley said, "It's still worth discussing, just for the tax advantages. But you're right, his death could change things, depending on what his son decides to do. One thing he's already done is throw his stepmother out. I've got her staying in my guest house."

"You're kidding!" Joe exclaimed. "He just kicked her out?"

"That's not the bitterest part so far as she's concerned. When she and her first husband got divorced (and he, by the way, is also over at the guest house) she got a cash settlement and turned it over to Azoli. He put it into the property here without giving her anything—no promissory note, no transfer of a share of property, nothing. So Charles, he's Azoli's son, says she can't prove he owes her anything."

"Was it a lot?" asked Elena.

"Depends on what you call a lot. I'd call a hundred thousand a lot."

"My Lord. Can she get it back?"

"Oh, I suppose there'll be bank records. The movement of the money can probably be traced. Of course, the intent may not be easy to establish. There's only her word for that. Conceivably Charles could claim she gave it to his father as a gift."

"Poor thing." Elena shook her head. "You just can't win with men like that, can you?"

"You say her ex is over at your house?" asked Joe.

"He spent the night there. Evidently she's been meeting him down in the gravel pit, ostensibly to discuss their kids. She has custody, but Azoli didn't want them and her ex-husband did . . . does."

"Did you just come over to share the local gossip?" asked Joe. "Or did you have an ulterior motive?"

"I need to find out if either of you ever saw Rima and her ex down in the old gravel pit. J.Q. and I are trying to establish a pattern for their meetings."

"We've seen a car in there several times," Joe agreed.

"Red car. It was there the day I got back. And I've seen her walking along the road at various times. I'd say she's probably spent some time there every day since I've been here. Sometimes A.M., sometimes P.M. Why do you care?"

Shirley shrugged. "Just that they didn't see whoever shot her husband. So they say. They heard the shot, though. A shot, I should say. They were there an hour, which could mean he was shot an hour before. J.Q. says their testimony should exonerate me, since I was up the hill in the other direction an hour before, but I'm afraid I'm not as hopeful about that as he is."

"You haven't decided who did it yet?"

Shirley snorted. "At last count, I had over a dozen suspects."

"Was that counting you and J.Q. and the two of us?" Joe asked curiously.

"No. If I put us in the pot, that'd make at least sixteen. And I have no idea which of them—us—if any, is guilty."

She set her cup down firmly. "And I don't want to talk about that now! I've brought over some papers." She handed over the fat manila envelope she'd brought. "Last couple of years' papers on the apartment houses in Washington. Profit and loss statements, occupancy records, income and expenses, that kind of stuff. We can go over them now, if you don't mind, because I promised to pick Rima up at the Azoli place, and it's probably a good idea not to make her wait too long."

Three-quarters of an hour later Shirley drove down the Azoli road with considerable misgivings. Everything she saw grated on her. The bare, chemically sterilized gravel of the roadway; the ranked buildings with their tinny roofs and the ubiquitous machinery, which was more typical of construction projects than of agricultural ones; even the house itself, which was the old Jewell house stripped of sheltering trees and surrounding foliage, the old porch ripped away and replaced by a concrete slab, the whole cleaned and neatened and oiled until it resembled nothing so much as a plastic model house, made to sit in a hobbyist's diorama. One expected the model train to come chuffing by at any moment.

Rima was seated on the front step with three suitcases piled beside her and Charles Azoli standing above her in midharangue.

Shirley pulled up, got out, and hefted the largest of the suitcases. "You ready?" she said, ignoring the raging man.

"I'm talking to her!" Charles shouted.

"I'm ready," murmured Rima. She was very pale, with a spot of hectic red on either cheek. "I'll get the other suitcases."

"You'll leave when I've finished and not until," Charles went on.

"She'll leave when she likes," said Shirley, stepping up onto the stoop to tower over the angry man. "She'll leave, and she'll talk to you through her lawyers, and you can find somebody else to holler at."

"I demand the right to look through those suitcases!"

Shirley's jaw dropped. "What do you think she's taking?"

"She might have anything in there. Things that belong to me! Things that belong to my mother. I demand—"

"Oh, go sit on it," snarled Shirley. "You little cock-a-doodle. I hope she does have something valuable, just to give you fits. I never met your father, for which I am now eternally grateful to a merciful God, for if you are an example of the bloodline, his death may be explained as a righteous act which can only improve the species. Whoever extirpated him deserves a vote of thanks from the human race." She turned on her heel, her glance sliding across the amazed face of two jeans-clad men who were coming around the corner of the house, got into the car, and took herself and Rima away in a flurry of gravel.

Rima was crying and laughing. "Did you see his face?" she sobbed. "Did you see that! Honestly. Extirpated. Why can't I ever think up words like that! It was almost worth it just to see his face." The sob turned into a sodden giggle.

"Who were those men coming up when we left?"

"The one in front was Ralph Moody. He runs the big

161

machine. And Harry. Harry was El's helper. Followed him around all the time like a dog, fetching things.''

"Pity I didn't know. I could've spared a few words for them, too. By the way, what is in the suitcases?''

"You mean besides my clothes?'' The giggle broke into a hysterical cackle. "I packed all the registration papers on the cattle. I figured I need something to hold for ransom until I get my money back. El had me do all the registrations and paperwork, so they were right where I could lay hands on them. There's about a hundred thousand in cows and bulls in there.''

"Sounds sensible to me,'' Shirley agreed. "Lord, what a twerp. Do people say twerp anymore? My dad used to say that. Twerp.''

"Isn't it nerd these days?''

"Nerd? I don't think that fits, but I'll have to ask Allison.'' She swung the Wagoneer into her own driveway. "Are you and your ex going to get back together?''

Rima started sobbing again. "He's . . . he's been so nice to me. I'd forgotten how nice he can be. He's the way he used to be when we were first married.''

"So?''

"I don't know.'' She mopped her eyes with a damp wad of tissue and fished in her pockets, trying to find another.

"Glove compartment,'' said Shirley, waiting until the woman had found herself a dry tissue and blown her nose. "Why don't you know?''

"Oh, Shirley. It's just everything! It's like I'm crawling back to him. If I had the money, at least, it wouldn't be so bad! But just to go back like I am, without a cent . . .''

"But he wants you to.''

"Oh, yes. Oh, he really does. If I didn't know Paul better, I'd say he did it himself, just to get rid of El so I'd come back to him and the boys.''

Shirley was shocked into momentary silence. Though it was a motive she hadn't considered, it wasn't the motive so much as the woman's matter-of-fact statement that surprised her. Wasn't Rima aware of the implications?

"But you do know Paul better than that?" she probed tentatively.

"Oh, Paul would be hopeless killing anybody. He can't even hit a nail with a hammer. I don't know how many times I've seen him smash his thumb instead of what he was aiming at." She wiped her face as she got out of the car. "If you don't mind my staying here for a day or two, I'd like to do that. Just until I get my head straightened out. Paul will take me shopping for groceries this afternoon, so I won't impose on your hospitality. In a day or two I should be able to make up my mind. Maybe Charles will agree to give me my money back. That'd make it easier."

"By all means, stay," Shirley told her. "J.Q. and I will go on about our business as though you weren't even there."

Which business, she found when she entered the house, included several phone calls, including both a call and a call back from Inigo Castigar. The lengthy message in J.Q.'s best engineer's lettering, firm black pen strokes on lined yellow paper, said that Inigo had been apprised of Shirley's question re Charles Azoli; i.e., when had he arrived in Denver? Inigo had been so concerned on Shirley's behalf that he had immediately solicited information from the airlines, thereby learning that no Azoli had arrived from anywhere on Wednesday night or Thursday. An Azoli had, however, arrived via United on Tuesday afternoon. This information was followed by three thick exclamation points.

"He was already here!" Shirley exclaimed.

"Who was?"

Shirley turned to find Allison peering cautiously through the doorway at her.

"Azoli's son. He was already in Colorado when his father was killed."

"Did he do it? What do you call that? When somebody kills their father. I know there's a word for it."

"It's called patricide, but I wouldn't accuse him of it yet. Not that I wouldn't love to pin it on him, the little cockroach!"

"You don't like him."

163

"I think you could say that. He was giving Rima a hard time."

"Well, you know, he probably blames her for being the lady who ran off with his father." Allison sounded quite depressed about it.

"In the first place, he's a grown man, not some kid who should blame a woman for his father's acts. I doubt if anyone could have run off with Azoli. In the second place, from what Rima says, his mother left his father. Then his father went after Rima."

"Yeah, but she might have just said that. Maybe she was carrying on with him all the time."

"Carrying on?"

"You know. Having an affair." She gave Shirley a sidelong look, one that Shirley was completely unable to interpret.

"It's possible, I suppose. Somehow the other version sounds more likely. More . . . consistent."

"What're you going to do now?"

Shirley glanced down the yellow tablet. The next number was familiar: the sheriff's office. Please call. Below that was a message from the district attorney's office in Columbine. Delbert McInery, the DA, had called. Would Ms. McClintock call his office to make an appointment for an interview?

"Much though I hate to do so, Allison, I'm calling the sheriff."

Allison hovered as Shirley dialed.

"Ms. McClintock," he said heavily. "Thank you for calling. Since you've been sort of helpful to me a time or two, I thought it would be only right to let you know the DA intends to bring you in again."

"What do you mean, bring me in?"

"Arrest you, Shirley. That's what I mean."

"You already arrested me, Botts."

"Yeah, and you got out. The DA, he thinks he can get your friendly judge overruled and either keep you in or get a high bail set."

Shirley felt herself going cold. The current district attorney had been assistant to and a political buddy of the previous district attorney, whom Shirley had been somewhat instrumental in removing from office. At least, she'd helped Botts Tempe get the evidence that had removed him.

"He should be grateful, the son of a . . ." she muttered.

"Who?"

"McInery! He'd wouldn't be district attorney except for me, and now you say he's going to arrest me!"

"He thinks you're dangerous, Shirley. At least, that's what he tells me. Look, I'm in the middle here. If you ask me do I think you shot El Azoli, I'll have to say no, I really don't think you'd do that. At least not until you'd done a lot of other nasty stuff first. But you had a motive and you were there, and Del McInery thinks he can make it stick, at least for a while. Me, I wouldn'ta felt right if I hadn't told you."

He hung up, and Shirley found herself mumbling into the dial tone. She turned around to meet Allison's apprehensive stare.

"Are they going to arrest you, Shirley?" she asked in a panicky voice.

Shirley hugged her. "Botts says they're going to try. That doesn't mean much, though. It's not time to scream and hide under the bed yet."

"What're you going to do?"

"I'm going to call Numa Ehrlich and tell him everything I know about everything. I'm going to suggest that Numa bring all this information before both the sheriff and the DA, together with the suggestion McInery and Botts had better investigate somebody besides me as a politically smart move. Or maybe a religious duty."

"Is it a religious duty?"

"Lord knows, child; I don't. Maybe it could be construed to be part of not bearing false witness or something. At any rate, if I'm lucky, Numa should chase Botts and the DA off in several directions and give me some room."

"You really don't know who did it, not at all?"

Shirley fell into a chair. "I really don't, Allison. I am baffled. Lots of people have lots of reasons for having wanted the man dead, but nothing really zings at me, you know? It's all sort of fuzzy and just barely possible and not quite believable. I mean, who could believe Marmot Marquez? You've seen him!''

''He doesn't look like much.''

''No, he certainly doesn't. I don't think the DA is going to believe he did it. Or that Bonifacio Labolis did it. *I* can't believe Joe or Elena had anything to do with it. Horace and Marthine don't look like killers to me. And that's the way it goes. I'm longing for one real villain to stick his head out of the grass and hiss, just so I can say 'Aha' or 'Eureka,' but Azoli's son Charley is the only one who fits that description. He's a snake if I ever saw one.''

''Would you rather he did it?''

''Oh, I guess. Charley's a stinker. I don't know him or his family, so my loyalties wouldn't be affected. Also, it would be understandable. It's always nice to have an understandable motive on the part of somebody you don't much like.''

''Will Sheriff Tempe go after him?''

''Charley won't talk to me, so if anybody goes after him, it'll have to be Botts or McInery.'' She sat forward and fished a pad and pencil from the shelf below the phone. ''Give me a few minutes to gather my thoughts so I can call Numa.''

Allison obediently departed. Shirley scribbled a lengthy list of facts and surmises, then called Numa, who, fortuitously, happened to be in his office and free to talk.

''Numa, the DA wants me to call him.''

''McInery? Don't call him. I don't want you talking to him; you'll just make him madder. I'll call him.''

''Well, I thought you ought to know what I've found out.''

''Proceed,'' he said crisply. ''I will record what you have to say.''

Shirley started at the top of her list, finishing fifteen minutes later with a dry throat. None of it had sounded very convincing.

''What motive do you ascribe to all these LALA people?''

''Politics, I suppose. If you can call terrorism politics. And that would apply to the EGN people, too. You know as well as I do, Numa, that when ideology takes over, facts take a backseat. El Azoli may not have oppressed a single minority person, but he was identified as an oppressor, and that may have been enough.''

"How about the ostrich farm people?''

"The Rodwingers' motive would have been to protect their investment, and that might apply also to Joe and Elena, even though I don't think they had any more to do with it than I did.''

"And the motive on the part of Charles Azoli?''

"Maybe he wanted to keep the foundation money from being dissipated. Maybe he found out it had already been dissipated and was furious. Maybe he hated his father for mistreating his mama. I don't know, Numa. It just seems to me his pretending he wasn't in town when it happened is pretty fishy.''

"Paul Howard's motive would have been to get his wife back?''

"Right. And Rima might have had a motive, too. Maybe Azoli threatened to divorce her once too often. And, finally, there's this business of their hearing the shot without seeing who fired it. Maybe Azoli wasn't even killed when we thought he was. I'd sure like to know.''

Numa sniffed, one of those patience-tried-to-the-limit sniffs with which Shirley was fully familiar. "Ah. Well. Let's see what I can elicit from the coroner or from Sheriff Tempe. He's not unreasonable.''

"Ha! I'm not worried about Botts. I'm worried about Delbert McInery.''

"Delbert McInery is a toad.'' Numa sniffed. "The second batrachian in a row to occupy the post in Ridge County. His grasp of the law is slightly inferior to his knowledge of quantum physics. Besides which, he has no love for any person of principle, which definition must, however eccentrically, include yourself, I suppose. Patience, Shirley. I'll call you when I have something to tell you.''

She hung up and turned to find J.Q. leaning against the wall, watching her.

"The part I heard was lucid," he said. "Intemperate but lucid."

"I don't feel temperate."

"Obviously. Do you feel like lunch?"

"We just ate."

"We ate at eight o'clock this morning. It is now almost one o'clock in the afternoon. I intend to have a large ham sandwich and a bowl of chicken soup. Shall I make you a sandwich, too, or are you fasting?"

"No. I'm not fasting, but I'm not hungry, either. I'm upset. I'm annoyed. I'm frustrated. I'm still scared."

"Take Zeke out for a ride. That usually settles you down. Either that or Glenfiddich."

"It's too early to start drinking. You're right. I'll go riding. Maybe it'll help me think. I'll see if Allison would like to go along." She went in search of Allison, finding her at last in the barn where Beauregard had his capacious stall.

"I thought maybe you'd like to go riding with me," she said.

Allison gave her another of those strange sidelong looks. "Sure. Where shall we go?"

"Oh, no place special. We'll ride up into the west pasture, go through the gate onto the back road, maybe go up into the hills a little way."

"Can I have a sandwich first?"

"You can bring one along. You go get whatever you want while I saddle the horses. I'll meet you at the house."

Allison ran off at top speed, shirttail flapping. Shirley saddled Beauregard and led him out into the paddock, whistling for Zeke as she went. He came trotting across the meadow as she went back into the barn for the saddle and a pocketful of horse candy—the same compressed alfalfa cake doted on by the cows, the goats, and sometimes even the dogs. While Zeke munched and nuzzled her pocket for more, she saddled him, mounted, and rode through the open corral gate and across the driveway, leading Beau by his reins. At the porch steps she dismounted, letting Zeke's reins drop while she tucked in her shirt and tied a kerchief around her hair under her hat.

J.Q. and Allison came out the door, each carrying a thick sandwich as they murmured to one another with conspiratorial looks at her.

Something hit one of the porch pillars within a yard of Shirley's head, making a loud splat.

"What the hell!" shouted J.Q.

Shirley, who had dropped when she heard the sound, rolled over and screamed at Allison, "Get down."

Allison got down. "Is somebody shooting at us?" she cried, sounding more surprised than frightened.

Another something hit the house.

"Call somebody!" Shirley shouted, hearing the screen door slam as a punctuation to her own shock. Beauregard reared, whinnied, then cantered toward the barn. Zeke whickered in his throat and stayed where he was as Shirley crawled up the steps, hunkered behind the low wall that surrounded the patio, and scrambled from there across the porch. "Stay down and crawl in the house, Allison. Move! Quick!" She pulled the door open by its bottom edge and lay where she was while Allison scuttled to and across her, then pulled herself through the door. J.Q. was on the phone, his voice raised in anger or excitement, she couldn't tell which.

"Damn fools," J.Q. muttered, slamming the phone down.

"Who'd you call?"

"Sheriff's office. Who else! Idiots thought I was being funny."

Through the screen door came a muted howl, an ominous and threatening presence, like the return of an avenging angel.

"They've started up that damned machine!" said J.Q., outraged. "What the hell?"

"Is somebody coming from the sheriff's office?" Shirley cried. "Did you tell Botts we're pinned down?"

"Oh, sh—I told them we'd been shot at. I told them so far as I knew the shooter was still out there."

"Why is somebody shooting at us?" cried Allison. "We didn't do anything! Is Beauregard hurt?"

"Shhh, honey. Settle down. Beauregard's fine. He was just getting himself out of the line of fire." Shirley pushed the door closed, moved back into the room, and stood up, peering through the front windows at Zeke, who was still calmly chewing.

"Shirley, don't."

"It's all right, Allison. I can't be seen in here, we're in shadow. Now, who in the bloody hell. . . ?"

"Maybe you were getting close," muttered J.Q. "Maybe somebody thinks you know something."

"I don't know anything," she shrieked.

"Don't yell. I only said maybe."

The phone rang. Shirley picked it up.

"Shirley?"

"Joe?"

"Is somebody up there shooting at something?"

"Joe, somebody up here is being shot at, namely, me. Did you hear shots?"

"Two of them. Sounded close."

"Too close! Make a note of the time, will you, Joe. I'll send whoever comes from the sheriff's office down to see you as a witness."

"Don't need to. Elena and I are coming up there."

"Be careful!"

"We'll be careful."

She turned from the phone and remained standing, still peering out. "I can't see anybody moving around. Whoever it was had to be shooting from down near the road."

"Are you sure Beauregard's all right?" whispered Allison.

"Beauregard has just rejoined Zeke, and the two of them are standing out there, wondering where the hell you are," J.Q. replied. "They're fine. Don't worry about them."

"Whoever's shooting might hit them by mistake."

"Whoever's shooting is a lousy shot," snarled Shirley. "Of course, at that distance, most everyone is. It's six hundred yards to the nearest good cover." She tensed, then relaxed. "Here come Joe and Elena."

The small brown truck that turned into the driveway came quickly toward the house, kicking up a cloud of dust that settled slowly as it went on around the house. Shirley went toward the kitchen door. "Smart people," she called. "They're getting out of the line of fire."

"Sheriff's man is here," called J.Q. "Flashing lights coming."

"He must have had a car nearby. There's been no time to get anyone here from Columbine," Shirley opined, opening the door for the Ramirezes. "Come in," she urged them, leaning out to look around at the familiar farmyard. Everything peaceful. Everything quiet except that screaming machine from over the way.

In the kitchen Shirley echoed mutters and exclamations. In the living room a deputy tried to make sense out of Allison's tumbled words and J.Q.'s laconic phrases. After momentary confusion, the two groups melded and Shirley gave a brief and blasphemous account of the incident.

"And where'd you say these bullets came from?" the deputy asked.

"Since both of them are embedded in the front of my house, why don't you go check them out and see?" Shirley snarled.

"Sheriff's coming. He'll probably want to do that himself."

"Well, hallelujah," muttered Shirley. "You suppose his approach guarantees our safety sufficiently we can unsaddle the horses?"

"I'll do it, Shirley," said Joe. "You sit tight."

"Sheriff'll want to talk to you," said the deputy to Joe's retreating back.

"Sheriff'll find me in the barn or here," Joe replied. "Keep your shirt on." He went out the front, shaking his head.

Shirley watched through the window while he led the two animals back to the barn.

Allison said, "Does he know where Beauregard goes?"

"Why don't you slip out the back door and help him?" Shirley said. "I'm sure your marksman has removed himself by now. If he has any sense at all."

"If he exists at all," said the deputy. "Sheriff didn't sound like he believed it much."

"I heard the shots myself," cried Elena. "And they didn't come from up here. They came from down by the road somewhere."

"Well, somebody from up here could've . . ."

"There are three people up here," said J.Q. "Shirley, and Allison, and myself. All three of us were together, on the front porch, when the bullets hit."

"Yeah, well," muttered the deputy. "I'll go see when somebody's going to get here." He stumped back out to his patrol car, which sat, engine on and lights flashing, near where the horses had been.

"Why?" demanded Shirley. "Why us? Damn it."

"Joe said you'd probably found something out about who shot El Azoli."

"Elena, I know less about who shot El Azoli now than I did before he got shot. Honest to God."

"Drinks," said J.Q. firmly. "I need a little something, if you don't mind."

"I wouldn't mind," murmured Elena. "If Shirley's having something."

Joe and Allison found them at the kitchen table gathered around a bottle of Glenfiddich.

"Me, too," he said.

"Glass in the cupboard," muttered Shirley.

"I wish I was old enough to drink," Allison said, staring at each of them in turn. "If it makes you feel better."

"Well," Shirley commented, rubbing her forehead. "Come to think of it, I feel rather more relaxed than I did half an hour ago. There's something rather factual about a bullet. Surprisingly enough, it feels easier to handle being shot at than it does to deal with being suspected of murder."

"Since you are too young to drink scotch, why don't you have a root beer," J.Q. suggested to Allison.

"Shirley lets me have wine."

"Right," Shirley assented. "With meals. As a gustatory adventure, not as a relaxant."

Allison went to the refrigerator, asking, "So what're you all going to do now?"

The adults around the table exchanged glances and raised eyebrows.

"Wait for the sheriff," J.Q. responded. "For whom I believe Shirley is storing up several well-chosen paragraphs."

6

A TWO-CAR SHERIFF'S convoy drove in, sirens shrieking. As the sirens died, the phone rang. It was Numa once again, and he exclaimed loudly when Shirley told him about the attack, going on at considerable length about the state of a world in which such things happened.

"That's not why you called, Numa," she said impatiently, peering through the kitchen window at Botts Tempe, who stood straddled on her porch, looking insufficiently impressed by the bullet holes in her house. "You had a reason to call."

"Correct. I thought you'd want to know the results of the autopsy, which my assistant just inveigled out of the coroner's office. You know, we tend to underrate Botts at times, but in many ways he's quite competent. In any case, he saw to it Azoli's body was examined within twenty minutes of the time you were there. It had, at that point, been dead less than an hour, so the report says."

"But that's not possible!"

"Possible or not, so says the official report. When you got there, Azoli was a very recent corpse, Shirley."

174

"I was very nearly a recent corpse myself," she said bitterly, reintroducing the topic of her own narrow escape.

"It sounds to me as though you have a sniper up there," Numa offered.

"A random killer, you mean?"

"Unless you can think of some reason why someone would want both you and Azoli dead, yes."

"I can't think of anything I have done in my entire life that would put me in the same category as that . . . that man!"

"Except that you live where you live. So did he."

"A random killer wiping out ranchers? Maybe a militant vegetarian? An animal rights activist, maybe? A terrorist for bovine separatism?"

He sniffed. "I have no idea, Shirley. Since you've got the sheriff there as a captive audience, I'd suggest you go talk to him about it. Call me later if you need me."

The phone clicked gently, leaving Shirley with her mouth open, still trying to think of any category that would legitimately include both her and El Azoli.

She joined the others on the porch, everyone standing around in an attitude of interest while one of the deputies dug out the bullets to leave one neat hole in a porch column and one rather raggedy one in the siding beside a window.

"Came from down the hill," grumped the sheriff.

"Of course it did," Shirley growled back. "If it had come from uphill, it would have been in the other side of the house."

"I don't suppose you saw anything?" Botts looked around the circle, receiving an assortment of shrugs and grimaces. "You two heard it?" he asked Joe and Elena.

"I was outside," said Joe. "I started for the house when I heard the first one. The second one came right after. Normally, I wouldn't have paid that much attention. People out here do shoot at coyotes."

"Wild dogs, mostly," amended Shirley. "Coyotes keep their distance."

"Well, right. This time the shots worried me, because of

what happened to Azoli, so I called Shirley, and she said she'd been shot at.''

"Hmnph," Botts grunted, glaring at the bullet in his palm as though he expected it to stand up and declare its point of origin. "Looks pretty much like the one we took out of Azoli."

"Rifle bullets do look pretty much alike," Shirley growled. "After they've smashed into something."

"You any idea why anybody would shoot at you?"

"I do not," she said emphatically. "Numa thinks we may have a sniper, and I'll tell you, Botts, that makes as much sense as anything else."

"Have to talk to Del McInery about this," he said. "Might change his mind about you. Might not, too. He'll say you coulda set it up."

"Yeah, well. Del McInery is an ingrate and an idiot."

"You figure he ought to think he owes you, right?"

"Well, if his predecessor, Cravett, hadn't been convicted on a drug charge, McInery wouldn't be DA. And if it hadn't been for me, you wouldn't have known anything about Cravett's involvement. I put you onto him."

"McInery still isn't fond of you."

"All that does is make me wonder what he's up to! If he's honest, he ought to love me to pieces. Anyhow, you do what you have to do, Botts."

"Never had a sniper case."

"Neither have I."

"Never could figure out why anybody would do that."

"I think snipers are usually judged to be mentally unbalanced."

"Yeah. That'd do it. Well, I'll tell you the truth, Shirley. I'd rather the killer wasn't you."

Shirley felt herself blushing. "That's really nice of you, Botts."

"Yeah. You'd be a pisser to prosecute. And that lawyer of yours is a pisser, too. I'd rather it was somebody who wasn't so much trouble."

He turned and went back to his car, leaving Shirley silent, with her mouth open.

"What'd he say?" asked J.Q.

"Never mind," she snapped.

"All right." He stood watching as the sheriff's cars turned and sped back down the driveway. "I guess the law is going to go look around along the road. So what's next?"

"I'm going in and finish my drink. You, Elena? Joe?"

"By all means," Joe answered jauntily. He followed her back to the kitchen and seated himself as before, giving Allison a friendly punch on the shoulder as he went. "Well, kid, that was exciting."

"That was scary!" she objected, wiping her eyes with the back of one grubby hand. "I don't like getting shot at."

Joe gestured ebulliently. "Yeah, but look. It got Shirley off the hook. You like that part, don't you?"

Allison nodded doubtfully. "Did it?" she asked Shirley. "Did it get you off the hook?"

"It may have helped," she admitted. "But it won't last unless we find out who did it."

The phone rang yet again. Shirley swore at it impatiently, threatening to pull it out by the roots, while J.Q. picked it up in the living room. He came to the kitchen door with Elena behind him. "Neb Bostom wants to talk to you, Shirley."

She hitched her chair over to the kitchen phone and turned into the corner, the phone propped on her shoulder. "Hello, Neb?"

"I saw the sheriff's car go up there, Shirley. Are you all right?"

She kept her voice casual. "Oh, somebody was shooting up the country, Neb. They just came out to see who."

"Nothing to do with you?"

She had no intention of worrying him. "No, Neb. Nothing to do with me."

"That's good. I was wondering. . . ." There was a long pause.

"Wondering what, Neb?"

"The other day, you offered to help."

"What can I do?"

"It's just . . . I've been so preoccupied. I've been writing checks to this one and that one for weeks now, but I keep forgetting to make a deposit. I'm afraid I'll be overdrawn. Mike would go to town for me, but I'd rather . . . I don't want to be alone just now. I was wondering . . . could you drop by the bank this afternoon and make a deposit for me?"

"What bank, Neb?" She looked at her watch. Two-thirty. The banks in Columbine stayed open until five on Fridays.

"First National of Ridge County," he answered.

"You want me to pick it up now?"

"No . . . no, Shirley. I'll have it ready in about half an hour, if that's all right. And when you get there, would you ask for Evelyn? I've called her. She said she'd post my deposit today. So I don't get overdrawn."

"Half an hour, Neb. Right." She put down the phone with a frown. He'd sounded so . . . so strained, so very weary. Well. If it would help him feel better, she'd make a bank run.

"Allison, we need to do a neighborly duty. Go wash your face and hands, put on a clean shirt, and we'll run down to Columbine to help Neb Bostom out. J.Q., have we got anything good in the freezer? Anything Neb and Mike might relish—that the granddaughter can cook?"

Twenty minutes later, clean and combed, the two of them set out, bearing one of two pans of frozen lasagna J.Q. had discovered lurking in the freezer. The other pan was defrosting in the oven following J.Q.'s invitation to Joe and Elena to join the family for potluck.

"What does Mr. Bostom want us to do?" Allison asked as they drove down the driveway.

"Take a deposit into town, to the bank. Neb's afraid he'll be overdrawn."

"That's a funny thing to worry about. When your own wife is dying, I mean."

"Maybe not so strange. I think when you're terribly grieved or worried about something, your mind actually takes refuge in less important things."

178

Long silence. Shirley cast a sidelong look to see a very thoughtful face. "Yeah," whispered Allison.

Now, what was all this? "I remember when my second husband was dying, I'd find myself worrying about the strangest things, like where I could get curtains cleaned or whether people would understand if I didn't accept an invitation to dinner. I'd lie awake at night, worrying about things like that, just to keep from thinking of the things that really mattered."

No response this time. Oh, well. Later, maybe. She eased the car across Old Mill Road and into the Bostom driveway.

"Was he nice, your husband?" Allison asked suddenly.

"Both my husbands were very fine men. I remember them fondly."

"Oh," said Allison.

Now, what had that been about? Shirley tucked it away for further rumination later, for Mike was waiting on the porch. He came down the wooden steps, leaning heavily on the railing, and reached an envelope through the window. "Here it is, Shirley. Dad says to remind you to give it to Evelyn."

"Your dad sounded so tired, Mike."

"I know. He fell asleep on the couch when we got back from our walk and slept until the sirens went by. I think they woke him."

"How did he hear them over that machine?"

"Oh, the wind shifts. Sometimes it's more intolerable than other times."

He raised a hand in farewell and stood back, a big man grown gaunt in late middle age, his face graven in grieving lines. "Thank you, Shirley."

"Tell Neb I'll bring the receipt, but it'll be a little later. I'm going to stop for groceries."

"That's fine. Fine," he said, waving. She waved in turn as she went around the big tree in the drive and headed out the way they had come.

"He looks so sad."

"Well, Mike was always very close to his parents. They had one of those storybook families, the happy-ever-after kind. From what Neb said to me, they've been sweethearts ever since they were kids. It's like . . . losing the greater part of your life, I suppose.''

As they went up the hill, the noise of the machine grew more shrill and vicious. Looking to her left, Shirley saw it had returned from the vicinity of the ostrich farm and was now plowing its way along her own fence line, eating through the last few remaining copses of scrub oak. Down at the barns, a figure she recognized as that of Charles Azoli strutted along a fence line in the wake of the jeans-clad flunky Shirley had seen earlier. Charles paused at a gate to write on a clipboard while the other man leaned over the fence, one hand extended, obviously counting cows.

''Inventory,'' Shirley said crisply as she turned right, onto the county road. ''The little twerp is taking inventory.''

''Dweeb,'' said Allison.

''What?''

''He's a dweeb, not a twerp. Nobody says twerp.''

''Dweeb? Let's see. Part dimwit, part feeble?''

Allison shrugged.

Shirley mused, ''Whatever he is, wait'll he tries to find the papers on those cows. Rima's got them.''

''Can't he sell them without papers?''

''Might be hard. Papers on a registered cow are like the title on a car or truck. Maybe he can get duplicates, but if Rima puts up a fuss, maybe not. She could claim her money bought the cows, and that might stall things a bit.''

They drove down the county road, took the exit onto the highway, and speeded up to match the traffic moving around them. Fifteen minutes later they entered Columbine, moving slowly into the shopping center and around it.

''I thought the bank was on Main Street.''

''Mine is. This is Neb's bank. First National used to be on Main, but they moved over here about two years ago.'' She parked, put Neb's envelope in her pocket, and crossed the parking lot with Allison at her side.

''Which one's Evelyn?'' Shirley asked a clerk at a desk in

the front window. Lines of customers waited in front of both tellers.

"Down at the far end," she was told.

"I'll wait here," said Allison, her eyes on a tank of bright fish set against the lobby wall.

Shirley joined the queue, one of her least favorite activities, while she reflected on the natural law that made neighboring lines always move faster than one's own. Normally she planned trips to town when no one else was there: early Monday mornings or during the dinner hour on Thursday nights. The woman ahead of her bought a quantity of traveler's checks in small denominations, making slow work of it. Eventually she moved away, fumbling with the checks, her purse, two shopping bags, and a child's stroller. Shirley presented herself.

"Evelyn? Neb Bostom told me to bring this deposit to you. He said he'd talked to you."

"Mr. Bostom?" she chirped. "Yes, he did call me. So awful about his wife. Is she any better? His wife?" While she spoke, well-schooled fingers opened the envelope, tallied the checks inside, popped a blank form into a machine, and tapped keys. "I told him he didn't need to do this. We'd have honored his overdraft. Nebraska and Oriana Bostom have been customers of this bank for over fifty years. We're not likely to charge him for a little overdraw."

She smiled brightly and handed the slip to Shirley. "You tell him I'm thinking of him."

"I'll do that."

Allison was still standing in silent fascination by the fish tank.

"Can I have one of those?"

"A fish?"

"An aquarium like this."

"They are fascinating, aren't they?"

"The fish are so bright! Like they were painted."

"We've got an aquarium somewhere out in the barn. Twenty-five or thirty gallons, I think. It's a freshwater tank, not salt like this one, but there are freshwater fish that are just as bright and a lot cheaper. If you want, we'll dig the old tank out, clean it up, and you can shop for fish.''

''When, Shirley? This afternoon!''

The eagerness in her voice reminded Shirley that Allison had not recently sounded either eager or cheerful. ''Well,'' she replied, ''the closest place to get a good selection of fish would be in Lakewood, and we don't really have time today. However, we can get a heater this afternoon, and a filter and some plants. As I recall from my son's time, you're supposed to let the filter run a few days before you put the fish in, anyhow. That gets rid of any chemicals in the water and lets the plants get started.''

''Where can we get the stuff?''

''Right next door, as a matter of fact. The pet store.''

''I didn't know they had fish.''

''All they have are goldfish, I think, but they've got aquarium setups in the window.'' She led the way to the pet store, where Allison took her time inspecting a tank of minuscule guppies, a gerbil, a pair of fluffy guinea pigs, and a sad-eyed cocker puppy before settling for a packaged aquarium kit: filter, aerator, heater, and a sack of white sand, plus half a dozen water plants in a Ziploc bag.

''Groceries next.'' Shirley watched Allison, who was busy reading the installation instructions on the back of the box. She seemed so concentrated, almost as though she, too, wanted a distraction. ''We'll move the car down near the Safeway.''

In the supermarket they plunged into the Friday afternoon shopping mob. Almost an hour later they emerged, Allison pushing a heavily laden cart, which they unloaded into the back of the Wagoneer.

''Okay. You set?'' Shirley stretched before folding herself onto the seat. ''You want those chips to eat on the way back?''

Allison shook her head, no.

''Do we need anything else in town?''

No again.

They settled themselves and headed back for the ranch, joining thickening lanes of highway traffic: commuters who

182

lived in the area combined with Friday afternoon traffic from Denver, weekenders headed for the mountains. Friday and Sunday evenings were always thick with traffic, going or coming, and Shirley snarled at speeders and dalliers both as she tried to avoid RVs while dodging sports cars that seemed to come out of nowhere. Too many people moved to Denver and brought their Boston or New York driving habits with them. They drove as though with blinders on, no peripheral vision, only straight ahead at top speed, swooping in and out of traffic, and the devil take the hindmost.

When they turned onto the county road, she sighed with relief, and as they approached the turnoff onto Old Mill Road, habit made her sit forward in anticipation.

"What the hell . . ." she muttered.

Old Mill Road was solid with cars and flashing lights. A helicopter painted with a red cross crouched in the neighboring field.

"A helicopter!" said Allison unnecessarily.

"I can see it," said Shirley. "Who could miss it!"

"Ma'am, you'll have to go around." An officious uniform leaned down to her open window and made dismissive gestures.

"Around where?" she demanded. "There's one road into my place, and this is it." There was another way in, but it would mean several miles on back roads to get there. She saw no reason to mention it.

He turned away, mumbled to a colleague, trotted down the road to speak to someone else, eventually returning out of breath.

"You'll have to wait until somebody moves something, ma'am."

"I can see that. What happened?"

"Some fellow got shot. He was alive, so they called the Flight for Life, but he was dead by the time the chopper landed."

Shirley moistened a dry mouth. "Who? Who was it?"

"Some fellow owns a ranch here. Over there by that barn."

"My Lord," Shirley whispered, awed. "Charles Azoli. They got father and son."

Allison's eyes widened, but she said nothing. She gripped Shirley's hand in her own, and they sat. Before them people moved here and there, groups coalescing and separating. After a time Botts Tempe came from behind the helicopter and stumped his way purposefully toward the Wagoneer, where he leaned through the window as the deputy had done.

"Shirley, mind telling me where you've been for the last hour or so?"

"Grocery shopping," she said. "Pet store shopping. Stopping at the bank for my neighbor."

"Down in Columbine?"

"Right. I went by here on my way out about three."

"She with you the whole time?" He jabbed a thumb in Allison's direction.

"She's a sentient being; ask her," Shirley snapped.

"I was with her the whole time," Allison said in a dignified though slightly apprehensive voice. "We picked up a deposit from Mr. Bostom. We went to his bank for him. We went to the pet store. We went to the grocery store."

"Who'd you see?"

"Teller named Evelyn at First National of Ridge County," Shirley answered. "Bald fellow at the pet store, the owner, I think. He sold us stuff for an aquarium. I didn't know the checkout gal at the Safeway."

"Her name tag said Betty Braun," Allison offered. "She has red hair and three earrings in her left ear."

Shirley threw Allison an astonished glance before turning back to the sheriff and asking sweetly, "Would you like to see the register receipts? Honest to God, Botts. This time we've got an alibi."

"Looks like it, don't it?" He stared at her broodingly from his baggy bloodhound eyes. "Damnedest thing."

"Was it Charles Azoli?" she asked.

"How'd you know?" he demanded.

"The deputy said a ranch owner. He's the only one it could be."

"Well, it was him. Shot. Just like his daddy. And we can't find his stepmomma."

"She's probably asleep over in the guest house at my place. He threw her out."

"Did, did he? Well, now."

"Forget it, Botts. She's not the type."

"You still think a sniper?"

"I never said I thought that. I just said it was possible."

"How come he's such a good shot aiming at Azolis and such a bad shot aiming at McClintocks, huh?"

Shirley shook her head, baffled. She hadn't thought of that. "Longer range, maybe?"

He snorted. "I'll tell Jerry to move that truck. You go on home. I may come over later."

Shirley waited, fidgeting, as the truck was moved, then drove past the clustered vehicles, down the familiar hill toward her own place. Once they were past the cars and trucks, it became very still.

"No machine," said Allison. "It was running when we left."

"Right," murmured Shirley. "I guess what's his name stopped work out of respect for the dead."

"Maybe with both the Azolis gone, he didn't know who was going to pay him," said Allison. "And that's why he stopped."

"Entirely possible." Shirley swung into the Bostom driveway and slowed down as she wound between the willows to the circle before the house. When she got out of the Wagoneer, something stopped her in her tracks. Some aura, some essence of the place that seemed stifled or withdrawn. She went up the front steps and knocked lightly on the door. After a long moment Mike opened it, his face streaked with tears.

"Shirley. Ah. God. Come in."

"Your mother?" she asked, hushed. "Oriana?"

"Gone," he choked. "Just a few minutes ago. Dad's in there with her. The . . . the people are on their way. How did you know to come over?"

"I didn't know. I just came by to drop off your dad's deposit slip. I won't stay. Tuck this away somewhere where it won't get lost. He may ask for it."

She gave him the envelope, patted him wordlessly on the shoulder.

"She was asleep all morning," Mike said, trying to clear his throat. "She wasn't in any pain. After you came, I fell asleep while Dad stayed with her. He woke me just a little while ago. She just . . . just stopped breathing." He leaned his head on his hand. "We were expecting it. But still . . ."

"But still, Mike. I know. If you need anything at all, you or Neb, you call me. I'm five minutes away, anytime." She patted him again and went back to the car.

"Did she die?" asked Allison. "He was crying."

"Yes, honey."

"I'm sad for them."

"Well, I am, too. I'm saddest for Neb. I don't know how he'll get along without her." She felt tears welling, remembering her own loneliness in the past. "Maybe we can include him in our family for a while. Suppers, maybe. It's hard to think of eating, sometimes, when you're all alone."

Silently, they drove back to the house. The Ramirez car was gone. The guest house was quiet, seeming untenanted. J.Q. was nowhere to be seen, which meant he might be out checking on cows. Shirley and Allison unloaded the car and put groceries away. It was almost six. Time for supper.

"I thought Joe and Elena were going to have dinner with us," Shirley remarked.

Allison opened the oven door, peeked inside, then shut it again. "The lasagna's bubbling in there. I don't feel much like eating anything, though."

"I know. Me, too. Nonetheless, I had no lunch and your sandwich was, as I recall, interrupted by our being shot at. What about I make a big salad to go with the lasagna. Spinach and cucumbers and green peppers and croutons and good stuff."

"I'd rather have lettuce than spinach."

"Spinach has more vitamins."

"Spinach is spinach," she said firmly.

Shirley got out the lettuce and put away the spinach. The ranch truck drove into the farmyard. Dog barked. After a moment J.Q. came in the kitchen door.

"Do you know what happened?" he asked.

"You mean Charles Azoli?"

"Right. Joe and Elena and I saw the flashing lights from out in the pasture, so we drove over there. He's dead."

"Allison and I were stopped on our way home. We went by Bostom's to drop off the deposit slip. Oriana died this afternoon."

"Oh." He dropped into a chair. "Well. Poor Neb."

Shirley began cutting peppers. "Did Joe and Elena change their minds about staying to dinner?"

"No. They'll be up in a minute. Elena wanted to shower and change her clothes."

Allison was already setting the table. Without comment she added two places.

There was a lengthy silence, broken when J.Q. asked, "Have you formed any opinion about this new shooting?"

"Numa said a sniper," Shirley answered as she put the chopped pepper into a large salad bowl.

"That's crazy!"

"I thought so, too, when he first said it. But you know, we've got these two nutty kids, Bonifacio and Marmot. They could be gun-crazy types. If so, maybe they went after Azoli, and then when I came along asking questions, they decided to do me in as well. They missed me, so they went after Charles. Does that make sense?"

He shook his head. "Not to me, it doesn't! However, there's enough possibility there to make it a priority finding out where they were this afternoon."

"Speaking of where people were—where was Rima?"

"Her ex picked her up right after you left. Her and her suitcases."

"He did, did he? Now, that's interesting." She looked at the table, where Allison was setting the knives with mathematical exactitude. "Wineglasses, Allison. We got any Chianti left in the cellar, J.Q.?"

"Always," J.Q. assured her as he went below.

Dog barked twice, his "known persons arriving" yap.

"There they are," said Allison. "Shirley . . . could I please have supper in my room?"

"Had enough of grown-ups?" Shirley asked, troubled but sympathetic. Damn it, if things would just quit happening so she could concentrate on Allison.

"It's not that. It's just . . . you guys have things you want to talk about. I thought I'd just curl up and watch TV."

"You do that. We won't be staying up late ourselves."

She removed Allison's place setting from the table and put it on a tray, adding a glass of milk and a candy bar from a secret cache Allison pretended she didn't know about. Allison was departing with her tray when J.Q. returned, bearing a dusty bottle. He looked after the girl, raising his eyebrows.

"Too many people dying," Shirley said softly. "It's like a war zone around here."

"I should think she'd want company."

"You and me, maybe. Not outsiders. Maybe she wants to cry a little, but not in front of people. Maybe she just feels sad and uncomfortable, which is about the way I feel. Or maybe it's just whatever's been bothering her, which is beginning to bother me more than a little." She grimaced. "There's our guests. My hands are all oily from the artichoke hearts. Can you let them in?"

J.Q. met them at the door, sharing the news about Oriana Bostom.

"Well," Elena murmured. "We knew it was coming. But poor Neb. Should we go over?"

"Not tonight, I shouldn't think," Shirley remarked. "Mike's there, and one of Neb's granddaughters. Tomorrow morning, maybe. From what Mike had to say about the granddaughter's cooking, we might make a point of taking prepared food over for a few days. I imagine other family will be arriving for the funeral."

They sat at the table, picking at the food without appetite.

"What do you think about this new shooting?" Joe asked, refilling his wineglass for the third time.

Shirley shook her head. "All J.Q. and I could think of was to find out where Henrietta's son and his buddy were."

Elena flared up. "You can't think that Henrietta—"

Shirley patted the air, calming her. "I don't think Henrietta anything, Elena. But her son might have been in on something. Or known about it."

"If anybody's going to question her," said Elena, pushing her chair back, "I'll do it. Better me than you."

"I don't care who calls her," Shirley rejoined. "Find out where Bony was Wednesday afternoon and this afternoon. Find out what she knows about his buddy, Marmot."

Elena left the room, making a point of it, and after a time they could hear her voice in the living room, rising and falling in exclamation and complaint.

When she returned, her mouth was set in grim lines. "Henrietta says Bony was up here," she said. "Wednesday and again today. He was up here visiting his pal Marmot."

Shirley and J.Q. exchanged glances.

"How'd she find that out?" asked J.Q.

"She threatened to throw Bony out on his ear unless he told her the truth about what he'd been doing. According to him, he took the bus to Columbine and Marmot picked him up, Wednesday and again today."

"You told her there'd been another shooting?"

"I did. Now she's scared to death he may have had something to do with it."

"What does her son say about that?"

"Bony says he just went to the ostrich farm with his friend, and they hid out in the barn and smoked dope. According to him, he paid no attention to the phone call when he was in the LALA office, and he had no idea who Azoli was or where he lived. She thinks he's telling the truth, if for no other reason than the fact that no one in her office discussed exactly where Azoli lived. The phone call simply informed them he'd moved to Colorado. It was later Henrietta found out exactly where."

Shirley leaned back and emptied her wineglass. "What do you think about it?"

Elena grimaced. "I've met the kid a few times. I'll tell you the truth, Shirley, I always thought he was just useless. One of those . . . I don't know. Do-less people. Short on vocabulary. Short on ambition. Not the kind of person who would ever do anything significant. In the context of racial . . . well, what would you call it?"

"Terrorism?"

"Unrest," she corrected firmly. "In that context, he might do a little graffiti, maybe some minor vandalism, and he'd probably yell slogans and insults, but I can't see him pulling off a killing. I certainly can't see him getting away with it. He'd fall over his own feet trying to run away."

Since this more or less confirmed Shirley's own impression of both young men, she couldn't argue. "How about someone else, someone they may have told about Azoli?"

"Henrietta says she really doesn't think Bony knew enough to tell anyone."

"You're reducing my suspect list."

"Not by much."

"By quite a lot, actually. You and Joe were with J.Q. this afternoon when Charles was killed. J.Q. and Allison and I were together when the shots were fired at us, and Allison and I were in town when Charles was shot. That lets us out. If Bony and Marmot's alibis check out, if they alibi each other, which seems probable, that lets them out. My original list included Charles Azoli; he's out." She counted on her fingers. "My list is down to nine!"

"Who's left?" asked Elena.

Shirley raised two fingers. "Rima and her ex-husband. Then comes X—" Another finger. "—which stands for an unknown but militant member of EGN or LALA who might have been informed by either Father Cisneros or Olivar Desfuentes—" The remaining finger and the thumb. "—both of whom are also on the list. Then there's the former Mrs. Azoli, plus Horace or Marthine Rodwinger, and finally your friend Henrietta."

"How about Rima and Paul's sons?" asked J.Q.

"We can check, but I think they're back in Baltimore. Besides, they're too young."

"I don't think much of your list," snarled Elena. "I know Henrietta, and she's just not capable. . . ."

Shirley grinned. "Well, I really took her off when Charles got it. She might have had a reason to do his father, but why him?"

"Thank you for very little," Elena snorted. "You're including the former Mrs. Azoli?"

"Her or some other member of that family. Someone could be here. We don't know. Charles Azoli was here before he said he was. Maybe some other relative came with him. We'd have no way of knowing."

"It's the same situation as Henrietta! Some outraged family member might have killed El Azoli, but what reason would they have had to kill Charles?"

"I'm merely going through my original list," Shirley said. "None of it made sense to me, either."

"And surely you don't really think Father Cisneros . . ."

Shirley howled: "I told you, I don't really think anybody, that's the trouble. Damn it, Elena. Don't pick a fight with me over this thing. It wasn't my fault! I'm not accusing anybody. But I know damned well I didn't do it, and for obvious reasons I'm extremely interested in who did."

"Calm down," J.Q. said, reaching across the table to pat her arm soothingly. "Rima and her ex left here right after you did this afternoon. I'm surprised you didn't pass his car on the road going out."

Shirley shook her head at him. "We stopped at Bostom's. They may have driven in while we were over there."

"Right," J.Q. continued. "The point is, we don't know where they went. We don't know what they did. Rima might have seen her disagreement with Charles over her money as a good enough reason to kill him. I know Paul Howard said he'd never shot a gun, but we have only his word for that. Also, you didn't include on your list the anonymous sniper that Numa suggested."

"So, add a theoretical sniper," she grumped at him. "It's always easier to arrive at a suspect if we don't need to be rational. Listen, people, I'm tired. I'm like Allison. I want to forget the whole thing for a while. Let's take our wine in by the fireplace and start a fire."

"Still too hot," murmured J.Q.

"I don't care. Open all the windows and build a fire. I need the symbolism. Hearth and home. Warmth and good friends."

J.Q. grumbled, but he and Joe brought in some wood and made a small fire while Elena stacked the dishes in the dishwasher and Shirley, after carrying the remaining wine into the living room, fell onto the couch and gloomed at the others, almost unaware of their moving about. Allison brought her dishes into the kitchen, said hello to Elena and Joe, then returned to her room, from which the sounds of a television game show came softly.

Though the sun had dropped low upon the western mountains to send slanting rays across the pastures, it was still full daylight. A cow bawled from somewhere nearby and was answered by a calf. A jay cried, its swooping flight carrying it past the windows on its way to the stream for an evening drink. The living room was dim behind the shadow of the deep porch, lit by the flickering fire. They opened another bottle of wine and sat sipping at it, saying very little as the sun dropped farther and the sky flamed in a blaze of salmon and scarlet that faded gradually to gray.

As though roused by the dusk, Joe stirred himself. "Let's get on home, 'Lena. Shirley looks like she's about to start snoring."

"Am," Shirley agreed, opening one eye. "But so are you."

"Sure," agreed Elena. "We'll talk tomorrow, Shirley. I've got to head back to Baltimore on Sunday."

"Okay." Shirley rose, yawning, and walked with the two of them out to their car. "Tomorrow I'll be in better shape to think about things. Maybe then we can make some sense of this."

She stood waving into the darkness as the taillights moved down the drive, joined by J.Q., who stood with one arm across her shoulders.

"This's been one hell of a long week," he offered.

"It isn't over yet," she murmured. "Tomorrow's only Saturday."

"You goin' over to Neb's in the morning?"

"Just for a minute. Find out when the funeral is, you know."

"If I'm around, I'll go with you."

"Sure."

Wordlessly, they turned to go back into the house as the stars pricked out in the darkening sky.

"Quiet," murmured J.Q. "No machine tonight."

"Would God it could remain quiet," she said fervently. "Would God that man had stayed in Maryland and done his damage to them, not to me."

"Selfish."

"Oh, indeed, J.Q. I cannot find it in my heart to be sorry he's dead."

"I know," he replied soberly. "Me neither."

Saturday morning, Shirley found Allison at the kitchen table with her aquarium kit spread out before her.

"We forgot that, didn't we?" she asked. "Completely forgot it."

"I thought about it in the middle of the night," Allison said. "So first thing this morning, I fetched it from the car."

"After I have a cup of coffee, we'll go find the tank," Shirley told her, stretching widely. "Where's J.Q.?"

"One of the goats got her head caught in the fence. She cut her neck, so he's out there putting stuff on it."

"Antibiotic?"

"That yellow stuff."

"We need to get rid of those last few stretches of six-inch stock wire," Shirley grumbled. "They will put their heads through, then they get their horns caught and can't get out. Bet you half a dollar it was Elena."

193

"I could bet you, but I won't. It was the black one."

"Elena's kid. Like mother, like daughter."

Long silence.

A very small voice asked, "Is that true?"

"Is what true?" Shirley was trying to see what J.Q. was doing through the kitchen window.

"Like mother, like daughter?"

The words created a convulsion somewhere inside her. Shirley took a deep breath, summoning all her good sense from wherever she'd left it when she'd let those words slip out. "In goats? Sure. In sheep, sure. In people, no. People have intelligence; they are capable of symbolic thought, they can make up their own minds about things."

"But you said . . . about Marmot Marquez, he must have got it from his father."

She breathed deeply, trying to remember what she had said. "I think Marthine said that, and I was quoting her. People say those things. It doesn't mean they are true. Not even when I say them."

"You didn't mean me?"

"Of course I didn't mean you, Allison. Why would you think I meant you?"

"Because somebody . . . somebody said something about my mother."

"Who?" Who would have dared! "Where?"

"At school."

"Over a month ago?"

"Well. Yes. It wasn't one of the kids. It was a parent."

"When?" Shirley asked, feeling anger surging.

"At the closing ceremony, before summer vacation. I heard two of them talking about my mother. About her being killed. About her being . . ."

Shirley sat down beside the child and held out her arms. Allison allowed herself to be hugged.

"Your mom wasn't very sensible, Allison. She never really grew up. You know that."

A mumbled agreement.

"But you weren't very like your mother even when you lived with her, were you?"

"The other night, when you were talking about . . . not letting women have babies. Maybe she shouldn't have had me."

"She wasn't a drug addict, Allison. She wasn't an alcoholic. You weren't born addicted or disabled. Your mother did drink a little, mostly out of loneliness."

"She was a . . . the woman said she was a . . . prostitute."

"Who were these people?"

"Benton's mother and grandmother."

"Benton?"

"Abschutz."

"Benton Abschutz's great-grandfather was a horse thief named William Webster. My father knew him. He was hanged in Granite County for killing a sheriff's deputy. His daughter married well, and she likes to pretend he never existed. So far as I know, her daughter, Benton's mother, and Benton himself are without flaw."

Allison sagged against her, bonelessly. "Is a prostitute worse than a horse thief?"

"Horse thief and murderer," Shirley corrected. "No. A prostitute is not worse. I'm not sure your mother could even have been called a prostitute. She was led into the behavior by someone else. She didn't do it out of moral depravity but out of that same childishness we both know about."

"But it's . . . it's the worst thing!"

Shirley rocked her. "Not really. People with sexual hang-ups see prostitution as the worst thing because they don't think any woman ought to be rewarded for having sex. They ignore the fact that for many women, marriage is a reward for having sex. We're a fairly puritanical nation—at least the male-dominated lawmaking part of it is. They pass a lot of sex-related laws, but in many countries prostitution isn't even illegal. In some cultures there are high-class prostitutes, or concubines or courtesans or whatever the Japanese ones are called."

"Geishas?"

"No, geishas are something else. Whatever you called it, the world is full of former prostitutes who now occupy respected positions in society and the arts and professions. I would not want any daughter of mine to be a prostitute, particularly not in these times of rampant sexually transmitted diseases, but I would not want any daughter of mine to be a number of other quite legal things, either."

"Such as?"

"Such as a salesman of bronzed baby shoes, fake Indian pottery, or 'collectibles'; a manufacturer of narcissistic toys for little girls or war toys for children of either sex; or a centerfold in a girlie magazine. I hope you have higher aspirations than that."

"What is going on here?" asked J.Q.

"I'm getting another lecture," Allison said impertinently, leaning bonelessly against Shirley's chest. "She's going on and on again."

"You want me to quit?" Shirley asked her, holding her tightly.

"Ummm. I think I know what you're saying."

"I'm saying you're you, Allison. Nobody else. Makes no difference who your parents were, who your uncle and aunt and cousins are. . . ."

"Yech."

"Right. You're you, perfect of your kind, and J.Q. and I love you very much just as you are."

"Yeah," she said almost contentedly. "I guess me, too."

"Well, if you're tired of listening to me lecture, go on out to the barn and open the door to that little room back behind the tractor. Look on the shelves along the back wall and see if that's where the aquarium is. You find it, maybe J.Q.'ll carry it in for you."

Allison promptly got up and went outside.

"Mrs. Abschutz's granddad, I seem to recall, was a county judge," J.Q. said with a stifled grin.

"Other side of the family was a horse thief," Shirley said

with a straight face, wiping her eyes. "I had it straight from my daddy."

"What started you on that?"

"Mrs. Abschutz and her mother, at the closing ceremonies at Crebs, happened to say in Allison's hearing that her mother had been . . . no better than she should be."

"Bitches," he muttered. "And Allison's been chewing on that ever since?"

"She has. And I've put my big fat foot in it at least six times since I've been home, making it worse."

"I've been afraid it would only be a matter of time until somebody said something to her."

"Not to her. Merely in her hearing. Abschutz is an attorney. Someone in his office was defense attorney in that case, which is how Mrs. Abschutz found out about Allison's mother. I'll give him a call later today, tell him to shut his wife up."

"You wouldn't!"

"I sure as hell would! Stupid woman."

"Hush," he said, gesturing toward the door.

Allison banged through the screen door, calling, "It's there, Shirley, but it's full of stuff and I can't lift it."

"Get it for her, will you, J.Q. I'll get breakfast started."

"What am I supposed to be getting?" he asked with ostentatious patience.

"An old fish tank. Used to belong to Marty. Allison has a craving for fish."

As he went out the door, she went after him, calling, "J.Q., is Rima back?"

"Nobody there," J.Q. said over his shoulder. "She didn't come back last night. I think we can assume she has departed."

"Interesting," Shirley murmured as she turned her attention to breakfast. "How very interesting."

The tank and the breakfast dishes were scoured at the same time, after which the tank was set up on a table in Allison's room. Allison was trotting back and forth to the bathroom with a bucket, filling the tank, when Shirley left.

"I'm headed for Bostom's," she told them both. "You want to come, J.Q.?"

"I'll stay here," he said meaningfully, looking toward the back corridor. "Allison may need help."

Shirley nodded in agreement. "She does need company. I'll find out about the funeral. Then I'm dropping by the Ramirezes' to talk about that property in Washington. Then the Rodwingers' to see if Mervin agrees with Bony about where they were. Then if there's time, I may drop in on Botts. I called him while you and Allison were fetching the tank. He says he'll be in his office this morning."

"Mending fences with Bottsy?"

"Well, he's not a bad guy, J.Q. He did call me to warn me about McInery."

"Still, take care. Don't go shooting off your mouth."

As she drove into the Bostom place, she saw Neb walking among the trees above the beaver ponds. Getting out of the car, she strolled quietly down to join him.

"Shirley," he said, raising one hand in greeting. He looked weary but peaceful, as though some long struggle had come to an end.

He led her toward the old bench above the pond, one that had been replaced bit by bit over the years, each slat being renewed as it fell apart, until it had gained a kind of immortality, and sank onto it beside her with an audible groan.

"Old bones," he said tiredly.

"I know." She smiled ruefully. "I feel 'em, too, Neb."

"Oh, hell, you're young yet," he said. "A mere brat."

"I suppose."

Ducks erupted from among the cattails across the pond, pursued by an angry Canada goose.

"Trespasser," commented Neb. "She's nesting late. Can't figure it out. Should have had goslings by April or May, and here she is setting."

"Maybe the nest got destroyed and she decided to try again," she offered. "Some of us . . . we do that."

"Could be."

Above them, from somewhere near the road, the liquid call of a meadowlark fell like limpid water into the day.

"Funeral's Monday," he said. "Two in the afternoon, from the Wilson funeral home in Columbine. There's a Stenger plot at the Columbine cemetery. She wanted to be buried there, near her folks. They saved me a spot, too, so I don't mind."

"We'll be there, Neb. Is more of the family coming?"

"Oh, yes. Marilyn's on her way in, and some of Mike's kids and their kids. Some are staying here, and some in town. I'll have plenty of company."

"My guest house is available, Neb, if it's be useful to you. And when they have to go home, you'll still have company, Neb. J.Q. and I are five minutes away. We want you to come over for supper as often as you can."

"Not too often," he said calmly. "Ori won't have to be without me long."

"Now, Neb."

"True." He smiled at her. "Kind of funny, actually. She had it, now I've got it. Quicker for me, though. So the doctor says."

"Cancer? Oh, Neb!"

"I don't mind. Kind I've got, it's real fast. Almost as though my body knew I had to do something, go after her fast, so she couldn't get too far ahead of me."

Shirley was speechless. He sounded so calm, so content, almost happy. He was eighty-five years old. Who was she to say no, now now, don't talk like that? He was old enough to talk like that if he liked! Who was she to decry his faith or mock his devotion?

She took his arm in her own and held it. He did not draw away but simply sat, the friendly warmth of their flesh mingling between them.

"Got to get back to the house," he said at last. "Back to Mike and Patti. They're real worried over me. You won't say anything to them, will you, Shirley? I don't want them to know. I don't want any fuss."

She cleared her throat. "Whatever you say, Neb."

199

They stood up and walked together toward the house. As they neared it, Neb leaned over and picked something invisible out of the grass. "Present for you," he said.

She took the mushroom he offered her. *Agaricus.* Pale ivory with salmon-pink gills, fresh and perfect and no bigger than her little finger.

"Never could pass them up." He smiled. "Even when I had a basket full."

He saw her into the car and waved good-bye. She laid his gift on the seat beside her and watched him go into the house before she turned the key.

When she arrived at her next stop, she found Elena sitting on the front porch alone, reading the morning paper. She set it aside and poured Shirley a cup of coffee. "Joe and I've decided we're very interested in your offer," she said. "I think the next step would be to see if the tax advantage is actually there. I'll ask my accountant at home, you pursue it here, and we'll call each other, okay?"

Shirley agreed that it was a sensible plan. "Where's old Joe?" she asked.

"Joe's down at the Columbine rifle range," Elena said with some asperity. "He found his old rifle in the back of the closet, and nothing would do but he go down and see if he can still hit a target. He's leaving this afternoon, so if you're going to town and want to see him, he'll probably still be there."

"He's going today, and you're leaving tomorrow?"

"Right. All the stock's gone. Chickens are gone. Gave them away. We're locking up the house, but I thought I'd leave you a key so you could check from time to time, see there's no leaks in the roof or whatever. If we haven't done something with the property by early fall, I'll arrange to have the plumbing drained down and the heat turned off before it freezes."

"You could rent it, Elena."

"Too much trouble. Tenants never take proper care of things. Hell, Mama didn't take proper care. And in any case, I don't want any long-term arrangement to worry about."

"All right, then. I'll look in on it for you."

Elena leaned forward and embraced her. "If I don't see you again before I go, take care, McClintock."

"Always do. And don't you go getting too involved in radical politics."

"Always do."

She laughed and waved. Shirley went back to her car, feeling somehow as though it were she who was leaving or had left. All the familiar, the dear, the well loved were shifting and changing around her, like chimeras.

The Columbine rifle range was only five miles distant, a not-for-profit, mostly weekend establishment run by the local chapter of the National Rifle Association. Shirley didn't like the NRA's politics, but she had no objection to their having a place at which proper handling of firearms could be taught. She recognized the truck parked in the lot, but there was no sign of Joe on the firing line. There were only two shooters, both with ear protectors and scopes.

She stood where she could be seen and waited.

The nearest rifleman put down his weapon, lifted a bulky earmuff, and said, "You looking for something, ma'am?"

"Joe Ramirez?" she asked. "His truck is here, but I don't see him."

"He's pulling targets for me. You know how to get out to the butt?" He pointed the way, far to the right, well away from the line of fire.

When she got there, she found a flight of cinder-block steps leading down into an eight-foot trench, dirt-floored and walled with more cinder block, its plane surfaces interrupted at intervals by the uprights of sliding target racks. Above the trench and behind the targets stood a long wall of earth fronted with straw bales, and behind that was a sheer arroyo wall. Joe was a hundred feet down the trench, busy clipping a new paper bull's-eye target onto a rack.

He looked up and saw her.

"Hey, McClintock! What you doing here?"

"Elena said you were leaving this afternoon. I wanted to be sure to say good-bye."

"I was coming up to say good-bye!" he said. "Hell, yes. I wasn't going to run out on you. Elena tell you what we decided?"

Shirley nodded. "Sounds good."

He grinned happily at her, hauling away on the target frame. It rose into the air above the trench and locked into position.

Almost immediately the shots came, slowly and deliberately spaced, the passage of the bullets overhead sounding as though the shots had been pulled off within inches of their ears.

Joe flinched. "Damn. I forgot my earmuffs."

Shirley had already started back. She treasured her hearing too much to stay in the butt when firing was going on. They emerged together onto the level. "What brought you out here?" she demanded, leaning close to his ear.

"Oh, I don't know. Old times, maybe. My rifle was pulling left, and I thought I'd sight it in. You going to be home later?"

She nodded, putting her fingers in her ears. "I'll see you later, then."

He grinned at her and went back toward the firing line.

It would almost make sense to go on to town and talk to Botts, but if she did so, she might miss finding Marthine at home. So, next stop, Rodwinger's, she decided, turning to go back the way she had come.

The ostrich farm was as she had seen it last. When she got out of the car, the big male, Hero, came to the fence and rested his chinless head on the top rail, peering at her, plumes aquiver. In the next pen the infants, already visibly larger than when she had seen them a few days before, peeped and pushed one another as they pecked up the grain from their feeder.

"Shirley McClintock?"

She turned to see Marthine coming toward her. "Hello, Marthine."

"How nice of you to come visiting."

"Not really, Marthine. I'm trying to find out about your son and Bonifacio Labolis. I hope you won't be offended."

Marthine's lips thinned. She put her hands on her hips and said forthrightly, "Bonifacio's mother has already called me. She wanted to know what her son had been doing yesterday and on Wednesday. Horry and I took Mervin to task and demanded a full accounting. He said they had been together, here, in the barn. While I cannot be absolutely positive, I think he is telling the truth. More or less."

"How did Bony get here?"

Marthine looked even grimmer as she responded. "As Mervin tells the story, when he was in town picking up grain at the feed store on Wednesday, he picked up Bony at the bus stop. Later that afternoon, according to Mervin, Bonifacio hitchhiked back to town. Their activities on that afternoon were, I suppose, relatively innocent. Nonetheless, I do not approve of the influence Bonifacio has on Mervin."

Which view Henrietta reciprocates, thought Shirley, wondering which of the two young men was actually the inciter or whether it was simply a matter of critical mass.

"Yesterday," Marthine went on ponderously, "Bonifacio phoned here with a spurious message from the repair shop that our television was ready to be picked up. When Mervin came back without it, he assured me the caller had been mistaken, the TV would be ready later in the afternoon. That allowed a return trip, to take Bonifacio back to Columbine, where he caught the bus. According to Bonifacio's mother, their accounts agree in all details except what they were doing in the barn. Mervin says they were just talking. About girls, he says. Bonifacio's mother says they were taking . . . drugs. I cannot believe after all we have been through that Mervin was once again involved with drugs!"

"My foster daughter saw your son carrying a rifle. I'd like to have a look at it, if you don't mind."

Marthine flushed. "It seems Mervin answered an ad in the local paper and bought this weapon so much down and so much a month. When we found it, I insisted that Horry return it. He couldn't get Mervin's money back, but that's all right. Maybe it'll teach him a lesson."

"He was carrying a shotgun the other day," said Shirley.

"Horry insisted we have the shotgun to frighten away predators. We no longer need even that. Now that that dreadful machine has stopped, we can put the chicks back in with their parents, and that will take care of the predator problem. Coyotes are no match for mature ostriches, I assure you."

"Marthine . . . I'm told your son has been in jail a couple of times for violent crimes. Honestly, do you think he could have shot Azoli?"

The woman looked at her feet. "I don't know," she said at last. "I'll look up the name of the man he bought the rifle from. I'll call you."

"Thank you," Shirley said in her most humble voice. "I do appreciate your help."

"I understand," Marthine said. "You have to eliminate all possibilities. I can't blame you for that." She turned to go about her business, making it clear that blamelessness was not equivalent to further friendship.

Ms. Minging's car was once more outside the school. Shirley hammered on the door and then spent twenty minutes on the subject of the Abschutz womenfolk, their flapping lips, and what effect their utterances had had on Allison.

"Why don't you let me handle it?" Ms. Minging suggested, when Shirley had run out of cusswords. "Why don't you stay out of it and let me do it?"

"Because it makes me so damned mad, is why."

"But you don't want the women angry with you. That might make them say something else nasty about Allison. You want them angry at themselves. I think I can manage that. All in the loftiest way, of course."

Shirley gave her a long look. Their eyes locked. Ms. Minging nodded slowly.

"All right, Xanthippe. You take care of it. But if either of those bitches says one word again, I will personally pull their tongues out by the roots."

She drove out onto the road. Now, time to go talk to Botts.

Though what she would say, she didn't know. She'd sic him on Marmot and Bony. Maybe, if someone confronted them with the rifle . . .

It didn't feel right. The shot that had killed Azoli had been clean, almost surgical. Marmot and Bony would not have been capable of that kind of action. Besides, thinking of them brought to book for the crime did not satisfy her. She still had that sense of violation and loss, with nothing to mitigate it.

Joe was leaving. Elena was leaving. Oriana was being buried. Neb was dying. Her beautiful place had been ruined and ravaged, and she couldn't even say why. Marmot and Bony? They might serve as a red herring, but no, no, it didn't feel right.

The wave of grief that burst over her was so intense that she pulled the car to the side of the road and simply sat, unable to go on. The pain was actual, physical. Like cramps. Like being poisoned. Her body rejected whatever it was, sought to cast it out, convulsed with it.

She took deep breaths, calming herself. Her hand came to rest on the mushroom Neb had given her. She lifted it before her face. So perfect. The texture like kid leather. The rosy gills, little-girl pink. Baby pink. Like something crafted, made by a master's hand, not merely sprung up out of nothing.

One couldn't say nothing, of course. Mushrooms did not spring out of nothing. Everything had a cause. Happenings, events, even little ones, didn't come out of nowhere. There was always a source, often a hidden, slow-growing source. Like public knowledge about Allison's family, a matter of slow rumor, months in the forming. Allison's painful reaction had been merely the fruiting body of that long, slow growth.

And Azoli's killing . . . it must have been the same, the murder being merely the fruiting body of a nature, a personality that had developed for years. El Azoli had germinated his own murder, had developed it slowly, had brought it to fruition by his own actions. It wasn't a casual thing. Not a

Marmot and Bony kind of thing. Not a whoop-de-do, let's take our new gun out and shoot somebody kind of thing. Not a yippie-ki-yi-dead kind of thing. Not messy at all. Very clean. Very sure.

She rolled the mushroom in her fingers. Perfect. Fully grown. And as she had explained to Allison, the larger part unseen.

Like a motive for murder.

Her hands went to the key, the steering wheel. The car began to roll, and she steered it back onto the road.

She was being silly. There was no similarity. The one was not a metaphor for the other.

Or was it?

Some people thought fungus inedible. The thought of mushrooms—or toadstools—repulsed them. They might kick a mushroom, but they wouldn't pick one. They wouldn't . . . treasure one.

But to someone else a mushroom, even a poisonous mushroom, might have its own perfection, its own acceptability. To be picked and examined and treasured for its own sake.

She drove to Old Mill Road, past the Azoli place, noting several almost identical cars near the house—rental cars, relatives, people arrived to handle tragedy. Tragedy that had sprouted inevitably. Tragedy that had been the fruiting body of something that had grown unseen.

J.Q. wasn't at the house. Allison wasn't at the house. Shirley went into her own room, her sanctum, sat at her desk with a yellow pad and three freshly sharpened pencils. If this, then what? If this, then that.

She heard a rustle at the door, J.Q. creeping up on her, cat-footed.

"Sneaky," she challenged him in a preoccupied voice.

"I thought you might be asleep."

"Not asleep. No. Thinking."

"You have that look around the eyes."

"What look is that?"

"The look a turtle has after it swallows a large worm. Sort of ruminative."

"Turtles aren't ruminants."

"Yeah, but your look is more omnivorous than mere ruminants can summon up. Have you figured out who did it?"

She nodded. He cocked his head at her. She swallowed deeply and nodded again.

"Are you going to tell me?" he asked gently.

"Yes. If you'll promise not to tell anyone else."

His jaw dropped. "You're still a suspect, Shirley! If you know who . . ."

She shook her head. "No. I'm not really a suspect, J.Q. McInery might like to harass me—maybe he even will, but I'm not really on the list. He couldn't make a case. Not anymore."

"So?"

"Where's Allison?"

"Where else? Over at Cavendish's."

"We got a while?"

"I should think. Long enough."

"Let's sit on the porch." She led the way out, moved two of the old wicker chairs around until they caught the breeze and missed the sun.

"This story starts with my dad," she said at last, when she was leaning back in the chair with her boots resting on the old wagon-wheel table. "Dad used to go hunting. He taught me to hunt when I was a kid, me and Sean."

"I know that, Shirley."

"Patience, J.Q. We used to get a deer or two, sometimes an elk, every fall. Dad always said the best hunters he knew were Nebraska Bostom and his son Mike. He had a lot of stories about Neb; he used to bore me silly telling them. Neb used to go up to Wyoming for the one-shot antelope hunt. You know about that?"

"I know what it is. You get one load for your rifle, and that's all. If you shoot and miss, you're out. You have to be good."

"Neb was good. He always got his antelope. There's a whole row of heads over there in his back room. He had the eye. That's what my dad said, he had the eye.

"He had the eye for other things, too. Mushrooms. He could see them when no one else could. Hummingbirds. He pointed one out to me the other morning. It was a hundred feet away, and I couldn't see it until it took off."

J.Q. regarded her speculatively. "So?"

"Mariposa lilies. He could spot them. Well, he was in tune, is what I'm saying. Eye, ear, hand, heart, all in tune with his surroundings, with what was growing and being and flying. And in tune with himself, too. Married his childhood sweetheart, went right on loving her, had a family, saw them grow up and leave, and stayed where he was because he loved where he was."

"And?"

"And his sweetheart fell ill. He went away with her to visit the family, and they returned home to find their home being despoiled. No matter. He didn't have to look at it. He could look at something else. But she . . . she wanted to hear the meadowlarks."

"That machine," breathed J.Q.

"Indeed. And the old gentleman, and he was very much a gentleman, J.Q., asked the man responsible for the machine to mitigate the injury. And the man refused, with rude words and sneers. And the time was growing short for Neb's sweetheart to hear the meadowlarks again."

"So?"

"So, while his sweetheart slept a drugged sleep, Neb went out of his house and watched the man from the top of Indian Bluff. He saw the man's wife meeting another man in the old gravel pit. I believe he saw the man himself sneaking down from his house into a gully where he could watch them, maybe listen to them. We ourselves saw this rather peculiar behavior, though at the time we didn't realize it because we couldn't see Rima and Paul from where we were. I believe the old gentleman may have seen it happen several times. I know he saw it at least once."

"While his wife was asleep, at home?"

"Drugged, asleep. She had so little good time. A few moments in the morning. A few moments in the evening. So the old gentleman put something in the gully or found something there—my no-trespassing sign—that he could sight on from the top of the bluff, and one day when the machine was loud, he sighted in his rifle by shooting the sign, twice. That explains the bullet holes in the sign. And that afternoon, when the man's wife was meeting the other man, the old gentleman waited until the red-shirted villain came sneaking down into the gully, and he put a bullet through his head.''

"But the shot! Rima and Paul said it was . . . oh. Oh, I see. . . .''

"Right, J.Q. I went to the rifle club to see Joe today. He was down in the butt, setting targets for some guy. When the shooting started, it was like the shots went off right next to me. When a bullet comes *over* you, if the conditions are right, it sounds right there!''

J.Q. nodded slowly. "The bullet exceeds the speed of sound. You hear the clap of the air above you before you hear the report from the gun. The report of the gun, if you hear it at all, is heard as an echo. Because it's above you, it seems close but nondirectional. But they never thought to look up.''

"Of course not. Not if it sounded nearby. But it's only a few hundred yards from the top of the bluff to the gully. Not even a long shot by Neb's standards.''

"And then?''

"And then his sweetheart had time to hear the meadow-larks. At least once, I believe. I hope.''

"And then?''

"And then the old gentleman found out the daughter of one of his oldest friends was suspected of the crime.''

J.Q. stood up and stared off across the valley. "He fired at you?''

"No. No, J.Q. He'd never have done that. Neb would never—Neb would never fire at anything unless he intended to kill it. No, what Neb did, he rigged me an alibi. He sent me to town on an errand. And while I was gone, he shot again. This time he shot the carbon-copy son, who had once again started up that damned machine. But he made sure I was somewhere else and I could prove I was somewhere else when he did it.''

"And now Oriana's dead.''

"Yes. Oh, I do hope she heard the meadowlarks, at least once.''

"Doesn't he care what's going to happen to him?''

"Nothing's going to happen to him, J.Q. He's got cancer. Some kind of fast cancer. He says he's dying. He told me that, almost gladly. I think he wanted me to know so I could . . . do whatever I needed to do when I figured it out. He put the solution in my hand.''

"And what was that?''

"A mushroom. I never even saw it growing there. He saw it. He stooped and picked it up. It was second nature for him to do that. He'd never pass up a good crop.''

"I don't get it.''

"Where did we find the *Lepista nuda*? Beside the ruts going down into the gravel pit. You said what? That part of them were fresh but part had been there for at least a day. Neb said he'd seen Rima's husband with her down there. He couldn't have seen them from the road. In order to have seen them, he'd have had to walk in at least as far as those mushrooms. He wouldn't have left them there. I mean, he would not. He couldn't have. It would have been absolutely second nature for him to pick them. Ergo, he didn't walk there. He saw Rima and her ex sitting on the stump, but he saw them from somewhere else. Where?''

"The only place he could have seen them on the stump from was the top of the bluff. But if he didn't fire at you, who did?''

She shook her head ruefully. "Who else but my old buddy, Joe? Joe did it. Scared himself spitless, too, because his rifle pulled left and he damned near hit me. This morning he said he was out at the range sighting it in because it pulled left, but how did he know that unless he'd fired it?''

"Joe? Why Joe?''

"He was . . . he was paying me back, for Orville Climp-

210

son. He was saving my ass because I'd saved his once, a long time ago.''

"Are you sure? Sure about it all?"

"J.Q., I have no proof whatsoever, and I am so damned sure, I don't even care where Rima and Paul are. I no longer think they could possibly be involved.''

J.Q. sat back down. "What are you going to do?"

She smiled ruefully. "Nothing. Not unless they arrest somebody. Maybe, when Neb's gone, I might tell Botts. And then again, maybe I won't. Let him think it's a sniper. Let him go looking at LALA or EGN or whoever.''

"And justice?"

Shirley looked across the green acres to the chewed brown hillsides across the fence where the squat yellow monster still brooded, needing only a human hand to begin its destruction again.

"I'm not real sure, J.Q., but it's just possible justice has been done.''

7

J.Q., ALLISON, AND Shirley went to Oriana's funeral, which was attended by people from all over Ridge and Granite counties, many of whom came back to the Bostom house afterward to share, as people did on such occasions, memories of old times. Nebraska Bostom moved among them, grave and content, so much so that Mike remarked to Shirley that his father wasn't taking it as hard as he, Mike, had feared.

Shirley smiled and agreed and uttered clichés about its being a blessed release that were echoed by others of the older people present. She was aware of an unaccustomed discomfort and had to concentrate on letting the occasion move around her, on not knowing any more than anyone else did.

Rima sent a thank you letter for the use of the guest house and asked if the shoes she'd left under the bed could be sent on to Maryland, where she and Paul were trying to make their marriage work again. By the way, she said, Clemmy had sent her a check for her one hundred thousand.

"Magnanimous of Clemmy," Shirley said to J.Q.

"She probably wanted to sever all connections," he replied.

A couple of weeks later the Azoli ranch was put up for sale, even though the realtors felt (so they told Shirley) the Azolis could not get back all the money El Azoli had put into it.

Allison returned to the subject of her mother several times, seeming less troubled each time. When school started, Ms. Minging called Shirley to say she thought Allison had weathered the crisis.

In mid-September Nebraska Bostom died after a brief hospitalization. A week or so later Shirley got a call from Joe Ramirez rather late one night.

"I keep up my subscription to the Ridge County paper, and I see in the obituaries that Neb Bostom died. Made me think maybe I'd tell you something about that day you got shot at."

"You mean that day you shot at me, Joe?"

"You knew it was me!"

"Well. Let's say I figured it out."

"Well, McClintock, it was only partly for you. It was mostly for old Neb."

"You knew it was him!"

"Well, sure, didn't you?"

"Not then, I didn't."

"You're slowing up, McClintock. If Rima and Paul were telling the truth about hearing the shot, then there's only one place the shot could have come from. Didn't you figure that?"

"Not until that day out at the rifle club. Makes me feel like a fool, Joe."

"No. You had a good reason not to think of it. You knew Neb, and you'd never met Azoli. But I had met him, Shirley. And Neb had for sure met him. And anybody who'd ever met him . . . well. Anybody who'd ever met him wanted him dead. So I had no handicap of disbelief to overcome." The words came out with an uncharacteristic venom.

She asked, "Do you think I ought to tell anyone? About Neb?"

"Hell, no. Let them go on wondering." A moment's silence and then, "You don't sound quite like yourself, McClintock."

She hesitated, then told him the truth. "I'm not, Joe. Ever since this summer . . . ever since all this happened, I can't . . . I can't get settled in. You know? The place doesn't feel as secure. Life isn't as . . . as immutable."

"It never was."

"It seemed so to me. Now . . . now I don't know. Now I have the feeling maybe . . . maybe I've cared too much. Sunk too much of myself into it."

"I used to feel like that sometimes. When I did, I usually did something else for a while. You think maybe you've gotten too settled? Maybe you ought to move on?"

"Move on? Well, maybe, Joe."

"Where, Shirley?"

"Somewhere. Somewhere where the destruction wouldn't hit me every time I look over the fence." Somewhere . . . different. Somewhere new. Someplace where discovery would take the place of . . . whatever.

"You won't want to trade those buildings, then?"

"I don't know, Joe. I might want to do a three-way trade, end up with something else, that's all."

"Let me know, huh, friend."

"I'll let you know."

He chuckled. "You knew what it was all about, didn't you? My getting the lawmen off you?"

"Orville Climpson, is what I figure."

"So we're even now."

"We've always been even, Joe."

She hung up and sat, looking at her bare feet.

"I take it that was Joe," said J.Q., lounging in the doorway, one moccasined foot resting on another, his pajama legs twisted around his bony legs.

"Yeah."

"Where does he think you ought to move on to?"

"He doesn't know, J.Q. Do you?"

"Wherever. So long as it's green. Am I invited along?"

214

"I wouldn't go anywhere without you."

"That's nice to know." He turned and wandered back down the hallway.

She sighed and looked out into the night. The moon was shining on the duck pond. An owl was hooting somewhere up the hill. The house was the house she had loved, had loved, had loved. It wasn't the house's fault it no longer felt like home.

ABOUT THE AUTHOR